A CABOT CAIN THRILLER

ASSAULT ON FELLAWI

ASSAULT ON FELLAWI
Book Four

CHAPTER 1

We came within sight of the last of the dunes at one o'clock in the afternoon, and the shade temperature—if there'd been any shade—was around a hundred and twenty-five. In the sun, it was a great deal hotter, with the soft sand still hot even at the depths to which our feet sank as we struggled over and through it.

The heat was bad enough; the physical effort of struggling up those powdery dunes was demanding in the extreme; the need to keep moving, to keep ahead of our pursuers, was powerful, because I knew what they'd do if they caught up with us. And *she* was the biggest headache of all; what do you do in a place like this, on the run, a million miles from nowhere, when you're dragging a naked woman along behind you?

The Bedouin call this place the Rub al Khali, the Empty Quarter, and empty it certainly is. For six hundred miles north to south; and for twelve hundred miles east to west, there is nothing but sand. Go southeast from Mecca for two or three hundred miles—if you can get through the terrible Jebel Hijaz—and turn to the east; and then, there's more than a thousand miles of the Empty Quarter, where *nothing* lives, no man, no animal, no bush, no weed. There's hot soft sand, and hot red lava, and hot grey rock, and nothing else.

Tihama, Yemen, Hadhramaut, the Trucial States and Oman, these are the quarter's borders, grouped along a barren and inhospitable coastline; and inland, there is nothing. It's as though the desert has driven its nomads out to its fringes, which indeed it has, where they sit by the tiny oasis and wait—for what? This has always been their life, and for the desert beyond the dunes they have nothing but the greatest respect.

And there we were, stuck right in the middle of it, as far from civilization as anyone can get, running for our lives from a group of horsemen who had broken all precedent and actually followed us into that terrible vastness where nothing could ever hope to survive.

They couldn't have been more than a mile behind us. The last I'd seen of them, the four horses had been floundering in the soft sand, struggling up to the fine dust at the top of the dune. The riders, dismounted now, were lying on the ridge and blazing away at us with American Garand rifles at a range of less than a thousand yards and still contriving to miss.

There was a time when the Bedouin carried an old Turkish musket that he merely had to point in the right direction and fire, and he was very good with it. But nowadays, every country that makes guns is falling over itself to give them to countries that don't; and one unexpected advantage of this is that the Bedouin are not sharp-shooters any more for a simple, though surprising, reason. The Desert Bedouin is accustomed to focusing his eyes on the far horizon, and a lump of steel foresight stuck up there under his nose, three feet in front of him, merely confuses him. And thank God it does, or we'd both have been dead by now.

Of course, it occurred to me that they could want us alive! Ahmed Fellawi was not the kind of man to take the insult I'd paid him lying down, and a quick bullet through the head wouldn't have been his idea of a correct solution to his problem. When he'd sold me the girl (sardonically enough, I'd noticed, and wondered about that at the time), it had all been a very simple matter of trade; but then, as soon as Tahari burst in, gun in hand, he'd known at once that there was a great deal more to this than he'd realized, and he must have known at once that I was after not only the girl but his blood as well.

Well, I'd got his girl. And he wanted my blood instead, and hers as well, no doubt. So we ran on, driven by that kind of desperate willpower that's a reflex to danger.

We stumbled along in the red-hot trench between the dunes, changing direction now to get round the horn of the crescent-shaped mountain of sand, struggling over its point and facing the next great dune—the last—that towered high over our heads. It was like being in a baker's oven. I heard a light plane flying high, and as we stood there, open-mouthed and gasping, it swooped down fast to take a look at us, and then was gone almost before I could get a good look at it, skimming dangerously low over the crest of the dune and disappearing from our sight. I brushed the sand and sweat out of my eyes and wondered if he was going to try and land. And who was he? Had he scared off the horsemen behind us? Or was he allied with them?

Here on the edge of the Rub al Khali, it had all the earmarks of a two-bit operation—a group of desert horsemen after the guts of two exhausted fugitives fleeing out into the dunes. But it was more than that; behind all this was a well-organized operation, and a plane could easily have been part of it.

When the sound of the plane's motors had played its amusing little desert trick of dying away completely, I pointed ahead and said: "The last one." I slung her over my shoulder and started the climb.

That was the arrangement. When we began to tackle the dunes, I said to her: "I'll carry you up, and you can slither down, it's the only way we'll keep ahead of them..." Her weight was nothing, a mere hundred pounds of angry, exhausted, woman, too tired out to argue, too tired to do anything more than roll with it, whatever I said to her; and too scared to worry about the loss of her dignity.

The sand was coming up to my calves now, with the added weight of even that slight burden, and at the top—it took twenty-seven minutes to climb up—I set her down again and said: "All right, start slithering. That's the last one, the rest is easy."

All she wore was my beautiful white silk jacket. When I'd bought her, she'd been quite naked. She'd cost me eight thousand dollars, American money, which is a hell of a lot more than the going rate even for young American girls. In theory, I'd done the job they'd given me to do—if I could get her out of this damned desert, a prospect which didn't seem very likely at this moment. All I had to do was send her home. But Fellawi had dropped too many hints, made too many covert boasts; and it seemed to me that I really ought to keep after him for a while.

My name's Cabot Cain. I work for myself, mostly, but once in a while Interpol comes along, points me in the right direction, and says: "Go get him, boy." And I go. The peculiar talents I have—does that sound immodest?—are too useful to waste when this kind of work has to be done.

Eight thousand dollars; the market price, they told me, was around five, so Fellawi had made a good deal. As for me, all I'd bought was a bundle of trouble; but she was sweet, in her own lunatic way.

Constance Penny Delorme, age twenty-seven, height five foot two, weight a hundred pounds, popular statistics 34-21-35, late stewardess with Pan American Airways, and more recently the property of one Ahmed Fellawi, en route to the slavers' staging area at the edge of that damned Empty Quarter.

We half-fell, half-walked down to the bottom of the dune, and looked at the flat lava rock spread out before us, and for the hundredth time she sank to the ground and squealed when she burned her bare behind on that red-hot sand, hot as the top of a stove. She had some sandals when we'd started running, or we'd never have made it even to here; and where were we? The sandals flopped on her feet like herring-boxes, but at least they kept the heat away, as long as she stood on them. In this part of the world, if you break an egg onto a flat piece of rock, it's cooked in two minutes flat. I know; I've tried it. Takes two minutes to cook a four-minute egg.

I said: "Keep on your feet, honey, don't touch that sand with anything."

She flapped my white jacket to try and make a breeze. "Are we nearly there? I can't stand much more of this."

"Nearly where?"

"Where we're going?"

I didn't like to tell her that I didn't really know just where that was. When you're getting *away* from something, it doesn't matter much, at first, where you're going to. I unscrewed the top of the cognac bottle, half-full now of hot water, that was all we had, and handed it to her. She took a few sips, trained already in this, at least; just enough to stop the dehydration from taking over. The heat was bouncing back at us from the lava like a blowtorch, and I stared out across the dark reds to where some huge flat rocks of green-blue-purple offered a different aspect and, perhaps, some sort of hope for us. I trained the Trinovids on the rocks and examined them minutely.

Some sort of hope? No, it was salvation. In the middle of the dark grey-blues and the strange, eerie orange-yellows, the flat rocks, a hundred feet high or more, were covered with a green and coppery sheen all down their sides, the color of sheet copper that's been weathered by time, but a little more blue. It could have indicated a deposit of silver, of course, but I thought not. Though no one in modern times has been around this area much, fifty-eight hundred years ago a certain King Seneferu made a long trek from the Sinai Peninsula right down to this corner of the Rub in his constant search for the miraculous new ore that began the age of metallurgy—copper. And though there never had been much silver here, there had been a long history of copper in all its forms.

It was the *blue* that excited me. The more I stared at it, the more I was convinced it was Cupric Sulfate, $Cu\ SO_4$, which is really common vitriol, and which crystallizes into $CuSo_{4.5}H_2O$—it is bright blue in color. If I were, right... There was a little bit of information tucked away there that had more or less been mislaid for some three thousand years; Moses knew all about it, but today they talk of miracles and ignore the importance of applied erudition...

How far was it? Three miles? Four? In the clear desert air, it was hard to tell.

Constance was looking at the water left in the bottle, knowing that when it was gone... She looked up at me and said somberly: "It won't last much longer, will it?" I could see her temptation to gulp it all down, and I admired the way she fought it.

I said: "No, it won't, and we've got to find water before it's all gone."

"Oh God! Here?" She looked over the frightening desert and said again: "*Here?*"

I nodded, but I didn't think it was going to be easy. I have a Doctorate in Hydrogeology, and the work I wrote some years ago on Hydrognosy has become a standard reference, so I was starting off with the proper knowledge, and I pointed to the great blue rocks and. said: "Over by the rocks there, there'll be waddies, gullies, cracks in the earth that'll give us a little shade to rest up in for a while. If we're lucky, we might even find a water hole."

Her voice was getting thick now. She said: "I'll settle for shade to die in. Anything to get out of the sun."

I could have wept for her. Her lovely pale eyes were squinting at me out of a once-white face that was red as a lobster now; soon, she'd have had bad trouble with the sunburn. All down the backs of her long thighs the color was the same, and it would be more painful than she could ever have known.

I said gently: "Let's keep moving, shall we?"

We struggled on together over the hard rock, and I was greatly relieved now. If Fellawi were still behind us, there'd be no tracks for him to follow. Not that I thought it likely; the Bedouin are too fond of their horses—because without them, they die—to bring them into this kind of wilderness. We found a small gully, but I wouldn't let Constance stop, as she wanted to, because although there was a bit of shade down one side of it, the distant blue rocks held more promise, and it was necessary to get to them before the real trouble started—the lack of willpower that dehydration brings on as its first casualty.

It's a progression: first, the strength goes, and it doesn't really matter because there's always the will to live that pushes you along. Then, and there's the danger, the volition is dulled, and you say to yourself: *the hell with it*. And then, lastly, you lie down and die.

So we pushed on hard, and the rocks came closer and closer, larger and larger, till we almost ran to the great patches of shade that stretched out to the north of them. They were great primeval slabs that were part of a small mountain, a mountain of red sandstone with not a thing growing on it, but split here and there into dark crevasses, some of which were several hundred feet deep; and there were great streaks of brilliant blue... Constance stood at the edge of one of these *wadis*, and stared down into it and said, like a child: "Will there be water down there? There must be! Oh God, there *must* be! Please?" Her eyes would have been wet, but there wasn't enough moisture in her even for tears. I handed her the bottle again and said: "Just a little, we're going to be all right."

She was still staring down there, fascinated by the darkness. I pointed to one side and said: "There, that's where we'll try for water."

We found a deep slice in the rock that was thirty or forty feet deep, with a great square patch of that sulfate glowing like polished shagreen, and we climbed down into it. It was quite narrow, the bottom of a small street with high buildings on either side, and the sun could not get down here. I sat her down on the hard sand—how cool it was!—and said: "Wait here. Don't make a sound, just rest. I'll be back soon."

She nodded, and smiled unexpectedly, and whispered: "It's like an icebox in here..." I found a smooth stone for a pillow, and put it under her head, and said: "Just rest, I won't be long."

Unexpectedly, she put out a hand and took mine, and said: "I'm a pain in the ass to you, aren't I? On your own, you'd have been out of here a long time ago, I know it. Anything I can do to make it easier for you, make it a little more comfortable..."

I said: "What a hell of an idea," and she said: "And what a hell of a time and place too." She sighed; and closed her eyes, and then opened them and looked at me and said: "You're a good man, Cabot Cain."

I said: "Yes. Not many of us left. Go to sleep, I won't be long."

I ran fast along the valley we were in, heading for a telltale patch where the bright blue was at its greenest; at close quarters, the color was not as bright as it had been at an angle and further away. And then, suddenly, the green-blue cupric sheen was all around me, covering the side of the cliff with a mellow, lovely patina. It was hard to the touch, hard, brittle—and cool.

All our troubles were over.

I found a stone, and hit the patina hard with it, just as Moses did with his rod, and when I'd chipped away an inch or so of copper-salt coating, the water started to trickle out, water that had been held here for centuries in the porous, honeycomb rock.

There's no trick to it—except to apply your knowledge of what it's all about; and knowledge is merely a matter of learning what other people have already found out for you; it's easy; I'm surprised more people don't take better advantage of seven thousand years of recorded experience.

Over the years, whatever water there is here, an inch or two of rainfall every seven or eight years perhaps, builds up in the rock wherever that rock happens to be sufficiently porous. It's like a giant sponge, or a honeycomb, and the water trickles slowly out of the sides, of course; but as it does so, it leaves a thin mineral deposit, like the caking on a filter, and in the course of time the deposit hardens and traps the water inside the honeycomb. As the years go by, the deposit creeps up the edge of the rock—it might take centuries—and at last the whole great honeycomb is sealed off, and it's full of water.

Moses knew this, and was remembered for it. The Bedouin know it, and accept it without wondering why. I knew it, and broke the coating now and it was going to save our lives.

I tasted the water in my cupped hand, and it was sweet and cool. I drank plenty of it, then guided the stream into the bottle till that was full too, and then ran back fast to where Constance was lying on the ground in the deep shade, her eyes closed. She opened them when she heard me coming, but otherwise she did not stir; she was too exhausted to move—until I held out the bottle to her. She looked at it dully for a moment, and then suddenly sat up straight and said: "My God, it's full!" She snatched it away from me and drank, and then looked at me in something like shame and said hesitantly: "Is there...is there more?"

I said: "Plenty. As much as we'll ever need, and more, lots more. I opened a hole in the rock, and the water will trickle out and go on trickling out for years, perhaps for centuries, before it seals itself up again for the next poor bastard passing by to help himself to. But don't overdo it, take it easy." She nodded, and drank deeply, ignoring my instructions and swirling the water around in her mouth before swallowing it. And when she'd taken half the bottle, she handed it back to me as though she still didn't believe it. I poured some over her head, and that's when she started to cry. And she couldn't stop.

I squatted there on the cool sand and waited, and when she'd finished she shook her head and said: "All I've got to cry about is a bottle of goddamn water."

She'd taken off my white jacket and rolled it up under her head to make the rock pillow more comfortable, and had been lying there long and naked and quite exciting, really, in spite of the grime and the sunburn. A soft pillow under her head, it was more important to her than anything else at this moment, a hand reaching out for comfort because comfort meant civilization and an escape from all this. I found it quite charming.

I said: "Put your jacket back on, and we'll go and get some more."

She climbed to her feet, unfolding herself, and I gave her the bottle to carry as another touch of that comfort she craved, and took her hand; and we hurried back to where Moses' rocks were. She slung the jacket over her shoulders, flapped her sandals, and hurried along beside me, all arms and legs and movement and sudden energy.

It's amazing what a difference some water inside you can make. Without it, you just slow down, imperceptibly at first, and then more and more, till you're not a moving man anymore, but just a shadow stretched out on the sand; and then, at last, a shell, dried out like an ancient mummy.

She walked quickly now, net panting or whining, not fighting the exhaustion because it just wasn't there anymore. And when the water came in sight, still trickling in a broad and gentle flow down the side of the rock face, she gasped and ran to it, and cupped her hands and drank deeply, and in a little while I took her by the shoulders and pressed her body tight against the rocks, letting the stream divert itself over her long, brutally-burned body. She fought the cold shock of it for a moment, but then stopped struggling and threw back her head and let it spill over her, and I said: "Hydrotherapy, it's what you need most now. Soak up the water from the outside." She nodded, shivering with the cold of it, and I said: "Rest here again, I'm going to find us a pool. Somewhere around here, there'll be a million-year-old waterhole, and we'll find it."

And I did, in less than five minutes. A little to one side, the cliff of the *wadi* curved itself into the ground, a fissure about fifty feet long and five or six feet high. And underneath it, there was the shimmering dark blue of cold water, deep in the shadow, barely visible from outside unless you knew where to look, a great wide pool in an overhanging cave. Somewhere else, the coating on those rocks, had cracked, or perhaps the water had filtered itself in the honeycomb till it was clear and free from the deposits which would form the sealant. And for how many centuries—who could tell?—it had been gathering here under the overhang. I tasted the water and found it sweet and fresh—with all that copper around it couldn't be anything else!—and I ran back and fetched Constance, and when I stripped off my clothes and hid them carefully—no good losing all sense of the danger now that we'd temporarily eluded it!—and dived in, diving down deep, deep, and deeper, I found that even though my eardrums were bursting I couldn't touch bottom. And it was so cold that I came up shivering.

Constance was splashing around at the edge of the pool, and she said: "My feet are freezing."

I told her: "Down deep, it's like ice. A million years, and the sun has never touched this pool, not once." I wondered if anyone knew of its existence, and thought it quite possible that no one did. In a land so dry that a man will kill for a goatskin full of brackish water, a Paradise like this—but a Paradise devoid of its garden—could go unnoticed for centuries. We were in the Rub al Khali; nobody ever passed this way.

We sat there, lounged there, swam there, filling our bellies and our pores with water, water that no one, in the whole of recorded history had ever seen or drunk, remembering the baking, blistering sun up there and knowing, even as we shivered down here, that sooner or later we'd have to face it once more.

To go where? It didn't matter for the moment. We were alone in an empty world, two stark-naked bodies rehydrating themselves and wondering what the hell would come next.

We trod water for a while, luxuriating in the silence, and Constance said at last, a trifle peevishly: "I suppose you wouldn't have anything to eat, would you?"

"Nope."

"No, I didn't really suppose you would. How long do we have to wait here?"

"You mean you'd rather be up there in the sun?"

She shivered. "God forbid." She looked at me sideways out of those pale blue eyes that seemed bleached out: "We *are* waiting for something, aren't we? Nobody in his right mind would sit around a godforsaken place like this all day doing absolutely nothing unless... Well, unless he had *something* tucked away up his sleeve."

I said: "Can you think of anything better to do? A brisk run across the sand dunes up there?" I didn't want to raise her hopes by telling her there was a small chance that...

She said: "And how long before that bastard finds his way down here?"

"Fellawi? There's no real reason why he should. Once we left the soft sand, there were no tracks for him to follow, even if he'd venture into the Rub, which I doubt. He might, of course, in which case we'll have trouble on our hands. But better to face trouble here, than out there. Out there, however he crossed the dunes, he'll be as close to exhaustion as a Bedouin can get, whereas we're fresh, and full of water, and fighting fit."

"So you're going to fight off four men armed with rifles with...with what?"

I said: "You've got a point there."

In the silence that followed we both, I think, thought about our predicament for a while. There was a faraway look in Constance's eyes, as though...

And then, she heard the slight sound the same moment I did. I saw her face go tight with sudden fear, I put a finger to my lips and jerked my head towards the interior of the cave, and slid along the water, dragging her by the wrist rather than letting her swim and make the noise she was sure to make, deep into the darkest overhang of the cave, the great dark curve of blue-grey granite that dipped almost to the water's edge. Only the edge of the pool was visible from the *wadi* outside, and here, deep in the cave, that edge was two hundred and fifty feet away from us, a broad gash of bright light that gave the water a pale blue, phosphorescent sheen that rippled with the movements we had made. We were in a long, low tunnel of darkness, lit by an eerie light that somehow seemed to tell the story of pre-history, the light dancing and shimmering around us, as though Hell were lit by neon signs, and the reflection of them was creeping up and brightening our strange and silent world.

I found an arm-hold and hung on to it, and held Constance tight against me with the other arm round her waist, pulling her cold body tight into mine and feeling her trembling. It was so cold and dark and silent in here that we might have been on another planet, with just the ghostly luminescence of the water around us.

We waited.

The sound had gone; or rather, had not come again. A water lizard splashed into the water close beside me, and I heard Constance gasp. It leaped onto the rock I was holding on to, and stared at me, quite unafraid. So there was life here, after all. But it had never seen man, or perhaps anything but its own kind, and there was no fear there at all as I reached out and grabbed it. It struggled wetly in my hand for a moment, and then kept still, its beady eyes questing, wondering, searching. I gestured to Constance to stay where she was, and I swam silently up to the entrance again, and tossed the little lizard out onto the rocks.

I heard it land with a soft thud, and saw it stand there for a moment, and then dash to the shelter of a small piece of sandstone, pressing itself underneath and peering out suspiciously, not sure that this intrusion of its lonely world was a healthy thing at all.

I heard Constance moving back there, and when I looked round, frowning, she was swimming slowly in, her white breasts, pink-tipped, picking up the strange glow of the water. I signaled her to go back, but I could see from the look in her eyes that she was too scared to stay far away from me. I signaled again, and she turned to one side and moved under the lee of the granite, out of my sight. I fancied I heard her scrambling onto a ledge, and wondered if the cave would magnify the sound or muffle it.

The lizard was still there. It poked out its head a bit more, and just stood there, peering at something that had attracted its attention.

And then, *he* moved.

There he was, moving in and staring down at the lizard that stared back up at him. He grunted, and began to turn around, and I thought that if only as a matter of principle I'd better get a jibe in first before he thought of something witty to say.

I said: "Well, I didn't really expect you to fall for that."

He turned and squinted at me, tall and slim and immensely elegant even here. Even here, dressed in a neat and well-made suit with hardly a crease in it, with a clean white shirt and a Charvet tie from the Place Vendome in Paris. My old friend Fenrek, Colonel Matthias Fenrek, head of Interpol's Department B7, and a long way from the hedonistic luxury of his Bois de Boulogne apartment.

He said affably: "Well, so it was you after all. I rather hoped it might be." It was as casual as though we'd happened to bump into each other on a stroll down the Boulevard de la Madeleine, and it was time for a cup of *filtre*; a little affectation of Fenrek's, never to lose his cool.

I said: "Nice to see you. How did you find this place?"

He shrugged: "The same way you did, apparently. I saw the copper sulfate on the rocks from the air, and knowing your quite extraordinary talent for hydromancy, I assumed that you'd be heading here too. I landed on the desert just this side of the dunes, and wandered over. Four miles, and it's *very* hot up there. How's the water?"

"Fine, come on in."

"Potable?" Anyone else but Fenrek would have said *drinkable*, and that's not just because he's a Hungarian, either.

I said: "Both potable and delicious."

"Good." He knelt down carefully on one knee, scooped up some water in his hand, and drank. He stood up then, and began stripping off his clothes, folding them neatly and putting them down on a rock close by, paying great attention to the neatness. He said: "There were some horsemen chasing you, all very picturesque and romantic. Did I recognize one of them as Ahmed Fellawi?"

"You did indeed. What happened to them?"

"From the air, it looked as though they were having trouble in the dunes. They turned back. The sand's terribly soft just there, and they may have gone back to get camels."

"Or perhaps you scared them off in your flying machine."

"Ahmed Fellawi? He's a cultivated man, my dear fellow, owns two or three planes of his own. He's not likely to be scared off by a Piper Cub."

"No, perhaps not. Unless he was worried you were armed."

I watched him test the water with the tip of his foot, saw his eyebrows go up at the cold of it. He said: "Strange how the skin always dries out faster than the belly. I've never been really thirsty before, and the craving is not to drink, it's to soak."

"After four miles? You're out of training."

"Yes, perhaps I am."

He was still testing the temperature of the water, reveling in the enjoyment and trying to prolong the expectation; anyone but a Hungarian would have been up to his neck in it by now, but not Fenrek, he'd want to prolong the savoring of it, heighten the expectation. Tall and straight, and contriving somehow to keep his elegance and poise without a stitch of clothing on him, he stood there on one foot, delicately testing, and I said casually:

"I've got a lady tucked away in the cave back there. She was afraid you might have been Fellawi."

"A lady? Oh my God." He slipped quickly into the water and stared at me, and I said: "Don't worry, she doesn't have a stitch on either. In fact, she doesn't even have any clothes. She crossed twenty miles of the Rub al Khali, in fourteen hours, dressed only in a floppy pair of men's sandals and my Brooks Brothers jacket."

He said again: "My God!"

I turned and called to Constance, and in a moment she was gliding towards us, blinking her eyes at the light after the dimness of the cave, her long fair hair streaming behind her, and her skin smooth and shining with all the red dust gone from it. She reached out and grabbed my arm to steady herself, and I said: "My old friend Colonel Fenrek, my new friend Constance Delorme."

It was good to see Fenrek's discomfort. It wasn't often he had difficulty holding on to his poise, and here, with the three of us treading water without a thread of clothing between us, that poise was almost—but not quite— disappearing. He inclined his head gravely and said: "Miss Delorme." He was holding on tight to his dignity, trying hard not to lower his eyes. He was always a man for the ladies, and Constance, even with the sunburn blistering her skin, was very good indeed to look at.

She said: "How in hell did anyone manage to turn up in this Godforsaken place? *Anyone?*"

Fenrek said, smiling, turning on the charm for her: "A plane, Miss Delorme, just a few miles away from here. Ready to serve you as soon as you're up to it."

She heaved herself out of the water with one quick movement, the movement of a young athlete, and stood there on the grey-blue rocks beside us. She said: "I'm up to anything, Colonel Fenrek."

I pulled myself out after her, sauntered over to where my clothes were hidden, tossed her the jacket, then slipped into the rest of them. When she had my coat on, and I was half-dressed, Fenrek said firmly: "Would you be kind enough, Miss Delorme?"

She grimaced and looked away while he climbed quickly out and got dressed. Even over his wet-through body, taut and muscular and efficient, far trimmer than you'd expect in a man fifty years old, his clothes hung on him neatly and properly; he even knotted his Charvet tie just so, and when he was ready, he said, smiling: "Well, shall we go? It's not very far, really."

We could have been on a picnic. We walked slowly and comfortably along the deep *wadi* for three and a half miles, climbed up the steep side again into the furnace that was above us—but noticeably cooler now, with the sun low down in the sky; soon, it would be cold even here—and struggled over the lava beds for another half a mile. The plane was there, just where Fenrek had left it, and the smell of it was alarming.

I stopped first—I've a good sense of smell—and Fenrek looked at it and frowned, and wrinkled his delicate nose, and when he started forward I said urgently: "No, wait!"

He looked at me and said softly: "There was a guard on it, the pilot..."

I said: "Wait here, I'll take a look." There was no cover of any sort, just red lava cooling off under the yellow sun. That terrible, frightening look had come into Constance's eyes again, and the sweat was pouring from her; she'd absorbed too much of that cool water.

Fenrek said: "My responsibility, Cain, stay with Miss Delorme."

He ran lightly over the ground to the plane, and we just stood there like idiots in full range of any gun that might be trained on us there. The flat little Beretta .32 he always carried, not much more than a toy except that he was deadly with it, was in his hand, but he put it away when he reappeared from the plane's cockpit and waved us over.

There was a great pink stain on the sand where the long-range fuel tanks had been drained, and he said grimly: "The pilot's gone."

I said: "Better gone than a dead body here. One of your men?"

"No, a charter from Assab, where I started catching up with

you."

We stood around and felt sorry for ourselves for a moment or two; the only easy way out of this damned desert had turned out to be a pile of useless machinery. Stalemate.

I said: "We need a minimum of two gallons of water to reach the coast. It's thirty miles to the nearest beach, if we head southeast."

Fenrek said: "And from there?"

I shrugged. "Sooner or later, even out here, we'll find a boat if we look hard enough."

"Yes. One of Ahmed Fellawi's."

"That's a chance we'll have to take."

"There's twenty gallons of water in the plane."

I said: "I'll take a bet there's not." He was courteous enough to look embarrassed; he should have checked.

We went on board and looked, and the tank had been drained dry; so had the little auxiliary tank, two gallons, bolted under the pilot's seat. It took us two minutes to unfasten it and fix it up with carrying-straps to go across my shoulders, and Fenrek said, hoping I'd refuse: "You're the athlete, but you've had a bit of a trying time, would you rather I went?"

I said: "Eight miles there and back, and I need the exercise, I'm getting flabby."

He looked pained, and agreed at once.

I started off back to the *wadi* where the water hole was, running fast and easily, and then scurried down to the bottom, filled the tank with water, hoisted it by its twin straps onto my back, and ran with it back to the plane; the whole thing took sixty-eight minutes by my watch, which wasn't bad, considering I had a twenty-pound weight on my back; in fact, I was rather pleased about it.

Fenrek was watching to see if I sounded out of breath, and I'm happy to say I wasn't. I said: "Two gallons, we can live for two weeks on it if we have to."

They'd spent the time I was away searching the plane for anything we might need on the trek. Fenrek had come up with an old blanket—the nights are very cold in the desert—and Constance, triumphantly, showed me a bar of chocolate, all melted and messy, she'd found on the floor somewhere. She said: "It all ought to be mine, because you're both gentlemen, but I'm going to share it anyway, you see what a friendly chick I am?"

We ate our little pieces of chocolate in silence, and set off for the shoreline.

The sun was turning from gold-red to pale-yellow, lighting the landscape with a brilliant, lovely sheen. The earth was a friendly place again, where kings had once ruled and built great cities, where the sand had once sprouted with fields of millet and corn and barley, where the great stone dams that King Seneferu built could still be seen if you were lucky enough to stumble on their outlines under the always encroaching sand, the blown sand that had put an end to the once great civilization that had flourished here.

Fenrek said: "We'll swing round a little to the east, Not too much, just a little."

"Oh? Why?"

He said briefly: "It's best." He wanted to keep something up his sleeve too. We had a long way to go, and within the hour it would be dark and quite cold. But we were headed for the sea, and when you're lost, it's always the sea that holds out promise of something at the other end of it.

That's the way it's been ever since primitive man first bound together bundles of reeds, and floated himself across the waters that were no longer to be a barrier between him and a better place to be.

CHAPTER 2

From the beginning, it had been difficult, sitting in my comfortable house in San Francisco, to realize that in these remote and hostile deserts—a long way in time and place from the Bay!—there are still slave markets to be found if you know where to look for them.

Slavery is still a way of life in some parts of the vast Arabian Peninsula, where the rule of the tribal Sheikhs is autocratic to a degree that makes the law of the Roman Emperors, by comparison, benign and democratic; they, at least, had a Senate to keep them in check, sort of. Although—let it be said at once—the slavery today is not as vicious a thing as it used to be; the slaves are well cared for, if only because they are so expensive to replace, and for the most part, they're fairly happy. I have seen slaves who didn't *want* to be freed, didn't want to be sent out into a hostile world to make decisions that had always been made for them, to fend for themselves when they'd previously always been fed, and housed, and kept busy.

It's perfectly understandable; how can a man who's always been told what to do and when to do it suddenly accustom himself to the rat race the world has now become?

Of course, knowing where these markets are is one thing; and actually seeing them is another. Get within a hundred yards of any of the three big markets in Mecca, and an Unbeliever's life is in immediate danger. If you're lucky—or unlucky—enough to see one of the caravans that cross the deserts by night, don't make the mistake of stopping to look too hard, because that'll be the last mistake you'll ever make. And if you inquire of the Governments concerned, you'll be met with a bland and polite denial—and you'll be watched thereafter until you're on the plane back to more enlightened parts, watched by a small group whose instructions are to take whatever steps might be necessary to see that you don't get too close, or learn to much, or even suspect.

I lost a good friend like that once. Harry Slovak, who'd made a deal with Life Magazine for a series of articles; he'd been foolish enough to strap a tiny Tessina camera to his wrist when his contact, heavily bribed but not as discreet as he should have been, smuggled him into the infamous market in Rassar, in what is still called, even today, the "Neutral Territory", to the north of the Rub; neutral because no one, quite literally, claims it as national ground. He went in, Harry, dressed as a woman, heavy black veil and all. Someone had talked, and before he could shoot his first picture, he was lying on the ground with a dagger in his back, and the Tessina was gone. That was the end of the series, and the end of Harry too.

None the less, there are markets in Brahimi Oasis, in which the slaves are habitually still kept in fetters; in Riyadh; in Suakin (specializing in young girls who have just reached the age of puberty); in Jedda and Medina, both for general merchandise, mostly men and boys; in Raifah, where a road has been specially built to accommodate the camels and trucks that carry the slaves there; in Dauga, women and girls only; and in Mecca itself, where there are no less than four markets functioning constantly, and five or six others that spring up from time to time.

At the other end of the main routes, in the High Volta, Niger and Timbuktu, there are a total of eight markets, mostly run on a wholesale basis; and one in Jebel Marra in the southwestern Sudan which is run as a school for concubines, black girls only, since many of the desert Arabs like the coolness of the black girls' skin in the hot weather; here, the children begin their training at the age of seven or eight, and are sold three years later to the caravans that pass through on their way to Arabia.

The main supply lines, as delineated by the Abolitionists' Conference of 1967, run from El Obeid in Kordofan across the Kassala Desert to the Red Sea and Mecca; from Bahr el Ghazal in the Upper Sudan across Lake Rudolph and the northwest Frontier area of Kenya and Somalia, up into the Mijertein, and across the Gulf of Aden to the southeast shores of Oman; and the longest, most prolific, and most tragic route of all—from the Upper Volta across the huge and empty deserts that lie to the north of Nigeria, over the barren, burned-out wastes of Chad, clear across Central Sudan (it's in the Sudan that replacements are taken for those who have died on the way, usually about thirty percent), to the staging area at the point where the Bahr el Azraq, the Blue Nile, crosses the Ethiopian border, and on by either of two routes—the northern to the Red Sea, or the dangerous dash across the mountains of Ethiopia and Eritrea, and across the water again to the Yemen. In all, this twin route is nearly eighteen hundred miles long and takes a little over three months. It's the oldest and most infamous of all the routes; if you fly over the area, you can pick out great stretches where a definite trail can clearly be seen from the air, white and shining; the white is bleached bones, dried out by the hot suns of more than four hundred years of human tragedy.

Nearly forty years ago, in 1923, the Emperor Haile Selassie of Ethiopia—he was the Regent, Ras Tafari then—had outlawed slavery and his Army was at constant war with the slavers; and because of this, the caravans preferred to use the longer route, even though it meant crossing the harsh mountains and dust-dry deserts of Kassala. But the destination was always the same, in this part of the world at least; the caravans, like arrows, were pointed at the great Arabian Peninsula; and once they hit the Red Sea, they were almost home.

There were men and there were women, and there were children too. The men to work in the date plantations, to dig the fields and to carry water; the women to fill the harems, or work the fields if they were too old for this; and the children to grow up to whatever fate their masters decreed for them. They came from Nigeria, from the Congo, from the Sudan and from Somalia. Once in a while, very infrequently, they came from the shores of the Mediterranean.

And now, they were coming from America. That was when Fenrek called on me for help.

We'd covered half of the thirty miles, and it was time to sit down and let Constance rest her poor bloody feet; in spite of the sandals, they were badly lacerated. She wrapped the blanket tight around her against the cold of the night, and sat there and shivered. She said miserably: "My God, all this brouhaha is on my account, and you know something? I was better off in that goddamn caravan. At least I had enough to eat. My God, they roasted the hump of a dead camel one day, have you ever eaten camel hump? Next to whale blubber and hamburger, it's the most disgusting thing there is."

They'd have fed her well on the caravan; she was a prized piece of cargo, and the potentates of Arabia like their women plump. One of them at least, Sheikh Abdul Karani bin Suleiman of the Ahmad Sharanis, once went so far as to offer to pay by the pound for the girls the slavers brought him.

Fenrek had been waiting for me to tell him what had been happening while he'd been sitting around his H.Q. in Paris, and I thought that now we were giving Constance (and him, though he wouldn't admit it) a chance to rest up, it might be a good time to put it all into perspective.

I said: "She left her plane in Khartoum, and I found out that she was last seen heading east on the road to Es Sufeiya, driven by an Arab whose name nobody seemed to know, in a beat-up old Buick taxi. It was another stewardess who saw her, wondering where she was off to, and with whom, and all I could get out of her was that the Arab was desperately handsome, black eyes, black curly hair, little black moustache, and that's a description that might fit almost any Arab of Fellawi's type. But it was the startling good looks that intrigued me— she made quite a point of it."

Fenrek was frowning darkly, groping for the map at the back of his mind; this wasn't really his territory. He said: "Es Sufeiya, isn't that the road that runs through Ethiopia, the road to Asmara? Surely they must know there's an Army drive going there now? Or would they know that? Maybe not. So you turned south, no doubt, where the road branches off to Reira, while they went on east to Kassala."

As usual, he was a guess ahead of me and getting it wrong. I said gently: "There's a small scale war going on around Kassala now, it would have been too risky for them. They'd have had to go south." In this part of the world, the roads—and they're only dirt tracks—are very few; and a Buick, off the road, would be in deep trouble. I said: "I bought myself an old military jeep for two thousand dollars, four-wheel drive and the tires worn smooth, which is the only kind of tire you want in soft sand. I struck off into the desert, bypassed Reira, where their scouts would have undoubtedly been waiting for anyone following them, and drove on to Gedaref, where the railway crosses the road. I realized that if they intended to cross the Red Sea—and where else would they be headed?—then they'd throw off pursuit, or try to, by moving in the wrong direction till they were sure it was thrown off."

He hated every minute of it. "The railway? You mean it's still functioning?"

"Why not? Rebels all over, and whoever holds the railway line for the moment is bound to keep it operating. It goes to Dilling, right in the middle of nowhere, twice a week to pick up cotton, takes it to the coast, goes back for more three days later."

He said sourly: "And some grubby little boot-black saw a kidnapped American girl pet on the train and head for Dilling, I don't believe it."

"Neither did I when I was told precisely that. Obviously sure they were now in the clear, they'd have gone in the opposite direction, for Port Sudan."

He thought about that for a while. A cool, faint breeze was blowing off the distant sea now, and the air was fresh and crisp. He said at last, uncertain: "Gedaref is on the oldest of all the slave routes, and the whole town would have a long history of, shall I say, co-operation with the slavers? *Fear* of them, if you like. So if you found someone willing to give you information on something they'd normally keep very silent about, there's at least a chance that he was telling the truth."

"No. Wrong information is always more successful than no information at all. He'd have been tipped off to point me in the wrong direction. If he'd clammed up, I'd have kept on trying, and I might have succeeded elsewhere. Ergo, I was pointed at Dilling. And ergo once again, I went in the opposite direction, driving off towards Dilling, of course, to convince them I'd swallowed the story, and then swinging round through the desert and heading for Port Sudan."

"More than four hundred miles. You must have known you'd

never make it, not through that sort of country."

"Ah, but I did. And I was right, as usual. They'd been seen at the checkpoint on the southern road, the one that goes to Suakin. Suakin, the old slavers' port itself."

He was getting terribly impatient. He said, worrying about it: "The checkpoint? If it was she, why the devil didn't she simply yell for help? She must have known that even if Fellawi had a gun in her ribs, he wouldn't dare to use it, not right outside a police post!"

"Yes, that's very interesting, isn't it? Why *didn't* she yell for help? An intriguing question, and an even more intriguing answer." He waited for me to tell him, but I thought I'd keep him guessing; Interpol are supposed to know about all the little human foibles. I said: "So—I abandoned the jeep and took a charter plane to Suakin, and I regret to say that they were still ahead of me. The port officer told me that a dhow had left for Jedda only two hours earlier, on the morning tide, loaded with bananas, olive oil and passengers, under the command of one Captain Tahari, a Somali from Mogadishu."

Now, at last, he sat up and took notice. He said, startled: "Hassan Tahari?"

"None other. The man we all know about."

And indeed we did. Tahari was an old, old man of immense vitality, a notorious slaver, a man who'd been reported dead four or five times; the last time was when, allegedly, he'd been marooned by his crew—he always treated them abominably—on one of the tiny islands in the Red Sea. Island? It was no more than a sandbar, and only twenty miles from shore, but it was the place where Tahari himself had marooned his own crew a few months earlier, the result of a squabble about who should get paid for what. There'd been a report to Interpol, who had long been interested in the Captain's activities, that a patrol boat from Yemen had found his body there—or what was left of it after the crabs had finished with it.

And now, Tahari had surfaced again, indestructible, wily, full of evil.

Fenrek sighed. "We'll never get rid of that man! Did you find out where he was headed?"

I couldn't help snorting at him. "How could I? As far as his official papers were concerned, he was headed for Jedda, but the bazaar gossip was that a delivery of slaves was being affected at Abu Raf, three hundred miles south of Jedda. It had to be the same one. If, indeed, Tahari's bananas were really the slaves he'd brought from the Sudan, including the young American from Khartoum."

Fenrek said patiently: "If, if, if! And suppose he had no intention at all of landing at Abu Rafa? Suppose he had already decided to change his mind once he was at sea?"

"The thought did occur to me, of course."

"And how come we're sitting in the middle of the Rub al Khali if our quarry is five hundred miles away on the coast?"

"*Was*, not *is*. It seemed to me that only one thing was certain. Tahari was taking his catch to one of the Sheikhdoms somewhere on the Arabian Peninsula..."

"All seven hundred and twenty thousand square miles of it."

"Not quite." Fenrek had forgotten something, they don't often do that sort of thing at Interpol, but this was a long, long way from Fenrek's beat; my own beat is the world, and even this sorry desert was part of it. I said: "The southern part only, the southern quarter even. Had he been going further north, he'd have waited another six weeks till the monsoon winds changed; in a dhow, he's dependent on the wind. And if he was going north, he'd have waited. Ergo, he's going south, and south of his port of embarkation there's not much of the Peninsula except the Rub al Khali. Now..."

I took a long breath, and Fenrek took advantage of it to say, grudgingly: "I'd forgotten about the monsoon. Tell the truth, I didn't know the change of direction was so imminent."

"Twelfth to the fifteenth of next month, the wind changes abruptly from south to north, and all the dhows that came south down the Red Sea with rugs from Persia, are heading north again, with bananas and skins."

"All right, all right, I don't need a lesson in geography. And we call it Iran nowadays, not Persia." I grunted; I prefer the old names.

Constance lay rolled up in her blanket on the sand, catching up on her sleep; she deserved it, poor dear. Her feet were sticking out, and there was blood on them. It's amazing how much a woman can put up with if she sets her mind to it, and I couldn't help admiring her fortitude.

Fenrek thought for a while and said: "And so...somewhere, you must have intercepted the caravan, or you wouldn't have found her." He looked at Constance's still body and echoed my thoughts: "She's had a lot to put up with, hasn't she?"

I said: "Yes, she's had a lot to put up with as a result of her own damn foolishness, and yes, I intercepted the caravan. It was a question not only of finding where they were going, but of getting ahead of them. So I joined a spice caravan, telling them I was an archeologist, and headed south. I assumed that even in Arabia a slave caravan would still have to travel only by night, a very slow business, and hide out during the day. I expected to get almost a week's trek in front of them. And I did. I went to Khadir Oasis, the last water hole before five hundred miles of desert whichever way they were going. North, east, south or west, if they landed in the southern part of the Peninsula and were headed inland, they had to pass through Khadir. So, I went there."

Fenrek said politely: "Most people who try to intercept the slave caravans finish up dead. How come you didn't? And I must say you had colossal luck if you really did find them there. Your whole argument is terribly tenuous."

"Just dealing in likelihoods, they're always very rewarding. And I wanted to see Khadir anyway, it's a place of immense fascination if you know your history. As an archeologist, I found a great deal to do to pass the time while I was waiting. You know how I hate to be idle."

He said: "Khadir; that's on the border of Arabia and Yemen, isn't it? And aren't the Yemenis and the Arabians border skirmishing again?"

"Yes to both questions. They grow excellent dates in Khadir, did you know that? They have the Zahidi, the Halawy, both of which really belong in Iraq, as well as the Deglet Noor and the Medjool. Over a thousand trees and only a few dozen families living there, plus, of course, the Sheikh's Guard on the water. The Guard, incidentally, is with the slavers, did you know that too?"

Fenrek: sighed. "The Guard is there to report on the passing of any caravans, slavers or otherwise, and to see that the water is not depleted in the dry season. And slavery is more or less legal in Arabia, as you must know."

I said: "More or less is the key phrase. Officially, it's not tolerated, because ninety-three percent of the Sheikhdoms' national revenue comes from oil, which means the West. And to avoid offending the West, slavery is technically outlawed, even though the whole world knows it's openly encouraged."

"And when the slavers' caravan arrived," Fenrek said sarcastically, "they didn't worry about your presence there in the least." He snorted. "It says in all the books that the man who sees a slavers' caravan on the march has seen his last sight on earth except for the knife that cuts his throat."

"Well, it wasn't exactly easy. I had a certain amount of lying to do. I had to set up a rather complicated cover. Do you, by chance, know about Siddakkus?"

Fenrek's impatience was beginning to show again. "I've read my history, for God's sake. Siddakkus died two thousand years ago, so what the hell does he have to do with this?"

"A little more than twenty-two hundred years ago, actually. But he left a few pegs in the desert for me to hang my hat on." It's impossible to goad Fenrek with enigma; he just sits there and waits, and all your pearls are wasted.

So I told him what happened at Khadir.

To anyone who moves more than a hundred miles from his own home town, in Arabia, every solitary traveler is an archeologist.

It's such a deserted area, with such an infinitely rich history in its past that Frenchmen, Germans, Swiss, Americans, and mad-dog Englishmen are forever pottering about looking for that past and the wealth and fame that go with it. Meet a lone stranger in his solitary tent, a million miles from anywhere, and the chances are—if he's not an Arab; the Arabs have more sense—that he's been sent there, God knows how many years ago, by one Archeological Institute or another, to find a little piece of the jigsaw that is history: a burial mound, the foundations of a palace, the dry-wall dams and sluices that once made this desert an agricultural center of enormous importance. They sit in their little white tents, and spend their days brushing delicately at the sand and turning up tiny shards of pottery, or pieces of mosaic, or once in a while a gold or silver coin, and they are piecing together the tapestry of the world's oldest civilization.

And there was enough around Khadir, neglected, unsought, unfound, to satisfy any casual observer that this was why I had come here.

Khadir itself was less than I'd expected. There were several thousand excellent date palms, three large water holes, one of them very deep, and a collection of fifty or sixty small huts, mostly made of whitewashed clay and covered with brown palm fronds. There were chickens and goats, and a few camels, and not much else except a solid stone building that housed the Sultan's Guard—fifty men under the command of a certain Lieutenant Osman. Osman was fat, gross and servile, and a nasty piece of work; but he was the man who had to become my friend. I went to see him.

His barefoot, ragged soldiers kept me waiting, because their officer was sleeping, but as soon as Osman awoke he was out there in the courtyard, staring at me in disbelief, still rubbing the sleep out of his eyes. He was dressed in a singlet and khaki uniform trousers, his skin white and soft and flabby. He stared for only a moment, and then abruptly turned on his heel and went back into the building without a word. I waited, understanding; first impressions are important to the Arabs, and he appeared again a moment later, properly dressed in his uniform with all his medals up, and said brusquely: "Well, what is it? I'm a very busy man."

He spoke crude French, though I'd addressed the soldiers, when I asked to see him, in Arabic. It was a good sign. *Any* contact with a foreigner, in these parts, can be usually profitable, in one way or another, and he didn't want his soldiers in too soon on any deal that might be cooking. Was I a merchant come to buy dates, perhaps? Why else would I be here?

The time to switch languages would come later. I said, pleasantly enough: "My name's Cabot Cain, and I bring you salaams from General Hishara in Riyadh."

His eyes almost popped out of his head. I'd never met the famous Commander of all the Border Armies, and if he knew I was in his territory without permission, he'd have had my guts. I was also pretty sure that so eminent a man as the General would hardly be in close contact with an obscure Lieutenant out in what could only be a punishment station, where unimportant officers were sent to be conveniently forgotten.

Osman automatically straightened his tie and stood a trifle taller. He was about to make some fulsome remark, but thought better of it, and said instead: "I am surprised, Monsieur Cain, that His Excellency the General even remembers me."

I said brutally: "Oh, he doesn't. But when I told him I was going to Khadir, he said: 'Ah, there must be an officer there, tell him you have my blessing. And, of course, give him mine.'"

He was wondering whether to believe me or not, and not daring to doubt. And he wouldn't dare, either, to get on the radio—if they had one—to check. But to make it easier for him, I spoke Arabic instead, and said easily: "The General and I are old friends. When he addressed the United Nations three years ago, I was his host in Washington. You know, of course, of his Excellency's interest in archeology. That happens to be my business too."

The light dawned. "Ah, yes, an archeologist. And how may I help you, *ya Pasha?*"

Ya Pasha... It's a good deal better than sir and not quite as elevated as my lord. So it was time to put myself on his level, once and for all, and I therefore called him *habibi*, my friend. "*Ya habibi*, I hope there is a great deal you can do for me. And perhaps there is a great deal I can do for you too." I threw a glance at the soldiers who were standing around gawking at my size, and Osman got the point and said hastily:

"But we cannot talk here in the sun, *ya Pasha*. Inside, it is so much cooler. And perhaps some coffee?"

"You are most kind."

We went inside the big, square building, its interior plastered with mud and whitewashed, and found Osman's office, and sat there on hard wooden chairs while a small boy, not much more than ten years old, made coffee for us at the brazier that stood in one corner of the room. He squatted on the ground on flat feet, his bony legs sticking up under his thin grey gown, and poured a cupped handful of pounded coffee into the *jezveh*, balanced it on the little fire, put his hands to his head, stared at the pot, and waited.

I said to Osman politely: "You have a good office, Lieutenant. One sees your importance."

He smiled deprecatingly: "A small force under my command, but perhaps, in time, the General will see fit to give me a larger command."

"I'm sure he will. Your family are well, I trust?"

"Thank God. And yours?"

"Thank God. And your health is good?"

"Thank God. Your health?"

"Thank God. And the world is good to you?"

"Thank God. And to you too?"

"If it is good to you, then it is good to me."

"Ah, thank God. By God, thank God."

We thanked God a dozen more times, saying *hami'd el Allah* over and over to show what civilized people we both were, and then the coffee was ready, bubbling up three times as the boy took the pot off the white ashes and held it gently back there for a moment or two, and then brought it to us in tiny eggshell cups, with a cardamom seed dropped in each of them. We sipped noisily, slurping up the strong, delicious syrup through our lips to show that we were not only civilized but cultured as well. And when we'd drunk three cups, we put them back on the tray upside down, and Lieutenant Osman settled back at his desk and said: "And now, *ya Pasha*, tell me about His Excellency General Hishara, I trust he is still winning all his battles?"

Ha! He'd made up his mind that he would have to find out from me if my credentials were legitimate, rather than risk the wrath of that terrible man by getting in touch and finding out at the source. And it made sense; the General was not a man to trifle with.

He was a legend in these parts, Hishara, and I hoped that one day I'd get the chance to meet him. Not only was he a fine, if unconventional, desert soldier, but he was also Arabia's leading poet; I once translated into Greek one of his immensely complicated epic poems on the defeat of the Sabaean Armies by Aelius Gallus in the year 24 B.C. He was a major linguist himself, and had written a standard reference work on desert warfare, with particular reference to horses and camels. It was said of him that when the Arab Command in

Riyadh had sent eleven tanks and twenty-four armored personnel carriers to help him in his battles against the Yemenis, he had scornfully sent them back because, he said, the stench of them polluted the desert air and annoyed his beloved horses. In his youth, he'd played polo for the U.S. team—he was at Harvard then—that beat the British in 1939. He was considered to be one of the greatest horsemen in the world. And his exploits with women were legendary.

I said: "He's knocking the hell out of the Yemenis, as always. He's back on the border now somewhere, so we can expect another glorious victory very soon."

Osman was beaming; there's nothing an Arab likes better than victory over another Arab. He said: "And in what way may I be of service to you? My house is yours, my strength is yours, everything I own, little though it is, is yours."

I said: "All I need really...I'm looking for traces of a fortress that was reputedly built here by one of Alexander's Captains. Alexander the Great."

"Ah yes, of course. We call him Iskander here."

"Yes, I know that. Do you know about Nearchus?"

"Of course, I am a man of great erudition." He didn't sound too sure on either count.

I said: "Nearchus was the man Iskander sent to circumnavigate this Peninsula, from the mouth of the Euphrates, through the Gulf of Aden, and up the Red Sea to the Gulf of Suez. An almost impossible feat under sail, as you probably realize."

"Yes, of course, the monsoons."

I wondered how much he really knew of his local history. He was a nomad, really, put down in a desert oasis and given a small and insignificant command. In spite of the military veneer (and in spite of the fat he'd accumulated as a result of it) he was still a nomad, a Bedouin. And to the Bedouin, history is legend, and the legends are told—sometimes with remarkable historical accuracy—by the itinerant troubadours who still wander from camp to camp across the impossibly empty spaces that the nomads call their home. They keep the legends alive, and the legends are the history that has been passed on for thousands of years by the soldiers, the priests, and the merchants who have driven east from the Mediterranean and south from Asia Minor since recorded history began.

Two thousand years ago, the land between the Tigris and the Euphrates was the center of the world; and even then, the desert that lay to the south, league after countless league of nothing but sand, was a barrier that intrigued the minds of the adventurous. It was Ptolemy—later to become Pharaoh of Egypt but at that time serving with Alexander—who planted the seed in the fertile mind of Nearchus, Alexander's Admiral, a seed that suggested there might be an alternate route to Ethiopia, "the land of the sunburned people", through the Arabian Peninsula, if a man could only survive its rigors. And one of Nearchus' Captains, a tough and wily adventurer named Siddakkus, set off from what is now Kuwait on the Persian Gulf, straight south into the desert, with a party of eight hundred soldiers and a baggage train of two hundred and thirty camels.

They were lucky. Struggling over the soft sand, in fearsome heat, they made less than ten miles a day; Alexander's marching quota had always called for fifty. And by the grace of whatever gods they worshipped, they hit the oasis that today has become Riyadh, after forty-seven days, their water almost gone, and even their camels dying. Today, Riyadh is one of the great desert centers (an oasis, like Las Vegas, in the middle of nothing) with a population of some sixty thousand or so; but in those times, it was merely a water hole fiercely held against all comers by a small tribe of Bedouin, who decimated the exhausted explorers, and drove the handful of survivors—Siddakkus, among them—south into the Rub al Khali to certain death.

Certain, that is, for men who were not built like these.

Incredibly, forty of them reached Khadir a hundred and fifty days later, with not an ounce of water among them; no one knows to this day how they did it. They fought a pitched battle with the nomads there, took the nomads' women and built themselves a fortress. They survived, and they began to prey on the caravans that came to the water hole—the only one for hundreds of miles—and in the course of time, their sons made Khadir Fortress into a palace and filled it with plundered riches, with gold and silver filigree, with beautifully chased vessels, with enamel work from Persia and ivory from India.

And when the old Siddakkus died, somewhere around three hundred B.C., the ever-waiting, ever-vengeful nomads moved in and destroyed the palace, beating it down into the sand that soon would cover it and hide it from the eyes of future generations. It is still there, somewhere under all that sand; it's never been found, though a dozen expeditions have sought to locate it and failed. Now Khadir is just a palm-filled desert oasis, and a few depressed families live there because this is the only home they've ever known. They live on camels' milk and dates, and a little millet they grow in the winter, and on the meat of chickens and goats.

I said casually, in French: "Why don't you send the boy away, *ya habibi*, and we can talk as befits new-found friends."

He threw me a sidelong sort of look, and hesitated, wondering what I was up to. But he nodded to the boy and said: "*Rub, ya ibn kalb*, get out, you son of a dog."

He turned and looked at me with a suspicious but not particularly hostile expression. There was almost a mocking look in his eyes, as though he could guess immediately what I was going to propose to him. Perhaps he could; if you take Arabia's archeological treasures out of the country without permission, you're liable to finish up in a very uncomfortable jail, for a very long time; and from Khadir, it was only eighty miles or so to the sea, where a dhow could, perhaps, be waiting? He found the idea intriguing, before I'd even broached it...

I said: "How long do you expect to remain here, Lieutenant?"

He shrugged. "I have been here a little over two years. Another three, perhaps. Who can tell?"

"Who indeed? And you like it here?"

The shrug broadened. "It is a job. A man must work."

"If he's to make money, he must work very hard. I expect to find Siddakkus' Palace, or what's left of it, and I expect it to yield quite a treasure. Apart from the mosaics and pottery, and the stones of the fort—all these things, you understand, of great historical value— there is almost certain to be coins, silver, gold artifacts, perhaps even jewelry. A lot of India's rubies once passed through Khadir on their way to Egypt."

He smiled. "That is why, in order to dig, you need the permits from the Government that no doubt you have."

"Uh-huh."

"As a friend of the General, you would have no difficulty in getting those permits. And, of course, as a matter of form, I shall have to see them before you are permitted to start work."

"Of course. But first, I have to locate the precise position of the dig. Not hard, not easy either. But it might take time."

"How much time?"

"I expect to be here for some six months."

"And do you have any special knowledge that will show you exactly where to dig? The desert is a very big place."

Lying brazenly, I said: "I know almost exactly where to start looking. I did some research in the Museum in Beirut, the old manuscripts... Yes, I know what to look for."

He took a deep breath and said: "It is my duty to warn you that the removal of antiques from the country is a punishable offense. Severely punishable."

I brushed it aside with a shrug. "Of course, it's the same everywhere. A lot of men have become rich, very rich, by stretching that kind of law a little."

He said nothing: He didn't have to speak at all. I could see the wheels turning in his mind. I kept quiet, and in a little while he said, enlarging on the theme: "For you, a foreigner, it would be ten or twenty years in jail, unless perhaps the General might intercede on your behalf. But for me, it would be my head, displayed in the public square in Riyadh."

I said, smiling at him: "But of course, we're talking in academic terms, are we not? The idea of our enriching ourselves, you and I, by any illegal action is ridiculous, isn't it?"

"Yes, isn't it? But it's pleasant to pass the time like this in idle chatter. The days are very long."

"And the nights are longer."

Ha! He was sure I was off on a new track now. His eyes had that veiled look to them; he was getting suspicious; I judged it time to pull back.

I said: "I noticed a couple of old trucks at the oasis. I wonder if I could buy one of them?"

He frowned. "There are three trucks here that work, two that don't. They use them in the season for carrying the dates. One truck can carry as much as thirty camels can, but they can only be used around the oasis, where the ground is fairly hard. Why would you wish to buy one?" He leaned forward suddenly and smiled, to erase any shadow that might have fallen between us. "So that I could help you; if it can be done."

I said: "We have to look for six fairly high mounds out there in the desert. Three running from north to south, three at right angles to them."

"Ah, the towers of Siddakkus' Palace, no doubt."

"Not quite. The burial chambers of his six Captains. They were roughly forty feet high, just outside the fortress, and where the gypsum rock walls will have worn away to nothing, the towers were built of granite, and should show up now as sand-covered mounds, perhaps as high as twenty or even thirty feet. They should be relatively easy to locate, if enough ground could be covered. On camels, it would take a long time, but a truck... You think I could buy one of them?"

He could smell the profit already. He said: "My friend Suliman Ibn Suliman has not used his truck for some time, he's gone back to camels. But I believe it still drives. A very good machine, it would be quite expensive. American, very good, very strong."

I said: "I wonder, is it asking too much? Could you possibly make him an offer for it? Whatever you think it is worth, or even a little more?"

He said gravely: "I will be most happy."

I laughed deprecatingly and said: "I should perhaps have made arrangements for transport before I came here. But I have a philosophy of my own; I believe that if a man carries enough money, he need carry almost nothing else, and that's so much easier, isn't it?"

"Ah, then you are a very fortunate man to be so rich."

"Allah has been very good to me."

"Thank God."

"Thank God."

I let it sit there for a while, and then I said: "You are really very kind to help me like this. At the risk of offending you, which I would not like, I insist on offering you a commission on the sale."

He raised his hands in a very creditable facsimile of horror. "But by God, I could not permit it!"

"If I were a merchant, I would expect to be charged ten percent for such a service."

"Never! I would be ashamed!"

"But surely..."

He shook his head, quite firmly. "I cannot allow it, *ya Pasha*. It is my privilege to help you. A friend of His Excellency the General..."

Oh, the cunning bastard!

I said casually: "Oh, he's not that close a friend." The wheels were turning again. He looked at me shrewdly, wondering just how much he could milk me for. I stood up to go, and he walked with me to the door. I said: "And I wonder, do you patrol the area around the oasis?"

"Oh yes, from time to time."

"Suppose you were to send some of your patrols out with specific instructions to look for those mounds I spoke of? Three north to south, three east to west."

He said, a little stiffly: "They are soldiers, it would not be proper to send them off looking for archeological remnants."

"Of course not. But you presumably keep your maps of the area up-to-date, and if they were looking for any unusual formations that might be noted on a military map, it could only mean that His Excellency would commend you for your zeal, particularly if I brought it to his attention next time we meet." It was just what he wanted to hear. I said; shrugging: "Of course, I realize that they would be working for me as much as for the Government, so I would feel obliged to compensate them, even if they didn't know exactly how they were helping me. If I gave you a few thousand *reals* to give them at your discretion, I'm sure no harm would be done."

He tried hard to conceal his eagerness: "They would be looking for just six mounds?"

"Each about twenty to forty feet high, covered more on the west with drifting sand, and in dead straight lines. It's always the straight line that gives an indication of human labor; there's no such thing as a straight line in nature, did you realize that?"

"That's very interesting." He still didn't want to appear too eager. "Perhaps after all, if it were kept a secret between the two of us...I would not like His Excellency the General to feel I had made a wrong decision."

I said clearly: "Anything you and I do together, my dear Osman, is nobody else's business at all. Nobody's."

I pulled out a bundle of hundred-*real* notes, not bothering to count them, and laid them on the desk so as not to offend his dignity by actually putting them in his hand. I said:

"You would be doing me the greatest favor if you would pay the men for me."

He tried hard not to look at the money; it was more than he made, legally, in a month, though I was very sure that his pockets were well lined by other means; the soldier who controls a water hole in these parts, where caravans of all kinds pass through at the rate of one or so every month... It was a likelihood that Lieutenant Osman was already a wealthy man, and likelihoods are what I deal in.

He left the money there where I'd put it as he walked me out into the hot sun again. He said, suddenly: "And where will you stay while you are here? A room in the barracks, perhaps? If I could offer you our hospitality?"

It was just a gesture; nothing could have been less desirable, either for him or for me. I told him I'd try to find a house I could rent, and he insisted, as I hoped he would, in helping me find one; such a friendly fellow!

We found a little one room shack where an old man lived alone, and he moved out and I moved in. Lieutenant Osman made the necessary arrangements, and I paid in cash to the old man, the equivalent of a hundred American dollars for the privilege of having a grubby roof over my head at nights. There was a glance between the two of them as I handed the money over, and the glance from Osman said: 'Report to my office and hand over ninety percent of that, and you may keep the rest.' Just a quick glance, but that's what it said.

And the next day, I was the proud owner of a fine American truck, a Dodge, 1932 vintage, with both fenders missing and the tires all patched with bolted-on pieces of other, older, tires.

That cost me twenty-five hundred dollars, American. I imagine that its fair price, out here, would have been a rough hundred and fifty. But I'd taken the first step; I'd established myself as the wealthy, eccentric foreigner, on the make a little bit, who wanted all kinds of useful things and was well prepared to pay for them.

And I needed the truck for another purpose.

It was on the third day that I took the next, and most important step. I'd have preferred to wait a little longer, but I had no way of knowing how far ahead of the caravan I was, just when I could expect it to appear.

I took Osman, a dear friend now, with all that money of mine in his venal pocket, out for a drive across the desert. There was hard lava rock, and hard red sand, and a lot of soft yellow dust where the truck sank up to its axles and simply stalled. I bogged down deliberately a couple of times, and we had to struggle to get it out, once letting most of the air out of the ruined tires and pumping them up again laboriously once we were on the hard stuff again, and Osman said: "You see, *Pasha*, it is quite impossible to leave the oasis by truck, except for that dirt track down to the coast. Even then... A long, hard journey, you must have many men aboard to push."

All round the oasis there were encroaching dunes which one day would swallow it up as they had swallowed up the test of the Rub. The net result was that except for the one track down to the sea, there was just no way you could get out of Khadir in a truck. If only a man could reach the mountain peak to the north, the way was rough but passable; except that the soft sand, almost quicksand in parts, was certain disaster for a depth of more than ten miles around the hard patch that was the Oasis itself, a barrier as formidable as a castle moat. And that one road; I'd seen, was heavily guarded. *Nobody* came or went around Khadir without Osman's agreement.

But like all problems, this one also could be overcome by learning, and learning is my strongest suit...

Some years ago, when I was invited to address the Phoenician Studies Concord in Baghdad, I met a Curator of the Izmir National Museum who had brought with him, for display to the more than eighty archeologists and anthropologists from all over the world who were gathered there, some excellently preserved extracts from the writings of King Hiram the First, who ruled the coast of what is now Lebanon (from the city of Tyre, which is now called Sur) from 970 to

936 B.C. One of his scribes had appended his own notes to the King's writings, and these were really the more important scraps, because they were written in the old, more or less pure Phoenician; the Phoenician language began to decay in the fourth century B.C., acquiring a much more cursive style and assimilating a great deal of ancient Hebrew, to which, of course, it is akin, being derived, as Hebrew is, from the ancient Canaanite.

One of the King's essays, which has been widely translated into a dozen languages, dealt with the excursion of his father, Abi-Baal, down the eastern coast of the Red Sea, and with the founding of the trading-posts there. One of the trading posts was at a water hole he called Khad-A-Rianu, which means "the gushing springs."

It's important to know that over the centuries the old names have changed, but that they have changed in accordance with fairly well defined trends. The Biblical Sidon has become Saida, Tyre has become Sur, Esh-Sham logically becomes Damascus, and even Ezion-Geber correctly becomes, if you know your languages, the town where King Solomon built his "navy of ships"—Eilath. And by the same derivational process, Khad-A-Rainu becomes the Oasis of Khadir.

I'd had a little time on my hands during the conference, and more as an academic exercise than anything else, I set about translating some of the scribe's notes. He wrote of a road that Abi-Baal built "straight as the flight of an arrow from the steps of the springs to the top most mountain peak in the north, a distance of seven leagues, on which we built a lookout for the raiders who came in from the desert. The road was of granite blocks, and was laid by four thousand men..."

Somewhere close by, leading out of the oasis, there was a granite road, nearly three thousand years old, that had not been seen or known in modern history until those obscure writings turned up and were then hidden away again in an equally obscure museum. There was not only historical excitement in looking for it; I had a strong feeling it might solve what was obviously going to be a tricky problem—the problem of getting out of Khadir in a hurry if any unexpected snag arose; I always like to have a trump card up my sleeve, and this just might be it. So I started searching, bogging down that damned truck every hour or two and knowing that while I was in sight of the oasis, Osman would be carefully watching through his binoculars to make sure I wasn't digging up the non-existent Palace of Siddakkus without him.

The steps were easy to find, they were still there, though the spring had changed its course and the great hole was now dry and full of sand; and looking north, there was only one point Abi-Baal could have referred to—the high peak at the southern end of Jebel Hijaz—some twenty miles, or seven leagues away as the scribe had described it.

On the first day, I began swinging the truck back and forth across this line, and bogged down in soft sand repeatedly for my troubles. But on the second, I found a patch where the sand covered a solid, rock-hard bed, that was buried not more than fourteen inches anywhere, and I knew I'd found Abi-Baal's granite road. From then, it was merely a matter of a few hours experimenting to find the course of the safe, straight line and of marking it here and there with a stone or two to make sure that, in a hurry, I'd be able to keep to it.

Five feet away on either side of its central line, the sand was impassable; but in that line, straight as the flight of an arrow, it was like driving along a highway. I practiced the run once, at speed, and only fell off the road once, where an underground disturbance, perhaps, had shifted it; I marked the point with a cairn, and knew that I was ready.

So on the third day, it was time to show Osman some color to illustrate my story of Siddakkus' Palace. And it was amusing to see how quickly he acquired the diggers' excitement, the enthusiasm for the undiscovered that might make history; it was a pity it was all such a sham, the whole lot of it. I eased the truck at one point carefully towards my secret road, and he stopped me suddenly: "No, *Pasha*, not that way. Quicksand, even a horse cannot live in it—a camel, perhaps, but not even such a splendid truck as this."

I nodded, swung the truck round, and headed back towards the oasis; it was getting late.

We drove in silence all the way back, and it was time for the crucial seed to be planted. I sighed, and said: "They are terribly long, the nights here. In daylight, there's always the excitement of the search, but at night..."

He nodded: "A vigorous man must have his wives with him,

that's what his wives are for."

I said: "When I was in Riyadh, I tried to find myself a woman to bring down here, but when she found out I was staying so long in Khadir, she thought better of it at the last minute, and left me. If I'd have been able to stay a while longer, I could have found a replacement, but the spice caravan was the last to make the trip for some time, and I didn't want to wait over such a trifle."

He was looking at me, wondering, counting the bank notes again, and I said: "Even the kind of money I was offering her... Women are getting terribly independent nowadays, the influence of the West."

"But surely..." He couldn't understand it; and no wonder, it was really a very unlikely story! There are more concubines to the square mile in Riyadh than anywhere else on earth. He said, puzzled: "Well, that really is astonishing."

"And here, there's nothing. I've taken a good look."

"Here? Nothing but goats and watermelons. I, of course, knowing I would be here for a while, made the necessary arrangements before I came. And the men..." He shrugged. "There are one or two camp followers, as you may have noticed, but nothing that would satisfy our tastes. I wish I could help you in some way. If we sent the truck to Qizar, perhaps? There's a brothel there, and we could easily arrange for one of the girls to come here."

"And she might look like hell. No, I'll have to face a long and unhappy time of celibacy, I'm afraid." He said nothing, and I added: "In Qizar, the girls will be so sick they can hardly stand."

"Yes, there is that, of course." He was musing, strangely reflective, and I hit it hard: "All that money, and I can't get the thing I want most." I wondered how much time I had; there was no way of knowing.

He said no more till we reached the oasis, and then, when we stopped outside the barracks, instead of getting out immediately he just sat there, and then he clicked his tongue sympathetically and said: "I will tell you what I can do. In a few days, I just might be able to help you." I looked a question and he raised a hand and said: "No, please do not press for any answers, a matter I really must not speak of. But as you say, there is no reason why a man whom God has made wealthy should not avail himself of all that God has to offer him. In three days' time, perhaps I will be able to do something for you."

I said eagerly: "Really?"

"It might be a little...expensive for you. The further one goes from the amenities of the city, the harder the amenities are to find, and therefore, the more costly, wouldn't you say?"

I said: "Osman, you've got something up your sleeve."

He said earnestly: "Yes, but please, no questions. It could even be dangerous. But...trust me."

The prospect of trusting this rogue was almost more than I could think of without laughing, but I said instead: "Three days?"

"Four, at the most. And the best. Really the best."

I said gravely: "*Ahsan minnak mafish, walla fi Misr*, I won't find a better man than you even in Egypt."

He beamed. "In a few days then."

He got out and went to his rooms. I drove slowly through the gentle palms, close by the edge of the water, parked the truck outside my hut, and went inside.

Things were moving at last; in three days, four at the most, the slavers' caravan was coming in. At the moment, that's all I wanted to know.

Up to now, that's what all this had been about.

CHAPTER 3

A small caravan passed through the oasis the next morning, but it was not the one I was waiting for.

There were some forty camels, and they were making the long haul down from Medina and Taif, calling in at all the coastal villages to supply cloth, and nails, and some foodstuffs to the scattered oases that were left without supplies when the monsoon was blowing the wrong way and the dhows couldn't make it. There's a surprisingly modern airport at Taif, and trade goods arriving there by one of the most modern means of transportation, the jet, would be offloaded onto one of the oldest, the camel train, mostly cigarettes from the Lebanon and Syria. But I was able to buy some excellent balls of cheese in olive oil, far tastier than the local product, some camel-hide sandals, and a large supply of Syrian cigarettes for Osman, who smoked incessantly, just to cement this unholy friendship.

His men were on guard at the water holes, and the caravan master was so blasé as to go into Osman's office with a thick wad of currency in his hand to pay the protocol bribe, without which his camels would have gone on their way with their bellies dry. Of course, there were official dues to pay as well, and I wondered what percentage of them would reach Riyadh. They also presented him with a young camel, born on the way, which he promptly sold to his friend Suliman Ibn Suliman, for nearly three times its value; he wasn't even trying to hide his venality from me now, and it was rather touching the way he offered me a small piece of green cloth that looked as though it had been cut from a looted billiard table.

He said, holding it out with both hands: "For you, *ya Pasha*, a piece of Holy Cloth blessed by the Khadi of Mecca himself. It will insure great fortune for you."

I said, taking it: "You're very kind, *habibi*."

He sighed: "Unfortunately, I had to pay rather heavily for it, the only piece they had that was truly blessed, but I thought: 'My good friend the *Pasha* must have this! So I paid for it, even though the man who sold it to me was a villain and a scoundrel."

I dug into my pocket. "Whatever you paid, I'm sure it was not too much for such a holy relic."

"Ah, but perhaps, since you are not a true Believer..."

"Even the Infidels, *habibi*, realize the worth of the True Faith. How much do I owe you?"

He said hopefully: "Three hundred *reals?* Was it too much?"

I said gravely: "A very fair price." I gave him the money and said: "I will carry it over my heart." He didn't even notice that I put it in my hip pocket, which was a pity.

The caravan stayed long enough to water its camels and fill its goatskins, and then it went on its way again, a slow, nostalgic reminder of a past that still lives, but only lives out here where history has not been destroyed by progress. The great ungainly beasts plodded nonchalantly away from the oasis, their bellies filled with water and camel scrub, their spreading feet floating over the sand, just as they had always done, along this very route, for all the five thousand years since the Sumerians first opened up the deserts to the south.

In all that time, nothing had changed, except now the priestly green cloth was torn from billiard tables where rioting students set the torch to everything that was alien.

And three days later, the slavers themselves appeared.

The first sign was the virtual disappearance of almost every man, woman and child from the dusty alleys of the oasis. Throughout the day, the women were there, prematurely old and haggard as they scrubbed their soiled clothes at the pool, and the men were picking the dates for His Highness the Sultan in his distant mud city, and the children were scampering in the dust, as children will wherever they live (if they're lucky enough not to live on concrete) throwing stones at the screeching chickens, chasing the goats among the tatterdemalion huts, getting themselves into all sorts of harmless troubles... And then, suddenly, they were all gone, gone to their huts to keep their eyes closed, because this was something it wasn't healthy to see, and years of training had taught them this.

A soldier came running from Osman's office, and said: "Better go inside, *ya Pasha*, better nobody see you here. The officer come to you soon..."

I said: "Visitors, *ya akhui?*" I addressed him as "my brother"; you never saw a scruffier-looking rogue, and the compliment pleased him. He grinned even more broadly, and said: "Better know nothing when it is good not to know."

I nodded and went inside, and waited until he had gone, and then ran quickly to the truck and drove it through the palms to the edge of the pool, and on through the other side, and round behind the back of a deserted, fallen-down hut that helped, but not much, to hide it; there was no one around, not even a soldier. I quickly checked that its tanks had gas in them (four dollars a gallon here, trucked up from the coast!) and that the four-gallon can under the seat was full of water. I hid the Trinovid binoculars, my money belt, and a few things I thought might be useful, under the chassis, and then ran quickly back to my hut and went inside and shut the door.

The day was hot, and inside it was like an oven. Through the tiny, glassless window, I could see the caravan coming in.

It was quite a sight; not only for itself, but for all its tragic associations—a sight that few men have seen and lived to tell about. It was hard to convince myself that this was the age of an enlightened social conscience, to remember that in some parts of the world, notably these, sociology and technology have always gone hand in hand—and here, painfully slowly.

And they came in an extraordinary optical illusion, one of the fanciful distortions at which the desert is so adept, and of which the mirage is the most common. It was strange to watch.

First, there was just the upper parts, the heads and long necks of the leading camels, to be seen, dark and eerie against the yellow sand. Then, as they moved on forward, the rest of the bodies became visible as they appeared from behind an oblique fold in the sand—the point of a dune. It was as though a great wall of sand had opened, at a slanted angle, to permit the upper parts of their torsos through first, and then the rest of them. Out of the yellow curtain they came, in an unending stream, less than a mile away. I counted thirty-seven of them. They were hurrying now. Not only could the animals smell the water—and after the long haul they'd be dry—but the drivers were beating them on with their sticks, knowing that it was not good to be moving in broad daylight, even though their scouts would have told them the road was clear, that everyone had been warned to keep his eyes shut...

As they came closer, I saw that the lead camel was blowing a great obscene balloon of throat skin out of the corner of his mouth, his anger with a hostile world for all the others to see. Some of the others showed their agreement, and blew out their saliva-wet balloons too, screeching the horrible camel anger as their drivers belabored them. Some of the animals had light framework sedans of bamboo and cloth over their humps, and I wondered what they contained.

And then...

Then came the line of slaves, a long strung-out thread of black bodies, half naked, men and women and children, their hands tied together and a long rope joining one waist to the next. They were stumbling along in the soft sand, trying to keep up. Three horsemen were on their flanks, and then a fourth appeared at the rear, light-skinned Arabs dressed in the *burnouse* of Algeria, but with Syrian *keffiehs* on their heads; they carried rifles, and there were long, curved, old-fashioned swords hanging from their ornate saddles. The horses were small, wiry, but well-fed and caparisoned in red and blue and green-dyed wool, with saddles inlaid with silver that flashed in the sun. It was a splendid thing to see the horses in all their finery; and a great tragedy to see the use to which such splendor was being put. Watching, I realized that this was a sight few men who were not of this desert had ever seen and lived to tell about—the same sad spectacle of human beings in chains that the deserts had been host to for as long as history had been recorded.

As they drew near, I pulled back into the relative darkness of the room, and watched. They passed quite close to my window, and I saw a woman open the drapes of the second sedan and lean out to look, a dark-skinned young girl with very bright eyes and a small black mark at each side of her forehead; an Ethiopian, then, and the daughter of a slave herself, that's what the marks were; I wondered how long she'd had her freedom, now lost again, probably forever. And then someone shouted out angrily for her to close the sedan curtain, and the face was gone. I heard a whip, and someone screamed, and there was a single rifle shot, though I had no idea what it meant.

I watched the line stumbling in. Most of the men were big, blue-black, from the Upper Sudan by the looks of them, with a scattering of lighter-colored browns who might have come from the northern borders of Ethiopia. I saw at least one Danakil, his matted hair hanging in ringlets over his eyes, those eyes peering through with an angry, savage glint to them; I had a feeling that he wouldn't last very long as a slave. As he passed, I saw there was a great red sword cut across his shoulders, and I wondered what sort of trouble he'd been giving them; you don't tame a Danakil very easily. They were all dressed in rags; some in remnants of their ochre waistcloths, some in tattered grey gowns, a few in khaki shorts, and one in what had once been a suit but was now a torn and filthy mess of pants and jacket.

The women were mostly young, but not all of them; some Sudanese, some Eritrean, and a handful I couldn't identify. One of them was nursing a baby, though she couldn't have been more than thirteen years old, a Somali with large hips and long legs and the delicate movements of a gazelle. I saw three that were obvious half-castes, one with quite fair skin and a hideous, pockmarked face, with henna-dyed hair that reached down to her waist.

And then they were gone, disappearing among the crowded palm trees, and I heard the shouting as the camels headed fast for the water, oblivious now of the yelling of their masters, concentrating on one thing only—racing to the smell of the water to get their empty bellies filled, ignoring the curses and the blows of their masters as they screamed their anger and their need; the most placid and easily controlled animal in the world—until he's thirsty and smells water, and then nothing will control him.

Four of the men were carrying huge bundles of shovels on their shoulders, bent double and sweating under the weight of them. I saw one man unrolling a long piece of red-and-white striped canvas that might have been an elongated flag, and I wondered what it was;

one of the overseers came up and yelled at him and made him roll it up again and put it out of sight. Two men were dragging a wooden crate at the end of a rope, struggling to get it over the sand, and another crate was being offloaded from the back of a screeching camel; the bindings were tangled, and the animal was refusing to kneel with the water so near, and the crate fell down and smashed open; not rifles, as I half-expected, but pick heads.

I wondered what kind of major digging was going on in Khadir Oasis that would require so many picks and shovels. It was a small point, but it intrigued me, and I wanted to know the answer. I even found myself wondering why it seemed so important.

I went to the string bed and lay down. There was nothing to do now but wait. In the course of time, Osman would be telling them—telling *someone*—that he had a wealthy customer for one of the girls, a deal that could be profitable as only a deal with a foreigner can be... Until then, it was a matter of patience.

I got up and did two hundred push-ups; inactivity bores me, and to date, in this damnable oasis, I'd had a bellyful of it. And then, refreshed, I sat down on the bed again, and listened to the sounds of agony out there, the muted moaning, the ululating cries of women, the hoarse shouts of the men... I couldn't get the image of the Danakil's black and savage face out of my mind; it was strange, but among all that tragedy, his seemed to me the most memorable, because I felt sure that soon he would be dead. The others might last a long, long, time, because there's nothing more resilient than the human condition; but not the Danakil; the next sword cut would be across his throat, even though they'd brought him, successfully, all this way.

And so, I did push-ups, and waited.

It was dark when they came for me. I heard three pair of feet approaching on the soft sand outside; and I slipped off the cot and stood behind the door, ready for anything untoward that might happen, though I didn't really expect it; because a man like Osman never killed a golden goose in his life, not until he'd taken every last egg from it.

There was a gentle knocking; they came in peace then, at least for now. A voice whispered: *"Cain Pasha?"*

I opened the door, and there were three of them, two of Osman's soldiers and one other man, a great bearded ruffian who might have been almost European, blue eyes, a thin straight nose, a tall, straight bearing. But when he spoke, I knew he was a Sennusi, from the Libyan Desert. He spoke Arabic, and expected me to understand quite clearly, so they'd already been discussing me...

He said: "There are some people who want to see you, come with me, leave your gun behind."

I said: "No gun, I never carry one."

For a moment, he looked as though he wanted to make sure, but he thought better of it, and satisfied himself with a look to the soldiers that meant keep your eyes open. They moved, all of them, with that furtive, slippery kind of walk that men get accustomed to when they have to watch out on all sides for trouble. We went over to Osman's rooms, the soldiers grinning at me ferociously; it must have been strange to them to have an American taken into their confidence.

Besides Lieutenant Osman, in full uniform with all his medals up and his long, long belt highly polished for the occasion, there were two other men now. One was small and wiry and quick and silent, dressed in khaki pants and shirt, with camel-hide sandals and a cloth cap, a caricature of a pirate with two old and unmatched revolvers stuck in his belt and a dagger as well. And the other—well, he was something else again.

The other was tall and slim, desperately handsome, with huge black eyes and finely-shaped features, a delicate, good-humored mouth, and a small, neat black moustache. He had the regal bearing of the desert Arab, the look of a man who is accustomed to sitting straight on a horse all day and riding hard. His movements were lithe and easy, the movements of the Bedouin; only the moustache was wrong, too neatly trimmed, too preciously elegant. A city man then, with a certain sophistication this little detail was meant to indicate. He wore the long embroidered robes of a sheikh, and the red-and-white checked *hatter* on his head told the world—and it might have been a lie—that he came from Hebron, near the banks of the River Jordan. It was bound with three white coils of camels' hair, interlaced with gold thread, that proclaimed his royal descent; and that might well have been a lie too.

As I entered, he was turning the wick of an old-fashioned

kerosene lamp, and he turned and smiled and said in immaculate, but affected English: "Mr. Cain? How very kind of you to drop by. I'm Sheikh Ahmed Fellawi, how do you do?" His smile was easy and relaxed; his face mobile, his eyes alert but full of friendly delight. There was little of the grave, serious hospitality of the Bedouin; this was something quite different, the meeting of old friends in a Via Veneto cafe, genial and outgoing.

He held out his hand, and his grasp was warm and friendly, and he hung onto mine a mite too long.

I said: "Sheikh Ahmed, a pleasure."

Switching languages, he said: "I understand you speak excellent Arabic. I wonder where you learned it? *Nahwi* Arabic, the classical language, they tell me."

I shrugged. "Here, there, everywhere. I used to teach it at the Calcutta Institute of Oriental Studies." I used the gutteral *rh* and *kh* of the Egyptians, and he smiled and said: "And studied, no doubt, in Egypt, how very interesting. And now, you're an archeologist searching out the fortress that Siddakkus built here. I'm surprised. there aren't really many Americans who know about the journey Siddakkus made across the Rub al Khali."

I said: "I used to teach Archeology too. I specialized in the Babylonian era." No good letting him think I didn't have any brains. Or, for that matter, that I didn't know just what he himself was up to, so I said pleasantly: "I saw your caravan of slaves coming in; did you have a good trip?"

He gestured elegantly, a shrug of one shoulder. "We lost rather more than usual after we left the Sudan. The Ethiopian Army gave us quite a bad time, I'm afraid." He barely paused. "The idea of slavery is quite repugnant to most Americans, you don't subscribe to those inhibitions?"

My turn to shrug, and I did. "Slavery is going to exist for as long as the good Lord makes one man better than another. In chains or out of them. A man can be a lot worse off slaving on an assembly line, wouldn't you say?"

He laughed, openly and cheerfully: "How very refreshing to hear you say that! A rationalization, of course! But then, I have the distinct impression that you are a very rational man indeed, am I right?"

"Is that bad? I didn't think it was."

"Of course not! We live in a difficult time. It's much easier to tolerate if we can brush aside the hypocrisies. As you say, Allah made some men better than others, and the weak must serve the strong, that's what ecology is about. And talking of hypocrisy..." He looked at Osman and turned back to me and said: "The mere possession of alcohol in Arabia is a punishable offense, and if you've been obeying our sectarian laws, you probably could do with a drink. It so happens I have some excellent Vodka, a taste I picked up at the Sorbonne." There was that mocking look at Lieutenant Osman again, and he said gently: "Some of us, Osman, are so holy that the moment alcohol touches our lips, it turns to water."

Osman looked stolidly at nothing and kept quiet, trying hard not to disapprove, and then thought his silence might be taken for disapproval and said hastily: "Of course, Excellency, I understand that."

It's a common enough rationalization among those Muslims for whom the proscriptions of the Koran, alcohol among them, are bothersome. But it was nice to know, none the less; it meant that we were indeed a long way here from any of the complications that the concept of law might entail.

Besides, I hadn't had a drink since I'd hit the shores of Arabia.

He opened a small, brass-bound trunk, made of polished teak with polished leather straps around it, his travelling case, and took out a bottle of Bulgarian vodka. He said: "Quite good, really. Of course, I prefer the Russian, but..." He sighed exaggeratedly. "I operate out of a town that has the best liquor supply in the world, but you still can't get Russian vodka there, the result of a twenty-year-old diplomatic squabble, one ship's Captain insulting another. Ridiculous, isn't it?" Osman obsequiously offered, with both hands, two of the little china coffee cups, and Sheik Ahmed accepted them with a curt nod and poured us drinks. He raised his little cup at me and said: "Are you a Harvard man, by chance, Mr. Cain?"

I said: "Stanford, Cambridge, and the Sorbonne. But I've lectured at Harvard. On aerodynamics, mostly."

He tossed his drink back in one gulp, and put down his cup,

and said: "Most archeologists are not particularly wealthy. They don't usually have enough even of other people's money."

I said: "Allah has been very good to me. I like, to think of myself as a rich man, it's very good for my ego."

He smiled. "In your religion, there's a rather trite cliché about the rich man, the camel, and the eye of a needle."

"As you say. Trite."

"In my own philosophy, I have observed that a rich man is seldom an honest man." He smiled quickly, making sure I didn't take it as an insult, and added: "As in my own case, for example."

I nodded: "Quite. And the one is so much more pleasant to live with than the other, isn't it?"

He was very happy. He said: "And who exactly knows your present whereabouts, Mr. Cain?"

I was half expecting it; *nobody* could have known where I was at this point, and that wouldn't have been a very good thing to let him brood on for too long. I said promptly: "The Institute for which I work, on a voluntary basis, of course, knows I'm in Khadir. The Museum of Riyadh knows I'm here. The Saudi Arabian Ambassador to the United Nations knows... Who else? Oh, my old friend General Hishara, of course. Why do you ask?"

That last name alarmed him, and he was taking pains not to show it. But he frowned. "General Hishara?"

I shrugged. "I like to know kings and beggars, as well as criminals and cops. Are you worried because I mentioned the arrival of your caravan? I couldn't help seeing it."

"Under normal circumstances, you would not have been permitted to see it."

"No, I suppose not. But what are the...abnormal circumstances you're thinking of?"

He said bluntly: "Osman tells me you might be a customer." As though ashamed of his bluntness, he added: "And Osman knows that I deal only with those fortunate enough to be blessed by Allah with enough of the world's material assets."

Matching his outspokenness, laying it on the line, I said: "I don't try to hide the fact of my wealth, but..." I left it hanging, and he said smoothly:

"I understand your concubine deserted you in Jiddah."

"Oh, that. Yes, that was a damn nuisance. It left me here with a minor problem on my hands. Not a very important one, really, but you'll admit that to a cultivated man, a place like this can get a little dull after dark." I shrugged. "I was hoping Osman could find me someone, but I hadn't really thought of...well, of a slave. Is that what you're suggesting?"

He smiled and said softly: "Better than the assembly-line, I think you said."

I took time out to think about it. I said at last: "And you think that among your women there might be something suitable? It's a novel idea. Different, at least."

"And it intrigues you?"

"It intrigues me. But I don't want any coal-black leper from the Congo."

He laughed, his white teeth flashing, his eyes alight with genuine pleasure, one of the group. He said: "I have a total of thirty-eight women. Of these, twenty or so can be eliminated immediately as far as you are concerned, they're fit only for the lesser Sheikhs of the Trucial States. Too scraggy, too ill-bred, too bovine... Among the remainder, I think you'd find about half too inexperienced, too frightened, or perhaps even...too *black*."

He put a great deal of contempt into the word; the racial distinctions have never been stronger than they are out here, and among the brown-skinned Arabs, the lighter the tone the better. If he's coffee-colored, he's a gentleman, if he's black, he's a slave, and it's not confined to color only—if he breeds horses or camels, he's upper-class, but if he breeds sheep or goats, he's lower. It's all very complicated, but not much different from the Western philosophies.

I said: "I'd prefer a lighter skin tone, of course. Would you by chance have any Circassians with you?"

The Circassians, strictly speaking, come from the Caucasus—Georgia, Armenia, Azerbaijan, these were once their homelands—but the term is used loosely here, and means a Turk or Persian or even an Iraqi if he's fair rather than dark.

It also means, even more loosely, anyone who *looks* half European but isn't, and it has come to be applied to almost any half-caste who takes after the lighter parent rather than the darker. They're regarded as a race apart, and they are greatly in demand, particularly their women. Their ruling classes, called in Tatar the *pshi*, were acknowledged as the best overseers if they were men, the best wives if they were women. Their nobles (in Tatar the *usden*), were the best possible craftsmen or concubines. And their *hekotl*, or peasants, were the best casual workers, whose women might, on the spur of the moment, be casually taken to bed.

Sheikh Ahmed switched back to his immaculate English and showed me some of his erudition, just in case I should take him for a mere pimp. He said: "No *true* Circassians, of course, but were you perhaps using the word in its vulgar sense?"

"I was indeed. A nice little half-caste would be very suitable."

"You realize how very valuable the Circassian women are among the desert rulers? My good friend Sheikh Yusuf Suliman ibn Kabbaj has eight of them in his harem. And he paid me five thousand dollars each for them, American money."

I said: "American oil money. His personal oil income is around three hundred million a year, so that's just a trifle for him. I wouldn't pay even a quarter of that."

He knew that I would. But it was merely a question of fixing a starting price, and twelve hundred and fifty was a good point of departure, I thought. He said: "What sort of price would you be prepared to pay, Mr. Cain?"

"For a Circassian?"

"Er...yes. And in what currency?"

I said: "I'm carrying American dollars, Swiss francs, and Arabian *reals*. And the price would depend on the merchandise. If I could perhaps see what you have to offer...?"

He was still not ready; nothing like a long conversation with a man to find out if he's on your side or not. He said:

"Suppose you tell me more precisely what it is you need. What age, for example? Is weight important? I suppose it is. What about intellectual capacity, does that count for anything?"

I said tartly: "I don't need a goat, Sheikh Ahmed. I need an attractive woman to sleep with, to talk to, to be there when I need companionship."

"Ah, the companionship of a beautiful woman... A wildcat?"

"No wildcats."

"And a very light skin, a Circassian?"

"The lighter, the better."

"...and, of course, the more expensive."

"I understand that. I'm prepared to pay a reasonable price."

The haggling could go on all night, but it was no good trying to hurry him, that's not the way they operate.

He said: "A virgin, necessarily?"

"Not necessarily. Virginity presupposes inexperience, unless she's been in one of your schools, and I don't suppose she has." The schools were all on the Arabian Peninsula itself; that's where the young girl-children were going. They'd be carefully trained, and then profitably sold.

He said: "And eventually, when you leave here? In six months or so, I'm told?"

I shrugged. "I could hardly take her home with me, so she'd be free to go. Or I could hand her over to Osman here, for possible resale or delivery to you next time the caravan came through."

He said abruptly, no longer the royal sheikh but just a slaver: "Five thousand dollars in American money."

"I don't buy anything, Sheikh Ahmed, without seeing it first."

He said thoughtfully, very slowly: "Y-e-s, of course. And you'd be prepared to pay that kind of money?"

"I would."

He looked at me carefully for a long, long time, and said at last, smiling to take the edge off the words: "I'm a little disturbed at your extraordinary readiness to cast aside the usual American inhibitions. Americans just don't buy slaves very often, not any more, it's not fashionable. Of course, in the oil fields, they do occasionally buy a girl, but their middle-west conscience always seems to bother them about it, even though its done with all the usual hypocrisy—a girl to make up the beds and wash the dishes, that sort of thing." He shrugged. "You seem to have very little of that hypocrisy, and it disturbs me. It's out of character."

"Without knowing my character better, you can't possibly make such a statement, can you?"

He nodded, and then fell into a kind of reverie, one finger gently stroking his long, aristocratic nose and sometimes delicately touching the ends of his moustache. For a long while, nobody spoke, and I was quite sure he was making up his mind to betray *someone*, even though I didn't know whom it might be. Not making it too obvious, he said at last:

"I have a young and very beautiful Somali girl, quite light-skinned, really, and with breasts as hard as young kohlrabis... I was very lucky to get her."

I said: "No Somalis."

"Then, a twenty-five year old half-caste Italian-Ethiopian, no darker than I am, and very, very beautiful. A noble's daughter, and not a mark on her body anywhere."

There was a fine point there, and he was pushing it. *"No darker than I am..."* That really meant, "forget your Circassians, I don't have any for sale." We could have been buying and selling a used car; white sidewall tires, power steering, power brakes... It was hard to realize that it was a woman we were discussing, a woman in the nebulous, abstract sense, but a woman who, when I met her, would have a soul and a past and a future all her own.

I said politely: "The nobility you suggest she has is really of no use to me. And somehow—call it an American inhibition if you like—I've got my heart set on a Circassian girl."

Again, there was that long silence. And then he smiled, and made up his mind. He said: "If you'll double the price, Mr. Cain, I'll give you an American girl, would you like that?"

I said: "My God, I don't believe it!"

He leaned in close, and smiled and smiled; and said softly: "And when you've finished here, you won't want to encumber yourself with her anymore, so you simply set her free and let her take her chances. Or hand her over to Osman to await my arrival on the next trip. He'll even give you a fair price for her."

I said again: "An *American* girl?" I sounded properly astonished, and a little bit incredulous as well.

He nodded benignly. "Tall and slim in the American fashion—too thin, of course, but that's the way your people like them, isn't it? We were fattening her up. Her skin is fair; her hair quite light and long, her breasts are excellent if a trifle small, and she's really quite skilled. She'll require very little training, very little indeed."

I looked flabbergasted a little longer, and then said: "Well, my God..." A rapid change of tone now. "She'll be a handful of trouble, no doubt."

"Only if you let her. It doesn't really matter how civilized a woman is..." he laughed shortly and said: "You and I know that *civilized* is not strictly the right word, but you know what I mean. However accustomed she may have become to a totally unfeminine position, all you have to do is show her the whip and she'll very quickly revert." I thought that was a very nice way of putting it.

I said, pushing for some answers: "How the devil did you manage to find an American girl, I can't believe it! And where, for God's sake, would you sell her, out here? I can't believe any of the sheikhs would be very interested."

He raised a finger at me and said smugly: "Then you know very little of your fellow man, Mr. Cain. There's suddenly become quite a demand for them. You may not know that the Sheikh of Najram actually married an American girl, while he was in the States for medical treatment, and brought her home with him. Now, all the other Rulers feel he's put one over on them, and they all want American girls."

"Then surely you'd be foolish to sell her to me?"

He shrugged. "One only, I'd be starting up a few more petty rivalries, and I can't afford to antagonize my clients. You see how frank I am with you?"

"And I appreciate it. Then, all we have to discuss is the price."

He stroked his little moustache again. "I have to take into account two opposing thoughts. Firstly, that however rich you may be, the oil Sheikhs are very considerably richer. Secondly, the Sheikhs are a long way from here, and there's always the chance of a death or two on the way there, even though we carry the...the special ones in sedans. In other words, Mr. Cain, a bird in the hand is worth two in the bush, so I'd be prepared to adjust the price downwards. Shall we say ten thousand?"

As a matter of principle, we haggled for a little while.

A little while? We haggled for half the night, I felt I had to.

And after three cups of coffee and another cup of vodka, the matter was agreed, subject to my approval of the woman. Eight thousand American dollars, and cheap at the price.

I said: "Do I have to confine her?"

He smiled. "Even an American woman has sense enough to know that she can't cross the desert. Where would she go? Obviously, she'd be far better off with you, even if you have to beat her regularly, than wandering around the dunes by herself. If you felt it advisable, you might point out to her what would happen if the Bedouin got their hands on her."

I said: "All right, I'll go and get the money."

"You don't carry it with you?"

I thought that was a very funny remark. I said: "The kind of money I'm carrying, I'd be foolish to invite a nighttime visit, wouldn't I? I think even my good friend Osman would cut my throat for ten dollars, if he were sure he could find my little hoard."

I was trying to prod Osman into saying something, but he still kept silent; he merely looked at me reproachfully. A question of gauging Sheikh Ahmed's relative importance, and a very small point indeed; but an important one.

I went out, and as soon as I was clear of the guards, I ran quickly, at speed, through the deserted fringe of palms to where I'd left the truck; it was still there, why shouldn't it be? And still half-hidden from inquiring eyes. I took out enough money from the bundles I'd hidden aboard, and then ran back fast, taking a short cut closer to the pool where the slaves were sleeping. There were guards all round them, but no one saw me; I took good care they didn't. I didn't want anyone snooping around the truck.

And then, unexpectedly, there was a shadow moving, close to my own shadow, a shadow so slight, moon-cast, that if it had kept still I'd never have seen it. But it moved, and I swung round ready. I reached out and grabbed, a throat in one hand, a thigh in the other, and pulled him in tight, with one knee on the ground so that I could up and hurl him away if I wanted to.

It was the Danakil, and he didn't utter a sound. His hands went swiftly to my neck and sank themselves in, and I rolled over with him on the silent sand and took the hands and crushed them just enough to release the grip, and I whispered to him in Amharic: "Keep quiet, I am not an enemy."

To the Danakils, all men are enemies. Through the long ringlets over his face, smelling strongly of cow's urine and ashes, the black, beady eyes held mine steadily, unblinking, I wondered how he'd managed to get away, even this far. Slowly, I released my grip, and he did not move. I whispered: "Stay here, I will help you."

As I pulled away, he made a sudden move, but I stopped him, and said again, savagely: "Stay!" It was like commanding a half-trained sheepdog. He lay there now, and did not move. I sneaked away and ran quickly, silently, to where the palms met the edge of the water, where the bushes were at their most dense. A guard was there, sitting with his back—foolish fellow!—to a date palm. I crept up on my belly, hooked an arm around, and put a heavy hand over his mouth, pulling his head back against the trunk with a dreadful thud. I hit him once on the side of the neck, and he went down and lay still, and I took his water-skin and his sword—but not his rifle, I didn't want indiscriminate firing all over the place tonight—and ran back to where I'd left the Danakil.

He wasn't there, of course. But I found him hiding in a clump of bullrushes. I held out the sword to him with both hands, and he took it hesitantly, and then swung it up and over to cut my head right off with one stroke. Patiently, I took his arm—it was like corded steel— and held it, and whispered again: "A friend, not an enemy! Go south, keep the moon in the corner of your hunting eye. Hide by day and travel by night..." And what then? I could only give him a sporting chance. I let go the wrist, and the sword went slowly down to his side. He couldn't understand what was going on; why should anyone, not of his tribe, befriend him? But then he recovered his wits, and touched the edge of the blade with a hoary thumb to test it, and nodded his approval. I held out the water bag, and he took it and felt its weight appreciatively, and then suddenly dropped to his knees and kissed my foot.

And then, he was gone, a shadow streaking away in absolute silence, like a black fox. I had a feeling that maybe he just might make it.

I ran quickly back to the barracks. And when I went into the room, she was there, looking bewildered and scared, hostile and resigned, all at the same time. All had to do was pay over the money, and she was mine. My own, personal female slave. American.

It was a stimulating thought.

CHAPTER 4

She was probably quite an attractive woman, but she didn't seem to be so at this moment.

First of all, she looked as though she hadn't had a bath in a couple of months, and her hair, which once might have been long and beautiful, was now merely long and unkept; straggling down over quite a delicate face spoiled by an angry curve to the mouth. Well, she had a right to be angry. And her eyes were red; she'd been crying. She was still, more or less, in her stewardess uniform, but her blouse was gone and she wore only the jacket and skirt.

Her shoes and stockings were gone too, and she wore great floppy sandals on her feet, and there was a blanket thrown over her shoulders.

She stared when I came into the tent. I don't suppose she was expecting an American, or perhaps it was just the usual thing, my size; a lot of people stare. She looked up at me wide-eyed—blue eyes, quite pale, much prized by the Arabs who would have been buying her—and said hesitantly: "They said you wanted...wanted to buy me. I don't...don't really believe it. Or have you come to rescue me? Is that it?"

I don't suppose the idea of an elaborate plot for rescue had entered Sheikh Ahmed's mind, and I didn't like the thought that she might have planted a suspicion there. I said: "Rescue? Not exactly. I need a woman, and you're for sale. But I think you'll be better off with me than with most people."

I had to see the look in Sheikh Ahmed's eyes; and as I expected, they were veiled again, thoughtful, wondering about that word *rescue*, I told him brutally: "Not too bad, but I'd like a better look at her before any money changes hands."

He said smoothly: "Of course."

It obviously wasn't the first time, because he merely nodded at her and she slowly began to take her clothes off. She shuddered a little, and then decided to challenge me about it, to make me feel bad; and when she was quite naked—except for those god-awful sandals—she held her head high and looked me straight in the face, standing there with her clothes in one hand, trailing on the floor, one knee slightly bent, looking like a statue by Maillol.

Fellawi still looked at me with those veiled eyes, and could feel them burning with all sorts of unanswered questions. I took my time looking her over. I said: "Turn around," and she did, then turned back to face me. I could see that she was dying to say something really nasty now that she was in the presence of one of her kind, but it seemed she thought better of it. I turned back to Sheikh Ahmed.

I said: "Not bad at all, what's her temper like?"

He shrugged; the suspicion was disappearing. "Really quite good. In two and a half months of travel, I've only had to beat her twice." He said hastily: "On the soles of her feet, you'll see there's not a mark on her skin anywhere."

"Good." I said adamantly, not to let those suspicions come back: "But the price is far too high. Seven thousand."

He knew I had the full price in my pocket, that it was merely a matter of procedure, of not giving in too easily. He smiled and shook his head, and we haggled some more, and finally I handed him the thick bundle of notes. He had the effortless grace not to make any attempt at counting them, but merely slipped them under his robe and said: "She is yours, Mr. Cain, and if I may say so, you've made an excellent investment."

The woman looked at me with a mixture of hatred and scorn. She said sourly: "Now may I get dressed, if you don't mind too much?" I nodded, not smiling at her, and she reached for her clothes to slip back into them.

And it was precisely at that moment that, without knocking,

Hassan Tahari came in. And he was already expecting trouble; his rifle was in his hand and pointing straight at my gut, and I saw that the safety catch was off and that his finger was on the trigger.

There was just time for a quick double check; I looked at Sheikh Ahmed and saw the look of furious indignation on his face where there might have been merely surprise; it was confirmation, if it were still needed, that this was the number one man whose activities had been interrupted by a subordinate. It wouldn't take long for Tahari to set matters to rights once more.

I knew Tahari, of course, from his photographs in the Interpol file. Unhappily, he knew me too. He said, not taking his eyes off me but addressing his master the Sheikh: "An archeologist coming down from Riyadh? There was a very big man, more than two and a quarter meters tall—"they always exaggerate, the Arabs—asking a lot of questions in Gedaref, a police spy. A few days later, he was in Suakin, asking more questions, always a jump or two behind the caravan. And now, another big man turns up in Khadir, a jump ahead of us, and we're expected to believe it's not the same man?"

I was glad he was so talkative. There was time to hook my foot under the brazier.

I threw myself at Tahari's knees, knocking aside the rifle as I went by. It fired, and I heard the bullet smash into the wall; and I also heard the red-hot ashes of the brazier scattering just around Osman's feet. I picked Tahari up by his belt—an old man, but tough as nails—and threw him at Sheikh Ahmed, and kicked the fallen rifle up into Osman's face; and grabbed hold of the woman's wrist and yanked. Her arm nearly came off with the speed of it, but she sort of flew horizontally through the door after me, and in a second we were heading for the trees. A startled sentry fired a hopeful shot or two in the darkness, and I heard someone staggering, stumbling after us; and a few moments later we were at the truck and in it.

I pushed the starter and it roared noisily into action, and we headed out of there fast, heading straight into the impossible desert, not caring about soft sand or hard rock or anything else. I pushed the accelerator pedal to the floor, and the noble old truck roared as only an old piece of machinery will. The gear lever fell out, but we were in second, so it didn't matter too much, and in a few moments I was able to wiggle it back into place again, and we bumped on crazily, wondering how long it would be for the horses to get after us. A moment or two for saddling, if they bothered to do that. We weren't doing much more than forty miles an hour, but it was enough.

The guards were running from the slaves' sleeping place, aroused by the shot, and I tore through them, paying them no heed at all, swung right by the edge of the pool, and headed for the broken pottery steps that the old King's scribe had written about, then swung the wheel hard over and headed due north. I felt the truck bump itself onto the hard granite road under all that blown sand, and then we were racing on, the wheels down deep but gripping on the roadbed, even when we passed the broad patch that I knew from my explorations to be quicksand; there was a steep dip down and up again where even the buried granite blocks had sunk until they found their own level. On each side of us, the soft sand was a barrier against pursuit; even the horses would have trouble there and would be slowed down to a stumbling walk; and it would take a long time to prepare the sleepy camels.

But they knew I couldn't get far in the truck; at least, that's what they *thought*. I watched for the cairns that marked the route.

Beside me on the seat, the woman was naked as the day she was born. I said: "Do you still have your sandals, at least? I didn't want to take my eyes off where we were going to look, but I struggled out of my nice white silk jacket and passed it to her, and she took it without a word of thanks. Instead, as she slipped into it, she said wrathfully: "If someone would kindly tell me what the hell is going on?"

I said: "We're heading for the sea, for the coast, where else would fugitives run for?"

"And then? What then, for God's sake?"

"Then we cut back towards the Rub al Khali, where no one is going to think of looking for us."

"The Rub al what? What's that?"

I said: "The Empty Quarter, so called because nothing can live there."

"Except us."

"Uh-huh."

She struggled with the door. "Let me out of here, I'm going

back, I prefer that punk of a sheikh to dying out there in the desert."

I said: "Sit tight, the time for foolishness is gone."

We came to a steep sandstone rise in the desert and climbed it, and I cut the motor once we'd passed it, and scurried back up to the top to listen. I could see the darker blob that was the oasis back there in the distance; dark against the pale grey sand, but there were no signs of pursuit. Fellawi was taking his time; he knew we wouldn't get very far in that beat-up old Dodge, and even less on foot.

The buried road came to an end at the cairn that indicated the beginnings of the foothills, and the truck slipped off it and deep into the sand, and sunk to its axles, and I left the engine running and the gear engaged and jumped out and said to her: "Get behind the wheel and keep her straight."

I saw her move over with a sigh as I ran to the back, put my shoulder against the bodywork, and shoved hard. The sand flew, and the wheels sank deeper, and then she was out and bumping along once more, and I ran ahead and jumped back into the driving seat and swung towards the coast; if and when they found our tracks, this was the way they'd expect us to go, and it didn't seem kind to disappoint them. It took a little time to find hard smooth rock to drive on, a mile or two further on, without leaving tracks so that we could change our direction when we were ready.

And then, the truck made up its mind for us; it blew a front tire. There was no spare, of course, so that was that. But we were facing the right direction, so I climbed down and said cheerfully: "Come on; honey, this is where we start to walk." She sighed, but followed me obediently down, and had the humor to say: "You bought me, a slave, so I'd better do as I'm told."

I checked to see that there was no soft sand to give away our change of direction, then took from the hiding place under the chassis the things that just might be needed—the marvelous Trinovid binoculars, my bankroll, the little flashlight. I took the water container, which was full, and a tight-packed mess of sticky dates, and an old bottle that was rolling around in the back—you never leave a useful container lying around in the desert, and what a lucky precaution that turned out to be!—and we headed up into the dark hills of the Jebel Hijaz, walking quite slowly and easily to conserve our strength. By my reckoning, we had about five hours to daylight, five hours in which to get well away from the truck and the oasis, and get ourselves safely hidden before sun-up.

And when we'd gone on for nearly three hours in near silence, she flopped down on the ground beside me and said, categorically: "You can do what you damn well like, you overgrown bastard, but I'm not walking another inch. Call me a cab, for God's sake."

Good. I hadn't wanted to start her talking until she'd recovered from the shock of what had been happening to her; I wanted to give her time to think a little, and now, it seemed, she was in better shape.

I said gently: "Just another couple of hundred yards, and you can rest. You see the rocks there? We'll rest there...and talk"

She hesitated just long enough, and then groaned and got to her feet, and went over to the rocks and found a place where we could sit in fair comfort, well under cover, with an easy way out if anyone should come along, though I didn't think that would be likely. The Empty Quarter was below us, we were at its edge; and no one would come even as close to it as this.

She flopped down and drew up her knees and pulled my jacket around them, and said, glowering: "My God, you *bought* me! *Bought* me, you bastard, like I was a piece of prime rib for roasting. You've got your nerve."

I said: "Would you have rather stayed? I imagine you must have had a change of heart somewhere along the line since you decided to set out on this caper."

Brooding, she said; "No, I wouldn't rather have stayed. But just try and screw me, you bastard, and I'll tear your eyes out, with what's left of my beautiful long nails."

She sat there huddled up and angry, angry and not understanding. There was a certain strangeness to her silence, as though all that had happened to her was unbelievable, and so she didn't want to ask any questions and be told of more impossibilities.

But there was one thing I had to know, I said: "You did start all this of your own free will, didn't you?"

She glared: "What makes you think I'd be such a goddamn fool?"

"There were a couple of places you could have yelled for help if you really wanted it."

She didn't answer; she didn't have to. Instead, she said, with a touch of astonishment in her voice: "That was a hell of a lot of money you handed over, how much was it? Just to make my day, tell me how much I'm supposed to fetch when *you* sell me. And are you going to make me take my clothes off..."

I said: "You don't have any clothes, only those beautiful sandals."

"...so they can all examine me? Look at my teeth, pinch my boobs, have themselves a good time and then say: no, the price is too high? My God, this could never happen in Wisconsin. And I'm thirsty, too. Not that I suppose that it means anything to you."

I held the can for her and dribbled water into her palms, and said patiently: "You haven't even told me your name."

"Connie, Constance Penny Delorme. And who the hell are you?"

"My name's Cabot Cain. At the moment at least, I'm with Interpol, sort of. Not very precisely, but sort of."

"Oh, a cop." There was the great contempt of the very immature.

"Not in the least, they're an advisory body, as a matter of purely academic interest. Officially, I'm not supposed to be doing this sort of thing at all. Officially, they don't even employ me."

She flared. "So why are you doing it?"

I said: "I just like running around the empty desert with naked women, it stimulates my imagination. Hungry?"

"Well, of course I'm hungry!"

I handed her some of the sticky dates, and she said: "Oh my God, dates again!"

I said: "Eat them. You're going to need all the energy you can muster very soon."

She grunted, and for a little while she fell silent. The night was cold now, though there was no wind, and the moon was rising; soon, in the moonlight and the crisp night air, it would be almost as light as day. All around us, the broken rocks were huddled together in weird and startling shapes, eroded by the dryness, standing guard over the sands below as though the proximity of that great dry expanse had withered them. There were no trees, no bushes, no camel-shrub, no weeds, nothing but hard dry rock that time had left alone, as though it were not worth bothering with.

She said at last: "I suppose I ought to thank you. Well, thank you." She didn't sound as though she really meant it; she would, later.

I said: "We're not out of the woods yet. Your troubles aren't exactly over, but they're...different now. At least we've a good chance of getting out of here alive."

"You know this part of the world?" She was trying hard not to sound frightened now.

"I know it."

"How do people live out here, for God's sake? Some of the things I saw..."

"I know. They survive, and that's what we'll do. It's just a question of knowing how."

"And you do."

I said: "Yes, I do. Survival is the oldest art in the world. And, take my word for it, I've studied it."

"Well, I suppose that sooner or later we'll find out how much of that is true, and how much is just bull, won't we?"

She sucked the sticky date sugar off her fingers, and then wiped them on my Brooks Brothers jacket, and grimaced at me and said: "They're good."

"They're Halawy dates, the sweetest of them all. Did you ever get a chance to talk to Fellawi on that caravan?'

"Talk to him?" She laughed. "Yes, I talked to the sonofabitch."

"But not, presumably, on a very intimate basis."

"Too goddamn intimate." Was there a bitterness in her voice?

I said: "I didn't mean that. I suppose he never mentioned anything that might relate to his plans for the future? It's not likely he told you much, but..."

She looked at me strangely. "Are you gunning for him? Is that it?"

"Not really. I just want to know as much about him as possible, he's up to something a trifle bigger than your...kidnapping." It wasn't quite the right word, but she didn't deny it. I said: "He's got something up his sleeve which just might turn out to be the same sort

71

of thing on a bigger scale. The rulers here have developed a fad for American girls in their harems, the new status symbol. And Fellawi is just the kind of man to cash in on that kind of fad. Unhappily, I wasn't able to talk to him long enough to find out what he's up to."

She gave me the impression of being an intelligent woman, and I told her so, and I said: "How come you walked into all this so easily? On the surface; it doesn't make sense, and I'd like to know more about it."

"To bolster your own intelligence?"

"No. And that wasn't a very kind remark. So tell."

"Well..." She lay down on her back and spread her long legs out carelessly, and said: "I was on the Kenya run, and we'd stopped over in Khartoum to change crews, and... Did you know they give us little pep talks, in the school?"

"The school for stewardesses?"

"They teach us how to serve two hundred dinners in thirty seconds, how to fill fat little salesmen from Ohio with bourbon without getting them drunk, how to brush off the Casanovas if we really want to. And my God, on any runs to Africa or the East, they teach us how not to be kidnapped for houris."

"For what?"

"Houris. You know, those harem girls."

I said: "For God's sake, *houri* is merely the Persian word for black-eyed, and by association, beautiful. It's not really a profession."

"Well, whatever. They teach us how not to be picked up by smooth-talking handsome beasts, and carted off to the sheikhdoms as high-priced whores."

"Very wise, I'd say."

"Anyway. In Khartoum, this gorgeous beast came up to me in a cafe..."

"Fellawi?"

"Who else? He's gorgeous, even you must admit that. He was very frank and open, and said a friend of his, a Sultan in Arabia..." She frowned. "Do they have Sultans in Arabia? I thought that was Morocco."

I said patiently: "It's merely the Arabic word for a sovereign. Do go on."

"Anyway, this gorgeous thing said a friend of his, the Sultan of somewhere or other, wanted an American wife. And by God, that would make me a Sultana, wouldn't it? Or is that some kind of a currant? In fact, he said *all* the Sultans wanted American wives, and would I oblige? I told him to get lost, Charlie, and he said I could have a contract, all signed and sealed and delivered, for three years as the Sultan's wife, at the end of which I could either stay or go home, whichever I wanted, and meanwhile I'd get a thousand dollars a week. Can you believe that? My take-home, for keeping two hundred lushes happy and comfortable, is a hundred and thirty seven bucks and forty-two cents, and here I would be getting a thousand for doing the same for one man. All right, for doing a trifle more, but it might surprise you to know that the trifle more is becoming very popular nowadays. It's very big with the Captains." She squinted at me and said: "But you wouldn't know that, would you? Aren't you a bit of a square, come down to it?"

I said: "Well, thank you. How kind of you to notice."

"Anyway. I was to get a thousand a week for being nice to this decrepit old bastard, whoever he was, and I mean, at that sort of figure, a girl couldn't hardly refuse, could she?"

"And you really fell for it? I can't bear to hear it."

"Are you kidding?" She had a sudden idea, and said pathetically: "It was all a line of bull, wasn't it? I mean, a hundred and fifty thousand dollars for three years is a sad thought if it really was there waiting for me."

"Just a line of bull. Go on."

"But they've got all that oil money. Millions of it."

"And they contrive to hang on to most of it. You were saying?"

"Anyway, I thought, well, why don't I ride with it for a while, maybe pick up a down-payment or something to teach this gorgeous punk a lesson."

"Oh my God."

"And so I agreed to meet him later that night to discuss it with him. We met in a very respectable cafe, and all I had was some of that Turkish coffee and some rose water, and the next thing I knew I was driving across the desert in the back of a beat-up old taxi. We drove and drove and drove, until the dust was coming out of my ears, and then we transferred to a truck, and then another truck, and then some more after that. My God, I never knew Africa was so big. We must have driven for ten days without seeing another soul on the road." She snorted, "Road! Just a ditch in the dust. Then we got to the Red Sea, finally, I don't know where exactly, and I was hidden in a godawful warehouse for three days, and one night shoved on board a boat, one of those Arab things, and off to...to wherever it was we landed. Then, for God's sake, they put me on a camel, just like in the kiddies Zoo."

I said gently: "Where did you join up with the blacks?"

"At Suakin. I recognized it, I'd been there once before on a side trip during a long layover in Port Sudan. My God, those poor bastards. I can't believe it's still happening."

"Nobody believes it. It would be too much trouble to believe it. They'd have to get involved, and that wouldn't do, would it?"

She was on the verge of tears at the thought of it, the memory etched into her mind. She said: "They used their whips on them if they even opened their mouths to ask for water. For me...I 'was obviously pretty special, they had two men standing guard, just standing there, no guns or anything, but somehow very menacing. I didn't dare yell, ever. When the blacks were on board, they shoved me on too, and..." She sighed. "That, I suppose, was that."

"And Fellawi was with you all the way?"

"Most of the way. He was in the front of the truck, I was in the back, a big bearded bastard keeping an eye on me, made me feel like...I don't know, like hell. But he was..." She hesitated, almost ashamed of what she was going to say, ashamed of herself for not hating him as she should have done. She said: "At first, he wasn't too bad, he gave me cigarettes, and a bottle of some godawful Greek wine, and gave me lots of *gazoz*, you know, that godawful pink lemonade they drink, and plenty to eat. Too much to eat... Then, one night, we were passing through a small town, I've no idea where it was, and I jumped out and ran, I thought I'd find someone who could help me. Anyway, I ran and ran, and someone caught me, and handed me back to them, just like that."

"No one tries to cross the slavers. No one."

"It was all right until the following day; when we were out in the desert again, and then..." Her lips tightened. "He didn't say very much. He just had two of his men hold me down on the sand on my back, with my feet in the air; and he whipped them, hard, on the soles, about twenty or thirty times. It hurts like hell, I can tell you."

"Yes. Yes, I imagine it does. You must hate his guts." It was a question; it seemed important to know the answer.

She shook her head. "No, not really. He had a...a sort of charm about him, does that sound silly?"

"No."

"He'd smile, and offer cigarettes, and light them for me. And the language he used, he sounded like...I don't know."

"And apart from that time, he never...mistreated you?"

"No." She hesitated, and then said: "Well, yes, a couple of times. He sort of raped me on the dhow. Twice."

It didn't seem the right choice of words, but I thought I knew what she meant. I echoed: "Sort of?"

A sigh. "It wasn't as bad as all that, really, I just said no, and he just insisted. Same thing used to happen at college, all the time, only he was a lot more gentle. Same thing happens with the Captains, some of them, just depends who you get as a skipper." She sighed. "Like I said, it's the new bag, I don't really mind it too much. Even with that punk Sheikh Ahmed, it wasn't too bad. Not really."

I didn't like the sympathy for him that she obviously had; the workings of a woman's mind are almost the only thing a man can't profitably study. I said, pushing her: "You know where you'd have finished up? In the course of time?"

She fidgeted a little, squirming on the sand then sitting up to look at me. "Some whorehouse, I guess. I'm grateful to you, if that's what you want me to say."

I had a nasty feeling that for some reason she wasn't grateful at all.

I said: "Some whorehouse is right. If you were lucky. You might have been sold off a dozen times before you got there. You'd probably never have left the Peninsula, finished up by working the fields alongside all the other old hags. Whatever made you think you could pull a trick like that on this crowd?"

She said 'tartly: "Because I didn't have any previous

experience of *this crowd*. And can you please tell me what's next on the agenda? Do we just sit here till the water gives out, and then lie down and die?"

It was good to hear the spirit in her, even if she wasn't particularly sure of herself. I said: "As soon as you've rested up, we'll be on our way."

"Where to, for God's sake?"

"I don't know where to. Just away from here. We have got to put space between us and them, and the sooner the better."

And then there was the sound of horses' hooves. It was muted and distant, but still distinct. I looked up at the bright moon and said: "Nice timing, if they'd come before moonrise I'd have been quite worried. Just sit quietly, and don't talk or move. Sound carries a hell of a long way in the desert, though we can hear them better than they can hear us, we're higher."

I went to the edge of the little cluster of rocks and lay down on the hard sand. The whole broken plain was there below us, with the oasis now quite clear in the moonlight. Further, much further to the north, I could just pick out, with the help of those oh-so-bright Trinovids, the outline of the truck, black against the sand. I swung the glasses round, and there, approaching the truck at speed in a wide arc, were fifteen or sixteen horsemen, coming in from the side where the ground was hard enough for them, at full gallop. They rode splendidly, the horses' manes streaming, the silver on their saddles catching the moonlight like sparkling drops of water.

Well out in the lead was Sheikh Ahmed himself, a solitary figure with the arc behind him, leading them, sitting straight and easy and riding magnificently. I saw him wave his arm; he'd sighted the truck. The arc swing round in obedience, and I watched with a certain respect as three men detached themselves from the formation and rode up behind the Sheikh while the others fanned out in almost military precision, skirting the dead vehicle like Indians round a wagon, not checking their pace at all.

And then, in a few moments, they were streaking off downhill towards the sea, the way the truck was facing. Two men, I saw, had detached themselves and were walking their horses, looking for tracks; but it was all hard rock down there, and I knew there'd be none. One man rode up to the Sheikh, and they rode together at full gallop for a moment or two, and then the man took off at incredible speed, flogging his horse and driving home the sharp spurs, at an angle that would take him, in time, directly to the little town of Qizan, a cluster of houses and stores by the sea where, if we'd been heading that way, we might just conceivably have found an anchored dhow we could have stolen.

It was good. They were all heading directly away from us.

But then... Not so good. I swung the glasses across the horizon, just to make sure, and there were four horses men heading our way, walking their horses and a good distance away still; they too were checking the ground for tracks.

I said to Connie, mildly: "We'd better get down into the Rub. There's a foursome headed our way, about half an hour's walk distant. We'd better increase that lead a bit."

She was scared again. I said: "No sweat, they won't catch up with us, not if we move right away." I wasn't quite sure; I was very conscious of the last stretch we'd covered, with the sand like dust under our feet. You can't hide tracks like those from a Bedouin for long.

I said: "We head straight into the Rub, the sand dunes." She climbed quickly to her feet and shivered, and I said: "You'll soon be warm, take my word for it." I took a quick look through the glasses at the horsemen, peering carefully over the top of the rise. Dammit, they were galloping; it could only mean they'd found our tracks. I said: "Let's move, fast."

We ran out of there, running easily down the slope towards the sand where the dunes began. I took her hand and pulled her along, increasing her speed, and in ten minutes we reached the first of the dunes; it towered high above us, fifty feet or more of shifting, slippery sand. We moved to the side and around its points at the lowest edge, and into the valley between that dune and the next, then around the point of that one too, and the third and forth the same way, pushing hard.

She was gasping now, and I said: "Now we're out of sight, but we've got to keep moving, and over the tops now, it's quicker."

We stumbled on, the sand up to our ankles and sometimes our calves, clambering up half on our hands and knees and slithering down the slopes on the opposing sides, sending up columns of fine dust that might have betrayed our presence. I warned her about it. I said: "At the tops, move carefully, the dust..." She nodded, too dry and too exhausted to speak. The water can was heavy, but it was a blessing. I gave her some to drink and took a mouthful myself, and we pushed on hard, and when daylight came we'd covered more than four miles and crossed over some thirty dunes.

Fifty more dunes, seven more miles, and poor Connie couldn't move another step. I couldn't blame her, she'd done marvelously well. I said: "I'll carry you up, we slither down."

She gasped out: "No, let me rest, let me die."

The water can was still half full, but I wouldn't let her take as much as she wanted, or even needed. It's the first rule of the desert; even if you're dying of dehydration, you never take the last half of the container, you still might need it even more desperately; you hang on and force the thirst away from you, and the thought of the water still left is what keeps you alive when by rights you ought to be dead, a mummy lying there in the sand.

I hoisted her onto my shoulder, a limp, unresisting bundle, and pushed on hard. It was so hot now that the air was almost unbreathable, and the sun bounced back at us off the white, red-hot sand like a blast furnace, the stifling, impossible heat that had made this the Empty Quarter; its fierceness was appalling, unlike anything I'd ever experienced before, and I know most of the world's dry deserts.

The horsemen caught up with us, almost, soon after midday.

Looking back constantly, I saw the plume of fine sand at the top of a dune less than a mile behind us, and we swung down and started going round the points again; they're lower, and easier to cross, but it's like tacking in a sailboat, zigzagging from east to west and back to east again and losing precious minutes all the time.

And then I saw them, all four riders; slithering down a dune, and a moment later they were firing at us, and not doing very well with their beautiful new rifles, though one bullet caught the water container and ripped it wide open, splashing its precious contents to waste in the sand, and sending me sprawling with a very sore shoulder at the same time. I swung round and doubled back, and passed them a dune and a half to one side, and made a wide, wide circle to put space between us, even if it meant going in the wrong direction. Sooner or later, I was sure, they'd give up, at least for the time being; the Bedouins don't like bringing their precious horses into this kind of wasteland, any more than back home a man likes to drive his beautiful new hunk of Detroit iron across a plowed, and muddy field, it's too precious to him.

But then? I got rid of the smashed container, a great jagged hole in its side more than four inches across, after pouring the little water that was left in it into the bottle; it didn't seem much to live on.

We struggled on. Connie was in semi-coma now and I stood her on her feet and slapped her back into consciousness, and made her walk a little to get the circulation going, then threw her over my shoulder again and ran on. And we lost them, or they finally gave up.

But it wasn't till four o'clock in the afternoon that Fenrek found us. "Look for water," I had told him, "and that's where you'll find me. Sooner or later, if there's water around, I'll find it. So be there."

I'd almost given him up.

CHAPTER 5

Fenrek said quietly: "If you want to sleep for a while, I'll keep watch."

I said: "Actually, I thought of doing a few exercises. Keep in shape, you know?"

He growled: "It was just an idea. What are we going to do with her?" He jerked his head delicately at Connie, stretched out there on the cold sand and as fast asleep as a woman can be and still remain alive, her blanket tight around her, one long leg incongruously stuck out at an angle and bothering Fenrek considerably; he never could resist a well-shaped leg.

I said: "Legally, in this country, she's mine, because I bought her. Actually, since I bought her with your expense account money, she's yours. So take her if you want to, dear fellow. If not, stop leering at that leg."

He said coldly: "I was worrying about that sunburn. She's going to be in agony tomorrow. And I repeat, what are we going to do with her?"

"I rather hoped she might help us, somehow or other. I've a feeling she could be quite useful, if only by publishing her memoirs as a warning for other young ladies straight out of finishing school. She'll never help us very actively in finding Ahmed Fellawi."

"Oh? Why not? I've been rather impressed by her courage."

"She has quite a warm feeling for him."

He said didactically: "That, of course, is the most ridiculous assertion I've ever heard." He thinks he knows a lot about women, Fenrek, and perhaps he does; he's had enough experience of them. He took time out to think about it for a while, knowing that I never made a ridiculous assertion in my life, and said at last, frowning: "A warm feeling for him? Surely not, not after what he made her suffer?"

"He sort of raped her a couple of times. The quickest way to a woman's heart."

He stared at me. There are times when Fenrek positively hates flippancy. He said: "And that's a ridiculous statement too, of course. Quite apart from the main question—how do you *sort of* rape a woman?"

I said: "I asked her the same question. Apparently you beat down the barriers, and then kiss and make up afterwards. Something like that. I'm told it happens all the time, even in the colleges."

"Good God! That's quite horrifying! So we'd better disembarrass ourselves of her at the earliest opportunity."

"You mean leave her here?"

"You know very well what I mean. As soon as we reach the coast and find a boat."

"Then the sooner the better. You think she's had enough sleep?"

"You know her better than I do."

I sighed. He was determined to be difficult. He'd been away from civilization for too long. Come to that, so had I.

We woke Connie up, and she merely groaned, and I said gently: "If we can reach the beach before the day gets too far advanced... That sunburn's going to give you a terrible time, I'm afraid." She nodded, and then promptly shut her eyes again, curling herself up and squiggling her hip into the sand to get more comfortable. I said patiently: "There's still a chance they might catch up with us here, you know, unless we keep moving. Down to the beach, and you can have a nice long swim."

She shuddered and shivered, but stood up and draped her blanket over her shoulders, and said "Just a goddamn chattel. I always wondered just what a chattel really was, and now I *am* one. God, what a thought."

We set out south, and she plodded along behind us, too

miserable to speak. Fifteen more miles, but the going was easy, and we covered it in a little over four hours. The sun was still low on the water, copper and red and glorious, its reflection almost as brilliant as the source itself.

And as we stumbled onto the beach, a great explosion tore the air apart.

Ahead of us, and a little to our left, the water went up in a great angry spout, and rocks were flying everywhere, and I yelled: "Take cover!" and grabbed Connie again, reflecting that I always seemed to be grabbing hold of this woman and yanking her somewhere. We threw ourselves, the two of us, under the friendly cover of some boulders, and I looked out and saw Fenrek just standing there, looking up in the air as a great hunk of solid granite came sailing down by him; he side-stepped neatly and efficiently, and it hurled itself into the sand close beside him.

There was a splattering of smaller rocks, and he looked at the two of us and said quizzically: "Just dynamiting, you know."

I said: "Yes, I can see that. But who, for God's sake?"

And then, a little way down the beach, someone yelled, and from behind the cover of the rocks a fat little man came running, perspiring heavily, panting, a look of anguished alarm on his face. He wore grubby white trousers and no shirt, and his skin was blotched with sunburn.

Stumbling over himself to reach Connie, he spluttered: "Are you all right, please? Are you hurt, no?" He stood there, panting, and said: "The flags, I didn't put them up, there's no one, no one here! Oh dear, are you all right?"

The last of the dust was settling, and I said: "No harm done, but what the hell is it?"

He took a deep, deep breath of relief. "I am to dynamite, we will build a wharf here, a small one, you understand, for the banana boats that come in here from Mogadishu, you understand?" The words were pouring out fast, and he was mopping away at the sweat, a flabby little man all full of apology and fuss. I helped Connie to her feet, and Fenrek brushed some dust from his jacket and waited, and the fat man smiled quickly and said:

"Hadkinjian, Arnold Hadkinjian, I make a small pier bring the boats in close, you understand? For the Sheikh of Hadramaut, a very progressive man, perhaps you know him?"

Fenrek wandered over and said: "Yes, I saw your boat from the air when I flew over a few days ago. I'm Colonel Fenrek, from Interpol, and this is Cabot Cain, Miss Constance Delorme."

The fat man said again, bowing: "Arnold Hadkinjian, a great pleasure." He seemed to realize for the first time that Connie had nothing on but my jacket and the blanket, and he goggled at her and blushed furiously, and I said:

"I'm afraid Miss Delorme lost her clothes, just one of those things."

"Er, yes, of course, how very untoward." I thought it was a nice choice of words. He said again, apologizing all over the place: "There is never anyone here, *never!* So, no flags, who shall I put up red flags for? My workers, they know."

The high rocks came down to the water's edge here, and he gestured beyond them and said: "My boat, perhaps I could offer you, I don't know, a drink, some coffee?"

I said: "I can't believe you've actually got drinks on board, in Arabian waters?"

He smiled, beaming now that he'd found something he could do to recompense us. He said: "Of course, when the Sheikh's men come on board, as they do from time to time, I do not let them know that I am carrying alcohol. I do not like to break the local laws, but..." He shrugged. "The work is so very hard here, and one must use one's own discretion, mustn't one? Don't you think?"

He, too, couldn't keep his eyes off Connie's long legs, and he danced round her and said, perspiring: "It is none of my business, of course, but perhaps, if you need something more comfortable to wear, I have a woman on board, a servant, you understand, but she might be able to provide something—not exactly suitable, but at least better than a blanket. Would you like that? I would be only too glad..." He was puffing along beside us, as we walked along the beach, and when we rounded the point, there was the most beautiful little yacht a man could wish for. Not aesthetically beautiful; it was grubby and ill-painted, and not particularly well cared for; but it meant, for a moment at least, a touch of relaxation and relative comfort, and that, to all of us, was beautiful.

It was an old coast guard cutter, which Hadkinjian told us he'd bought in Egypt; and fifteen minutes later we were on board, sipping *ouzo* and water, enjoying the clean, antiseptic taste of the milky liquid. There was even ice, from a small electric refrigerator. "Any fool can be uncomfortable," Hadkinjian said expansively.

He had a skipper on board, a surly, taciturn Greek named Pastroudis, a young Maltese mate named Sogo, a crew of four Somalis, and a young and strikingly attractive Ethiopian girl named Ngatua who, he claimed—casting a semi-apologetic glance at Connie—was his cook. She came in, bowing and smiling, all courtesy and shining white teeth, her hair piled high on her head in three concentric curves and fastened with beautiful ivory pins. Her skin was coffee-colored, her features delicately Hamitic, and her eyes had that fascinating slant to them that indicated an alien blood in her ancestry, probably Beja. Her movements were astonishingly lithe and graceful, and Hadkinjian beamed at her and said, in fluent but very incorrect Amharic:

"Guests, my little dove, and I'm afraid we have to find some clothes for this naked woman, you won't mind, will you? I'm afraid I promised. And some food."

He turned to me and said: "Amharic, she speaks no other language, so you will forgive me? I told her to bring food and clothing for Madame."

I said: "You are most kind."

She went out; and came back soon with some bread and some cheese and some hunks of freshly-boiled crawfish, and some tomatoes and green peppers, and she sat with us, smiling, and began to make sandwiches. And when she'd finished, she set them before us, and held out her hand for Connie, and made gestures to indicate that there was clothing in the other cabin. The two women went off together, and left us alone.

Fenrek said to our host: "I wonder if we could impose upon you...could we ask you to run us over to Aden? The nearest place we can get a plane. Would that be too much trouble?"

Hadkinjian was about to agree, and I said gently: "Not Aden. Djibouti."

Fenrek stared. "Djibouti? That's twice as far! Aden's less than two hundred miles from here, Djibouti's a hell of a way!"

I said: "Three hundred and eighty, roughly. But that's where we have to go, none the less."

"But why, for God's sake?"

I said: "Djibouti has the best supply of liquor in the world, only you can't get Russian vodka there."

Both of them stared at me blankly. I said: "The result of a twenty-year-old squabble. Nineteen fifty-one, three Russian ships put into the harbor, and the port officer refused to give them the correct salute, there was an indignant protest from Moscow, you remember?"

Fenrek sighed. He knew better than to argue. He said patiently: "All right, Mr. Hadkinjian, could you possibly take us to Djibouti? What is it in a craft like this, a day and a half's cruising? Would it be asking too much?"

Hadkinjian's smile was even broader. He said: "Such a nice town, Djibouti. For three weeks now I have been blasting these rocks, and it is time I took a little cruise. I can do some fishing on the way back, I will be delighted to take you there."

We sat and drank his *ouzo*, and waited for Connie, and he told us about his operation, chatting, amiably and gesticulating broadly.

He had a camp on shore, a little way further up the beach from where we'd arrived, with a crew of workmen provided by the progressive Sheikh, to assist in clearing a path for his new jetty. There was no road here, but it was equidistant from two small villages, villages that lived on the verge of starvation and were only there because of tiny fresh springs that bubbled out of the rock, the water so sour with gypsum that it was almost impossible for a foreigner to drink. A few coconut palms grew in these two places, and almost nothing else, and when there were no nuts, the villagers lived on bananas that came from Mogadishu to trade for copra. It was a hazardous existence at the best of times; and in the monsoon, when the boats could not land their cargo, it was the natural and expected thing that the old men, the women, and the children should starve. But soon, there'd be a wharf, and the boats could come inshore whatever the winds were like.

Connie came back with a brilliant red and blue cotton dress that reached a few inches down her thighs, her legs covered now with the white cream powder of lanoline lotion for the sunburn, which was atrocious. On an empty stomach, she'd had too much of the fiery *ouzo*, and was so drunk she could hardly stand, and she promptly went to sleep on the cabin's divan.

Fenrek said: "In Djibouti, we can put her on a plane for the States, there's a bi-weekly service." I said nothing, and he looked at me and scowled: "Unless you have something up your sleeve for her to do?"

I grunted at him, and looked at Hadkinjian and said: "Ahmed Fellawi's base of operations is Djibouti, that's why we're going there."

Fenrek was horrified. He threw an anguished look at Hadkinjian too, as though I'd broken security by talking in front of him, and then threw up his hands, the cat out of the bag, and said: "I find that very hard to believe. We have an agent in Djibouti, and if he really operated there, I'm quite sure we'd know about it. His trade is only legal in one country, and that's Arabia. Therefore, it makes sense that Arabia would be his base, not Djibouti, where the French police are both efficient, and ruthless with people of his kind. And moreover, if your assumption is correct, which I doubt, the last thing we want to do is expose that poor young woman to Sheikh Ahmed Fellawi once again."

There was a faint smile on Hadkinjian's face, telling me what I wanted to know, but to make it easy for Fenrek, I said to him: "I see you know Sheikh Ahmed, Mr. Hadkinjian. Or at least you know of him?"

The smile went quickly, and he looked at Fenrek and said: "Colonel, you must understand that a foreigner in Arabia, must, how I say it? Adapt himself to the way of Arabia. Yes, I know Sheikh Ahmed, a very bad man. Two years ago, when I was in Aden, blasting, you know, I met him and was able to do him a very small favor. He was generous enough to make me a present—something. I needed quite badly."

I said: "Let me make a wild guess. Could it have been, perhaps, the girl Ngatua? Your cook?"

She was there, sitting with us and not understanding what we were talking about. But when I'd mentioned the Sheikh's name, I'd seen the look of sudden alarm in her face.

Hadkinjian threw her a worried look. He turned back to me and said: "Er...yes, it was. But I am a cultured man, Mr. Cain, I pay her a salary, a handsome salary, like any other servant, and so... She stays with me willingly. I would even say eagerly." Blustering, he said: "If only you could talk to her, if only she knew your language, she would tell you!"

He was almost weeping.

I thought I'd practice my Amharic, and I said to the girl: "Your master thinks that perhaps we want to take you away from him, but if you are happy, then nothing is further from our minds. I see that he treats you well, with respect."

It is an important thing for the Ethiopians, the respect.

Her lovely eyes were wide and staring. She said: "He treats me well." Her hand shot out and took Hadkinjian's, a touching little gesture. She said: "He is my lover, why should I want to leave him?"

"I know that too. I want him to understand that we have not come to take you away. You know Ahmed Fellawi?"

She nodded. "A very bad man. He stole me from my village when I was fourteen years old."

"And when was that?"

"Two years ago, three perhaps. He was taking me to Yemen, he told me, but he gave me in Aden to this man, to my lover, and I am very happy with him. I do not want to go away. I will not go away." It was a flat statement of fact. I could almost feel the love she had for this fat and flustered and very human little man.

I turned back to him and spoke English again, for Fenrek's benefit. I said: "Two, three years ago, Aden was in turmoil. Off the record, would that favor have had anything to do with your stores of dynamite?"

He was nervous now, looking at Fenrek and getting ready to start lying. But Fenrek said smoothly: "Interpol is not really a police force, Mr. Hadkinjian. We merely coordinate other people's efforts. And I have no interest at the moment in whatever peccadillos you may feel guilty about."

"Pecca...peccadillos?"

I said: "Your criminal past, Mr. Hadkinjian."

He was scared now, more worried than he need have been. He

said quickly: "No, no, I assure you! I merely lost some dynamite, a considerable quantity of it, and the Military authorities believed that the man responsible was Ahmed Fellawi. But I refused to give any sort of evidence against him—a man must be careful what he does when he's away from home, is it not so? And so, Fellawi went free and chose to show me his gratitude rather than his enmity, which I would have greatly feared." He saw Fenrek's disinterest and plucked up courage. He beamed and said: "It is sometimes wise to be a coward, is it not?"

I said gravely: "The wisest thing in the world."

I was thinking; if he'd chosen to give evidence, the Sheikh just might have been behind bars, and all those sad wrecks of human beings... I couldn't get the memory of that caravan out of my mind, or the image of that poor animal Danakil, running for his life in a hostile country with nothing but an old sword, a water-skin, and his own native cunning. I wondered where he was now.

I said; "Well, I'm sure we can all forget about that." I sipped his *ouzo* and said: "Since you're kind enough to take us where we want to go, could we leave fairly soon, do you think?"

He beamed, the panic gone. "Give me a few moments to make arrangements with my foreman on shore, and we will leave whenever you wish. I would very much like to see Djibouti again, a splendid town."

So that was settled. "We took showers in the tiny bathroom while Ngatua was preparing a more solid meal, and by the time we sat down to eat—ice-cold sea urchins for hors d'oeuvres, chopped starfish poached in coconut milk, and a fine broiled crawfish flambé with Cognac—we were under way.

And as evening was falling on the following day, we pulled into the shark-infested harbor of Djibouti.

CHAPTER 6

It was good, among other things, to be legally somewhere for a change.

Since I'd left Khartoum, I hadn't once used my passport, though I'd been through the Sudan, Ethiopia, Hejaz, Yemen (just a few steps over the border, that night when we escaped from Khadir), Hadramaut, and Saudi Arabia. It was a pleasure when the Customs Officer and the Immigration Officer, and the Health Officials all wanted to inspect me; it made me feel part of society again. Though that might not be such a good thing either, come to think of it.

But Fenrek's pass got us through everything with a minimum of formality. He was eager to get into town, and it occurred to me that he'd raised very little objection when I'd suggested going to Djibouti. He didn't even voice his usual argument—that my reasoning was tenuous. After all, there might have been other twenty-year-old diplomatic squabbles, and other free ports where you couldn't get Russian vodka...

But it was a likelihood that I was right; give me a good likelihood and I'll go to the ends of the world to check it out. Of course, it's a delightful town—one of the few remaining bastions of the old colonial world where privilege still runs rampant and the way of life is relaxed, easy, and informal. They run a good little town, the French, even if it means getting tough with the locals when they have to.

And here Fenrek was, bustling around and keeping his eyes

very wide open as though he expected someone to come welcoming him the moment he arrived. And she did, too.

There's no one in the world quite as devoted to his trying work as Fenrek is. He's tough, and viable, and obstinate, and nothing will stop him once he gets under way. But he has his little weaknesses too, and the greatest of them all is an enormous appreciation for a handsome woman. He'd turn his own mother in if his work demanded it; he'd leave Madame Pompadour's bed if action were coming up; and the woman isn't born who could really take his mind off the intricacies that are always nibbling at the back of his brain.

But if he habitually visits Rome, or Berlin, or Stockholm, or New York, he does take certain pains that he won't feel too much alone there... Lisbon, Madrid, Istanbul, Paris (which is his home), and Budapest (where he was born)—in all these places I knew he had a little pied-a-terre, paid for out of his own pocket, of course, because he's terribly ethical, suitably inhabited by a charming woman for whom his love, at that moment, could never be greater.

He admits it. He doesn't even regard it as a weakness, and to tell the truth, he's probably right, because a weakness presupposes an ensuing harm; and Fenrek's women *never* get him into trouble.

But here, in Djibouti?

It's a nice little town, but it's a very long way from the rest of the world, and I don't suppose he'd been here more than six times in his whole long career.

So I was faintly surprised when he said, as we sat in the Cafe Oriental, sipping champagne out of tulip-shaped glasses (in a free port, champagne is as touting as beer, and a great deal better to drink at six o'clock in the evening): "I've invited a guest along, a young lady. You don't mind, do you? Our agent here, we have to keep her *au courant* with what's been going on."

I said: "I'll be delighted," and when she arrived, I was.

She drove up in one of those ridiculous little Citroens, the *deux cheveaux,* which looked as though some demented children had knocked it together out of bits and pieces of old corrugated iron; surely the most hideous car ever designed by man—and one of the most efficient. Where a mule or a camel can go, over ploughed fields or across the deserts; the *deax cheveaux* will bounce monstrously along, and get there when everything else, including the camel, has laid down and died. She had the piece of rag which is the top folded back and tied with its little rag straps; at seven o'clock in the evening, the humid heat of the day—and what a blessing that humidity was after the arid desert!—had changed to a cool and refreshing dampness.

She bumped twice into the curb, and once into another car as she maneuvered into an impossibly small space, and then gave up and left the little car there with its rear end sticking out four feet into the road, and eased herself out through the comic door that swung open on bare hinges, and came smiling over to meet us.

I was impressed. She was perhaps thirty-five or so, or a little younger, *petite et chic* in the old-fashioned way, with her black hair cut short and framing her face in a not very flattering coiffure that I suppose is fashionable. The tiniest, of figures, almost like a boy's, with no bust to speak of, and hardly any hips, but a vitality to her that was delightful. I suppose gawky would be a good word to describe her; but she was really quite charming with it. She had an interesting, rather than a beautiful face, with startling black eyes and that most-modern kind of make-up that tempts a man to turn his head and look twice. Her nose was small, her mouth was small, and there was a quick, alert look about her that intrigued me. Her steps were tiny too, and fast, very fast; she moved as if tomorrow were just around the corner and would be coming too soon.

And then her face lit-up with a smile of pure delight; she rushed into Fenrek, and threw her arms round him, and he lifted her off the ground and hugged her, and said, beaming: "My dear, dear Jo, it's been so long, far too long, it must never happen again, I can't bear to be parted from you!" It all came out in one breath, and she kissed him, and I stood there like an idiot, waiting for the fuss to die down, and looking covertly at Connie—still dressed in that ghastly mini-dress and those terrible shoes.

He hugged her and kissed her and embraced her and fondled her, and looked at me over her shoulder with an idiotic grin on his face, and you'd have thought it was Dante and Beatrice all over again.

He put her down at last, and grinned at me like a fifty-year-old schoolboy with his first love, and said: "Cabot Cain, Constance Delorme, my dear, dear friend Josephine St. Juste. Jo, Connie, Cabot, we're all very good friends." He squeezed her arm again and he just couldn't take his eyes off her. The sort of woman who grows on you, no doubt.

She wore a jet-black sheath with a high collar and an intriguing string of tiny ceramic' beads painted in once-bright colors and now faded to the palest blues and reds and greens; they were the vid beads the Portuguese brought out here in the late fifteen hundreds, trade beads for the Somalis to exchange for their hides and their incense, and they were rare and beautiful and very valuable.

I took her hand and sat down quickly; her head was not much above my navel, and it looked ridiculous, and she shot into a chair at speed and said: "I'm bursting with all kinds of news for you, but it will have to wait until the social amenities are over." She spoke French, and looked at Connie quickly, and said: "Not a strange language to you, of course?"

Connie sighed. She said in English: "Talk, honey, I'm just a load of baggage anyway," and the young woman switched promptly to English and said: "This champagne is quite undrinkable, so I'm going to have some Dubonnet Blonde." She smiled at Connie and said: "So much better for the figure, you have to worry about that, don't you?" All in a matter of seconds, her sharp eyes had taken in the tatty, over-colored dress and the patent-leather shoes, and Connie said: "Honey, they've just been fattening me up for the slave market, and the dress belongs to an Ethiopian tart because lately I've taken to running around the desert stark naked, and at better times I look a hell of a lot better than this. And I can cope with anything, doll, even with you." She spoke with a genial kind of veiled hostility which promised well, I thought.

Fenrek, pouring oil, said to Connie: "Jo's a model, she knows all the stores, and no doubt some of them will be open still."

Jo said: "The stores, no, they all close at five. But Madame Chanson, who happens to be a fat little fag named Jean-Louis Krok, will happily open up his salon for us whenever the evening is sufficiently far advanced. We have to go there anyway. He, or she if you like, is a police informer, though no one except him, or her, knows that I know that." She looked at Connie's dress again and said affably: "There's no reason at all why even an Ethiopian tart should have such atrocious taste, darling, is there? But don't worry, Madame Chanson will do wonders for you, though we might have to look for a girdle some place." All in one breath, she said: "And why were you running around the desert naked? The Bedouin chasing you? And that thing round your waist, darling, is definitely a curtain pull."

It was; off Hadkinjian's boat.

Fenrek poured some more oil and said: "She's had a terrible time, Jo dear, so don't be unkind to her. She was being sold, if you please, in a slave market."

"My God." I waited for her to ask who in hell would want to buy her, but she didn't. She said instead, politely: "Sold? To the Bedouin Sheikhs?"

I said: "No. To me."

"Oh, Well, I hope you got what you paid for, people usually do."

I was getting to like Jo more and more with every passing comment.

The waiter came and poured some Dubonnet, and Jo looked at Fenrek and said: "But first things first. How long will you stay in Djibouti?"

He took her hand with a sickening affection and said: "Not half as long as I would like."

I said patiently: "That wasn't the question."

"Oh," he threw me a look. "Well, possibly a day or two, possibly longer, we just don't know yet. We only arrived half an hour ago, a grubby little tug owned by a man named Hadkinjian, I wonder if by chance you know him?"

Jo had taken a gold-backed mirror from her bag and was critically examining her makeup. She said: "A name like that, he must be an Armenian. I try not to know any Armenians; next to the Hungarians, they're the most dreadful people in the world." Fenrek, more Hungarian than Bela Kun, beamed at her.

We called the waiter over and ordered dinner, and as we waited, Fenrek took her hand again and said: "Hassan Tahari has surfaced again, you remember him?"

She looked at him quickly, her eyes bright. "So he's not dead after all. I always half suspected he'd turn up again."

"With a man named Ahmed Fellawi, you know him?"

She shook her head, and I said: "I believe he was a desert Arab originally, perhaps from Syria, judging by his accent, though he wears a Hebron *keffia*, with the regal white and gold, if you please. But he is a well-educated man, and I have good reason to believe that this town might be his home base. If it's not...then we're wasting our time here." I looked at Fenrek and said: "Wouldn't you agree?"

He merely stared back indignantly.

I said: "He speaks excellent English and French, he's five foot eleven, weighs about a hundred and sixty pounds, has a cute little black moustache, and is desperately handsome. All the girls fall in love with him. He is a slaver."

Connie said nothing.

Jo shook her head, puzzled. "If he works out of Djibouti, I really ought to have heard of him. But I haven't. Perhaps Jean-Louis might know something."

The dinner came—partridge soup, *sole meuniere*, and venison steaks—and we chatted about nothing in particular until it was cognac time, and then Connie said pathetically: "Look, I don't have to sit here all night in this godawful dress, do I?" She turned to Jo, "What about this fag friend of yours? For three months now I've worn nothing but a tattered old uniform, or what was left of it, a white silk jacket that scratched my sunburn, and...and *this*." She made it sound far worse than it was, though it really was pretty bad.

But Jo was on her feet in a flash, a quite extraordinary movement. One second she was sitting down with a glass in her hand, and the next she was standing up and smoothing her dress over those non-existent model's hips.

I said: "What on earth does a model find to do in Djibouti?"

She looked at me, astonished, and said: "Would it surprise you if I said I modeled? We're a very civilized community here. And it's a free port, so the French fashion houses send everything to this part of the world. We send them on to Addis Ababa, to Port Sudan, Massawa, Asmara, you'd be surprised how many customers there are in Africa for good French clothes. You don't really expect an Ambassador's wife to dress like Tondeleo, do you? We have quite a flourishing trade here. I model, Jean-Louis sends off photographs, we both collect. And now, let us go and see what she can do for this poor, poor Connie of yours." Her eyes were hard on Fenrek.

I felt I had to come to his rescue, so I said, correcting her gently: "Of *mine*. My own personal property. I bought her, remember?"

She turned those startling eyes on me, smiled, and said: "Yes, of course, and isn't that absolutely marvelous for you? Come along, *mon petit*." She took Connie's hand in hers and dragged her off. They were already in that ridiculous car by the time we'd paid the bill and caught up with them.

Ridiculous is the only word Fenrek, a mite under six feet tall, could barely get into the back; I'm seven inches taller than he is, and forty pounds heavier, and it was agony, but it didn't last very long. We pulled up under a portico, bumped into a railing, stopped, and clambered out.

Madame Chanson's name was on an incised brass plate, with a whimsical little touch of her own underneath the name—a bar of music, 'the first seven notes of *Au Clair de la lune*. I thought it was rather sweet, and said so to Jo as we went up the stairway to the second floor. She nodded: "She's a dear thing, really she is, you'll love her." She stopped and looked back at me and said: "And you just might find her very, very interesting as well. There's absolutely *nothing* she doesn't know about what goes on in Djibouti."

She rang the doorbell, and as we waited, Fenrek said: "I told Jo on the phone what it was that brought us here. And she thinks that Madame Chanson might be able to provide a few answers to our questions. Don't ask me how a hermaphrodite dressmaker can know so much about the underworld, but..." He shrugged.

I said: "Security?"

"If Jo trusts her, we can. Take my word for it."

"Good."

The door opened, and a Somali servant, white gowned, a green *tarboush* on his head, bowed us in, and then Madame Chanson herself—it couldn't have been anyone else—came sweeping across the room towards us, his head on one side, his arms extended. A broad, broad smile on his pudgy face.

He was a man of fifty or so, plump but not fat, of medium

height, with long, very white hair elegantly dressed and trained, and he wore a burgundy-red velvet jacket, cut tight at the waist and sort of skirted, with yellow trousers that flared out at the bottom. Draped around the tight neck of the jacket were enough silver beads, and gold pendants, and finely-chased filligree-work, to make him appear a trifle top heavy. Just as Fenrek had done (I saw the frown on Fenrek's face), he lifted Jo clear off her feet with his hug, and said: "My darling Jo, how good of you, how nice, how delightful!" He set her down and looked at us, and she said: "Good friends, Jean-Louis. In the business, the Intelligence bit..."

Madame Chanson raised a horrified hand: "Please, my dear Jo, when there are guests, you must call me Madame Chanson, really, I insist."

Jo grimaced and sighed, and made the introductions: "Jean-Louis Krok, Colonel Fenrek, Cabot Cain, and Connie Delorme, whom we have to do something about." A sudden thought, and Jo looked at Fenrek and said: "We've plenty of money, I hope, haven't we?"

He nodded gravely. "Plenty."

Madame Chanson extended his hand, and I thought for one awful moment Fenrek really was going to kiss it, but he apparently thought better of it, though there was twitching at the sides of his mouth that made me realize he'd contemplated the idea. Jean-Louis put his arms round Connie and gave her a hug, too, then took my hand and said: "A great pleasure, and any friend of Jo's, if I may coin a philosophy..." He turned back to Connie and said: "Darling, you really are a mess, aren't you?" He looked at Jo. "From the bottom up?"

"From the bottom up. Everything."

"Excellent."

He looked at Connie again and squinted, and said dreamily: "I see you in gold lame, with just a touch of black, something quite modern, but not too sophisticated. A trifle *outré*, but not...not *wild*." He reached out and patted her hips and said: "Ah, you're really very lucky, this year it's all hips and breasts and curves everywhere. Poor Joe, she has neither, no hips, and no breasts at all, just little tips of cut lemons, I really don't know how she manages." He looked into my eyes, sighing, and said: "Have you seen her naked? I suppose you have, so I don't have to tell you how terrible it is. But she wears clothes nicely, bless her, and in our business, that's all that matters. And all the dear Consular ladies think they can look like her if they can hide their forty-four inch busts, and we really do try to help them, that's why we're here. It's so important to help people, isn't it? Even though sometimes it's hardly worth the struggle."

He looked at Connie again, full of professional admiration. He said, sighing loudly: "Really, darling, you must look absolutely marvelous naked, just the right lines exactly, the bust is what, seventy-five centimeters? That would be, ah, thirty-four and a quarter inches? And the hips...thirty-five, I'd say, no? But that waist, darling, at least an inch to go, will you do me a favor? Just one inch, two and a quarter centimeters, it would make *such* a difference."

Connie waited patiently while he looked her up and down, and then he said: "All right, everything off, *everything*, down to the bare skin and we'll start from scratch."

Connie murmured: "I've been through this routine before somewhere..."

Fenrek said hastily: "Jo tells me you have a private room here? Where we could talk?"

"Ah yes, of course, Jo knows where it is."

He minced across the room with one hand to his breast and the other held out, like an Infantry officer leading the charge, and Jo took us into an anteroom all done up in purple and mauve, and then into a small, windowless room that was painted black all over, even the ceiling, with a single dead-white skull-on a dead-white marble table, a single dead-white light shining on it. Fenrek stared and said: "Good God."

Jo laughed, her white teeth shining. There were four huge black plastic chairs, pneumatic, pumped up and looking extremely uncomfortable, which they were, and we sat down, and Jo said: "We have to wait one minute."

There was a discreet knock on the door almost immediately, and the Somali servant came in with a tray on which there were five bottles of cognac and one bottle of Creme de Menthe, three brandy snifters, and three liqueur glasses.

I said: "For God's sake who drinks Creme de Menthe here?"

Jo grimaced. "The dear girl, she'll always try to convert all her guests to her taste. She doesn't really expect us to drink it."

There was Remy Martin, and Courvoisier, and Martell Cordon Bleu, and Bisquit, and Gaston de la Grange, which I thought ought to satisfy everybody present.

The Somali said: "If you would like coffee, *'sieurs et dames*?"

Jo shook her head and said: "Nothing else, Abbed, and thank you." He bowed, and was gone.

She said: "Now. Ahmed Fellawi, who calls himself a Sheikh and wears the regal *hattar* and *agal* to which he is not entitled." She leaped up and went to the table and said: "Everybody for Remy Martin?"

On principle, since Fenrek nodded, I said: "Courvoisier," and she looked at me reproachfully with those lovely eyes, and poured me the Remy Martin anyway. She sat down again and said: "Four separate informants keep me posted on the activities of the slavers, and not one of them has ever mentioned the name. That does not imply that he doesn't exist, merely that he's very adept at keeping out of sight. One of those informants tells me the slavers are up to something quite big just now..." She broke off, frowning. "No, that isn't what he says at all. He says there's something very exciting going on, or about to go on... I think he was indicating a change in procedures, or routes—I don't really know." She wasn't a bit happy with her lack of knowledge; it was as though she felt personally responsible for the inconclusiveness.

I said: "Could it have been a change in the *demands* they have to meet? I'm told the rulers are looking for American concubines now; the new status symbol."

She nodded briskly. "Yes, it could have been that. Easily." She frowned, and said slowly: "The pieces are dropping into place. The Sheikh of Najran...while he was in the States to treat an ulcer recently, I seem to remember he married an American girl and took her back with him. Knowing the rulers, I'd say that might easily start a...a trend." The frown deepened, the black brows drew down tight. "No, that isn't right either, that was just the news release. The truth of it was..." Oh that concentration! "The truth of it was, he was on his way home, and he propositioned one of the stewardesses on the plane, a girl named... named...ah yes, Mary Lesteroff, I think. She resigned her job in Kampala, and went with the Sheikh to Najran, where she now lives in great luxury, the number one wife because she's still young and beautiful. No crime committed, of course, because she went of her own free will and hasn't, so far at least, had cause to regret it. Later on, no doubt, she will; when she gets a little bit worn out, and is put to work in the fields with the other ex-wives."

I said: "And it has started a fad. A fad for American concubines."

Jo blinked those great eyes at me. "Why Americans, why not French, or English, or Swedish? What have they got that we haven't?"

Nobody could tell her, so she went on: "In the general area of the Middle East and Africa, there've been, what? three or four cases of stewardesses leaving their planes and just disappearing, over the course of the last six months. It's fair to suppose that some of them, like Mary Lesteroff, have made some sort of arrangement that suits them, but...are we stretching a point to guess that one or two might have been headed for the harems, like your Connie?"

I said: "Not stretching a point at all, it's a likelihood. And it's too late to do anything for them now, but if we're faced with an increase in this sort of activity, then maybe we should increase our activities too. And the more vigorously, the better. You know the going prices?"

She looked at Fenrek, nodding. "After you called me, I did some quick checking of the facts and figures in the last report of the U.N.s. Anti-Slavery Commission. It seems that the going price for an able-bodied male slave in Arabia, almost the only country that hasn't ratified the Anti-Slavery Treaties and where, therefore, slavers can operate without too much interference, is now around three hundred dollars in American money. Ten years ago, the price was a little less, but the African governments weren't trying very hard to put a stop to the trade. Now, Ethiopia in particular, the Somalis in Somaliland, the Sudanese in Kassala, and the Egyptians along the northern shores of the Red Sea, are prosecuting their fight against slavery with a great deal of vigor. In other words, between the source of the slaves in Central and West Africa, and their ultimate destination in Arabia, there's a belt of prohibition extending from Egypt clear down to Somaliland. Which means that at three hundred a head it just isn't feasible any more to carry five or six hundred men and women in chains across nearly two thousand miles of Africa; the losses are too great now, and so are the risks. But... More cognac, anyone?"

She was on her feet again, pouring the drinks, and then she turned to me and said: "You *bought* Connie, you said. Do you mind telling us what you paid for her?"

"Eight thousand dollars. Circumstances dictated a higher than normal price."

"But if the fad catches on, the price will go up?"

"Undoubtedly."

"Then the picture's changing, isn't it? It's hard to hide a long ling of men in chains from a probing army, but a truck with two or three girls on board? More profit, less risk. Is this what your Ahmed Fellawi has seized on? Three or four girls, five or six, a dozen even... A rough hundred thousand dollars by the time he's finished, and the question is only one of supply. And we all know that the American planes carry- four or five young women each, all trained to be smart, attractive, efficient... And they're gullible enough..." She broke off and laughed shortly. "That's the reason why! Gullibility! A French woman would never fall for it! But in any of the duller towns where the planes change crews—Khartoum, Port Sudan, Kampala, Nairobi, the stewardesses are bored and ready for any Ahmed Fellawi who can smile at them and offer them a little excitement. A gullible woman can easily be persuaded, one way or another, to leave the security of her hotel." She shrugged. "A handsome young Arab, full of suave charm, like Ahmed Fellawi... It must be very easy for him. All he has to do is lure the girls away to an Arab cafe. Perhaps they believe they're seeing life as it really is in the Middle East. Perhaps they're looking for kicks. It doesn't really matter. All that matters is that he should lure them out of their hotels, slip them a drugged drink, and bingo! another five thousand dollars, maybe more, in the bag." She said with a sweet smile: "So all we have to do is catch Ahmed Fellawi, and make an example of him. Like by sliding him along that board on the guillotine."

Was this the smart, chic, and attractive young model talking? I could hardly believe my ears.

As though reading my thoughts, she looked at me and smiled. "Catch him, preferably, in one of the Somalilands, even French

Somaliland. It's still a capital offense in all of them."

She was right. The Somalis have suffered much at the hands of the Arab slavers, ever since they came to Africa in—when was it?—probably the thirteenth century, though nobody really knows.

Fenrek said, with a sigh: "Only problem—find him."

And then, right on cue, Madame Chanson and Connie came in. Connie was smiling a little self-consciously, and no wonder. She wore a silver gown with some white at her shoulder, all very elegant and shimmering, a very expensive lamé from Damascus. Her hair was piled high on her head, and her face had been done; she looked extremely attractive, even beautiful. And Jean-Louis was clapping his hands to his face and saying: "Isn't she absolutely *gorgeous*?" He looked at me and said: "I really must congratulate you, those breasts are a work of art, nothing less. When I see a breast like that, I sometimes wish I were..."

He sighed. "No, I'm much better off as I am. But she is gorgeous, isn't she? Isn't she?" He simpered and patted a stray hair into place, and stood there with one hand on his hip, and just *sighed*.

He fussed with the silver lamé and said: "A tiny bit in here, a tiny bit looser *here*, and it will be perfect. We must make sure it *drapes* properly, darling, the drape, it's important." He looked at the glasses and said: "Oh dear, nobody had any Creme de Menthe, I can't think why, it's heavenly."

Fenrek smiled, and said gently: "Why don't we all sit down and talk. And yes, she really is lovely." He looked hard at Jean-Louis. "Jo tells me you know a great deal about the local underworld, Madame Chanson. I'm interested at the moment in the slave trade. Specifically, a man named Ahmed Fellawi. You know the name?"

Jean-Louis sat down primly, his knees together, and sipped his beautiful green drink. He said: "Fellawi, Ahmed, calling himself a Sheikh, which he is not. Educated at Beirut University, then Harvard, then Cairo. He has an organization in Djibouti, but it's merely skeletal. He comes here once every three or four months, stays a few days, goes off again, no one knows to where."

Jo said, almost angrily: "Jean-Louis! You never told me!"

He smiled at her. "You never asked me, sweet."

"No. I suppose not."

Jean-Louis went on: "And there's a rumor going around that some of the slavers are in town again. Nothing very exciting, just a rumor."

He smiled, got up, pulled out a hidden drawer in the dead-white marble table, and pulled out a thick file. Waving it at Fenrek he said: "Sooner or later, the Somalis will take over this territory, as they have taken over the British and the Italian Somalilands to the south of us. It promises to be a very trying time for those of us whose income depends on our continued welcome here. So it has always behooved me to keep a file on just who might one day become whom in the local government and opposition. Ahmed Fellawi was assisting the Somalis in their anti-French activities a few years ago. He was deported to Aden."

I said: "Where, no doubt, he continued his nationalist activities against the British?"

He shrugged: "Very probably."

"It's a likelihood that it's the same man."

He was leafing through the file carefully. "He was thrown out of Aden once the local Arabs took over, too dangerous a man for them to associate with, and for a while he was running guns to the Yemeni Royalists, but Yemen got too hot for him too. There's a report that he ran a slave caravan from Kassala to Mecca last year, but lost his entire collection on the way through the northern part of Ethiopia—the Ethiopian Army ambushed him. He came back here last year, and tried to set up his old organization, pro-Somali and anti-French, but the Danakils across the bay in Tadjoura—the larger part of the territory—have come to realize they'll be worse off under the Somalis, whom they hate, than under the French, who leave them alone. So, they refused to listen to Fellawi and he had to give up. I'm told he went to Khartoum to try his luck there; so if this is your man..."

"Likely, at the very least."

"...then one of his wives runs the brothel on Guani." He made a delicate little gesture. "Part of the Arab philosophy, a man's wives should work for him."

Fenrek raised an eyebrow. "Guani?"

I said: "A small island, just a bare rock, really, ten or twelve kilometers off the coast. Technically, outside territorial waters, but the

French claim jurisdiction over it. It was an anti-submarine lookout post during World War Two." I asked Madame Chanson, and it seemed very important to know the answer: "How common is that knowledge—that the Madame of Guani's brothel is in fact Ahmed Fellawi's wife? Does everybody know that?"

He shook his head vigorously: "Nobody, nobody knows it, Mr. Cain. Nobody. I picked up the information fortuitously a few months ago, it's a very well-kept secret."

"Even from the police?"

"They're not really interested in Guani, and they know almost nothing about the slave runners, so... No, they don't know either." He patted his burgundy-red jacket to smooth away the wrinkles, and said dryly: "Of course, we're technically against prostitution here, but since we're a very busy port it's convenient to have somewhere close by, but not too close, where the dear sailors can amuse themselves without upsetting the sensibilities of the Consular wives. Oh, those poor Consular wives! You should see the way they *dress*!"

I said: "Tell me her name. And also—how *safe* a place is Guani?"

He looked me up and down with unabashed admiration, if not lust. He simpered: "How safe? For a man like you? Those muscles must be absolutely gorgeous! I suppose you're not gay, by any chance? No, I didn't think you would be."

I said: "Not safe for me, how safe for an unaccompanied woman to visit the island? A tourist looking for excitement?"

Fenrek was already a leap ahead of me, as usual; it's a disconcerting habit he has, reading my mind, born of long, long association. He said indignantly: "You are not, I hope, thinking of throwing Connie to them again?"

I said: "Why not? I'm sure she'd like to help us."

He was so upset he could hardly do more than splutter. I looked at Connie and saw what I expected to see; her eyes were cast down and she was smiling a secretive sort of smile which told me all I wanted to know and hadn't really been too sure about. A woman her age, these days, has all sorts of strange emotions, jumbled and incoherent perhaps, but making sense if you try and understand the gap, and the reasons for it, that exists between her generation and mine.

Brush away the very efficient training of an airline stewardess—which really bridges that gap, it has to—and you're left with the mixed-up but none the less logical instincts of the young and immature.

I said to her gently: "You'd help us, Connie, wouldn't you?"

She was smart enough not to agree too readily, and that was good too. She said: "Twenty two years old, and all my life I've never been in a whorehouse. You'd like to do something about that, wouldn't you? Just what, exactly?"

"Yes, I would like you to go there. Unhappily, I can't go myself, I'm too easily recognizable. Jo lives here, so she's known too. And as for Fenrek, I'd never let him take such a terrible risk."

Fenrek exploded: "Well, really! She is *not* going there, Cain, emphatically not! There's nothing she could do, anyway."

I said: "If she does what I tell her to do, she'll flush out Ahmed Fellawi for us."

"Absolutely not!"

I turned back to Madame Chanson: "You were going to tell me her name, Ahmed Fellawi's wife."

"Ah yes. She calls herself Leilani, Madame Leilani. And I am told she's a very competent woman, not at all out of the Arab world. In her late thirties, which is old for an Arab woman, but still attractive. And hard, very hard."

"And if I send someone there, how does she get there?"

Jean-Louis shrugged. "By boat, of course. Every hour on the hour, both ways. And there's one of Madame Leilani's men on the dock at this end, to make sure no one goes aboard who might make trouble. The clientele is carefully screened before the boat crosses the water."

"Do any women ever go out there? Alone?"

Again that exaggerated lift of the shoulder. "Of course. You must know what beasts women are."

Interesting. But it was going to make it somewhat easier for us.

I turned to Connie and said: "So that's settled. The ten o'clock boat, and I'll be there, one way or another, soon after, to get you out of the trouble you're going to get into. All right?"

Madame Chanson simpered again. He said: "Oh dear. You really are a terribly reckless man, aren't you?"

I said to Connie again: "All right? The trouble won't be insupportable. And it will pay off handsomely, for all of us."

Her eyes cast down again, that very secretive, I-know-something-you-don't-know smile on her face once more.

Connie said: "All right. Just tell me what it is you want me to do?"

Fenrek threw up his hands and said: "*Merde*!"

When we took our leave, I shook hands with Madame Chanson, and said: "You must come and visit me sometime. I'm staying at a place called the Hotel Moderne."

He clapped both hands to his plump face: "Oh, you silly boy! How could you possibly stay in such a dreadful place?"

I said: "I'm afraid Ahmed Fellawi might come looking for me. A waterfront dump like the Moderne is the last place he'll expect to find me. Good-night, Madame Chanson. And thank you."

Fenrek was staring at me, frowning.

But not Jo. She had at least an idea of what was going on.

CHAPTER 7

Fenrek wanted to take a boat and come along too; he was horrified when I said I was going to swim.

He said; "Good God, it's six or seven miles!"

"With the tide in my favor, that's a matter of two hours or less."

"Take a boat, for God's sake. We can rent one."

"No. Why should there be one of Madame Leilani's men on the boat dock?"

"Huh?"

"Obviously, if they're screening the visitors to Guani, there's something going on out there that doesn't bear inspection, and it's not just simple prostitution, because the government here tolerates it. Ergo, they have to keep some sort of protective measures going, and that will undoubtedly include a watch for any stray boats coming in. But if I swim, I can land just when, where, and how I like. And the *how* is undetected."

He stood there and looked at the waves rolling in and breaking on the shore. There were one or two dim lights out where the shark-fishermen were setting their great iron hooks. He made a last desperate effort. "The sea's crawling with sharks around here, you must know that."

I said: "Sharks don't crawl."

It was a risk, but not as bad a risk as taking a boat and being discovered. And the *carcharodon*, the great white man-eater shark, is not very common here anyway. The *porbeagles*, or *Lamnae*, are quite common here, and so are the threshers known as *Alopius*, but neither of these common types is much of a menace at night, when they tend towards somnolence. The only one I was worried about was the *Galeocerdo tigrinus*, or Tiger Shark if your Latin's not good; but the last Galeocerdo killed here was more than three years ago; they prefer the deeper waters of the Red Sea itself.

We stood in the darkness on the beach, a little way from the bright lights of the town, and waited until a passing fishing boat should get out of range.

I said: "You see? A bright night like this, a boat can be seen for miles."

He was still terribly worried, and I said: "I'm going to be all right, I almost beat John Konrad's record for the mile a few years ago. I met him in Australia, he gave me some very good pointers."

"There's a strong current sweeping up into the Red Sea."

I corrected him: "This time of the year, sweeping out into the Gulf of Aden."

"That's even worse."

I said: "I'll see that it doesn't carry me back to the Arabian Peninsula. I've no wish to see the Rub again for quite a while."

He raised his elegant arms and said: "The whole thing's impossible! I wish to hell you'd tell me what's at the back of your mind."

I shrugged. "Finding Ahmed Fellawi. We've precious little to go on."

"As soon as Connie starts asking questions, you know what they're going to do to her, don't you? And what was it you told her to say when she gets there?"

"She is supposed to ask for Ahmed Fellawi, nothing more."

"I'd say that's more than enough. If his visits to Djibouti are such tightly-kept secrets, then Madame Leilani is going to want to find out how Connie knew of the connection. That's very dangerous information for anyone to have. You've thrown her to the lions, Cain. They're going to beat the hell out of her until she tells them where she got her information."

"No. They won't dare."

"*Dare*? You're out of your mind!"

I said: "In spite of all that Fellawi did to her—or perhaps because of it, who knows the workings of a woman's mind?—Connie is more or less in love with Fellawi, didn't you notice that?"

He said stuffily: "I thought I detected a certain fascination."

"And it shows. Madame Leilani has got to assume that there just might be something serious between them."

"She's his wife, remember."

"*One* of his wives, not quite the same thing, and even if the question of jealousy arises, which it might, she's still got to leave the decision to Fellawi himself. Ergo, she'll send for him. And that's the point of the whole play."

"Tenuous. Very tenuous."

"Not in the least. Connie will be held prisoner, I will get her out, and Fellawi, knowing now that we're after him, will come looking for me. It's all very easy if you only apply your Hungarian sense of logic to it. For God's sake, if any Tom, Dick; or Harry can go looking for him at his wife's place, he's got to find out how come."

"You're risking her neck; and that's a terrible thing to do. And to tell the truth, I don't understand how she allowed herself to be persuaded so easily."

"No persuasion was necessary, didn't you notice? She *wants* to see him again. She's not quite in love with Fellawi, I think your word 'fascination' was the right one. But it's still a thing we've got to cure her of, isn't it?"

He fell silent, and I knew that he was trying to project himself into her mind; and failing miserably, of course. He knew that the reasoning made sense, but he couldn't convince himself of it because he'd had little experience of overly-impressionable women like Connie.

He said, shaking his head: "I can't really bring myself to believe it, though the indications... Yes, it looked like that. But it doesn't make any sense at all! Goddamn it, he *raped* her!"

"That's part of the reason. He beat her up, very callously, he raped her twice, and she pines for him. Don't try to understand human nature in women, it's indecipherable."

"And so, she goes willingly to whatever is waiting for her

there."

"And I'll get her out, whether she wants it or not, before any great harm can come to her."

The fishing boat had gone, and I stripped down to bare skin and put all my clothes in the heavy plastic bag Madame Chanson had given me. As I stood in the shallows, I said to Fenrek—looking more than usually miserable: "Come over on the first boat tomorrow if I'm not back. I probably will be, one way or another. With Connie."

He said grimly: "At the crack of dawn I'll be there, with a large force of the local police. If you're back before then, you know where to find me."

I said: "You made a good choice this time, give her my love too."

He said glumly: "I always make a good choice. Seven miles of shark-infested waters, you'll never get there."

I stepped into the water, tied the string of the bag round my waist, and set off with a six-stroke crawl. I can keep up the six-stroke almost indefinitely.

I had only one encounter with a shark, and it wasn't much to worry about. An hour and a quarter had passed, and I stopped the fast crawl—no good tiring yourself out—and turned on my back to rest for ten minutes. And then I saw him.

He'd probably been following me, though I was careful not to splash, keeping my feet an inch or two lower than usual and the curve of my back a little less. I lay still and watched. He wasn't very big, a matter of twelve or fifteen feet long by the look of his grey fin. He circled me slowly, and I watched him, and he came in closer and closer with each turn, not too sure of himself at all. I did nothing till he was less than six feet away, still circling warily, and then I changed my position and lowered my legs to give my arms more freedom. He promptly went back to a distance of ten feet or more and took to circling once again, closing the diameter of his circle, just slightly, with every turn, playing it very carefully. I kept very still, holding a lot of air in my lungs for added buoyancy; the water is very saline here, and it was quite easy to keep my shoulders clear of the surface, as they had to be, of course.

In the bright moonlight, reflected even more brightly by the gently-swaying water, I could see the spiracles, the gill opening behind the eyes, rather larger than I'd expected them to be; a bottom-feeding shark then, probably a *Squatina* or *Orectolobus*, up to the surface to see what the commotion was about.

He was back to his six-foot circle now, and slowing down, which was an indication he was thinking of charging in fast. I made a little movement, and it gave him pause. Then he began circling again, and I started to swing round with him, to make sure he couldn't twist on his side and go for my legs while he was behind me. I raised my forearms out of the water, and waited.

He came in a little closer; three feet now; I could have reached out and touched him, easily. And then he made up his mind and began to roll and to dive, so I hit out hard with my right fist and punched him square on the nose; it was like hitting a concrete wall, and I hit him so hard that I broke the skin on my knuckles. There was a flurry of water, and he was gone, straight down to the depths that were his proper home.

I went on with my swimming, switching now to a four-stroke; no need to break your neck just because you're in a hurry. And fifty-five minutes later I was crawling up onto the little rocky beach, of Guani.

It wasn't much of an island; about a mile and a quarter long by five or six hundred yards broad, mostly sandbar, with a few scraggy coconut palms growing on it, self-seeded probably, washed in on the tides, with a small rocky plateau at one end on which a single building stood—a long, low, tile-covered house with a single red light visible over what appeared to be the front door. There was a glow beyond it, which I assumed came from the wharf where the nighttime boats would put in.

I unpacked my bundle and got dressed quickly, and stuck Madame Chanson's flashlight in my belt, and ran fast round the narrow sand belt at the base of the rocks to the other side. Yes, it was the wharf, a somewhat rickety but adequate affair of porcupine wood and coil matting, and just above it, at the side of the house, there was a pleasant little verandah, a patio, with a few tables under brightly-colored umbrellas and a bar running down one side, lit by a row of colored bulbs. I could hear the faint hum of the generator, muted and well-muffled.

There were two Somali waiters there, and half a dozen French Naval officers sitting drinking, with six or seven girls, mostly Somalis, though there was one there who might have been European—Italian, perhaps. There was a door in the stucco wall that led into the house, and it seemed that the floor level was five or six feet above the level of the rock—a cellar, probably, cut down into the rock below it. One wing of the house was lower than the main building, and seemed to consist of a row of small rooms; some eight or nine of them; the girls' individual quarters, no doubt.

Somewhere, a phonograph was playing, a pleasant sound; it was one of Mozart's *Divertimenti*, number seven, and very good to listen to. I sat and enjoyed it for a while, and when they switched to the Country Dances. I completed my circumambulation of the house, keeping well in the shadows of the rocks, and getting to know every inch of its profile. I found a barred window, about three feet square, set in the lower part of the building below floor level; the cellar, then. There was only the one window below the ground, and this, I thought, was the logical place for Connie to be—if, indeed, she'd asked the proper questions and had, therefore, run into the kind of trouble I expected her to find. Or perhaps it was a little too soon...

On the verandah, one of the officers finished his drink and went with one of the girls to the last room at the end of the row and shut the door; and then two more went off with their choices and the other three went into the main house. The two waiters stood, white robed and red turbaned, in a corner, whispering together, I went silently back to the barred window.

The bars were not very thick, and they were merely soft iron, enough to deter a Somali, perhaps, but not a man who keeps up his energy the way I work on mine. It took me less than five minutes to bend two of them apart, and in a moment more I had eased open the sash with the point of my pocketknife and was inside.

It was dark there, just a beam of pale light streaming in through the window; I didn't like the shadow on the floor of the bent bars, so I spent another five minutes or so bending them back into position, so that if anyone interrupted me the window would not show signs of interference; if I had to get out in a hurry, I could always use the stairs and go through the house, one way or another.

I took out the flashlight and let the beam wander round. Some cases of beer, about fifty or sixty, a large and well-filled wine rack against one wall, a long shelf, well-stocked with liqueurs, mostly by Marie-Brizzard, which is very popular here, some cases of champagne, and twenty-five large glass demijohns of the cheaper red and white wines which are mostly French mixed with Algerian and sell for seven or eight cents a liter.

There was a broom closet full of cleaning stuff, several unpacked boxes of wine glasses, a large wooden box full of tools—a hammer, screwdrivers, a saw, pliers, nuts and bolts all mixed in together—two heavy axes and a small chopper, three old but still sharp carving knives, three bottles of ammonia, ten long strings of onions, hanging from the ceiling, two sacks of potatoes and a cardboard box filled with garlic cloves, a barrel of olive oil, nearly empty, a sack of flour, three coils of barbed wire and a coil of half-inch manila rope, and a variety of bits of lumber, mostly doweling and harrow planks.

Facing the window, in the opposing wall, there was a small, heavily-barred door; it was locked. I found a piece of heavy wire, cut and twisted it carefully to shape, and twiddled it until the lock sprang open; it took three minutes. I noticed that the lock was properly oiled. Good. And there was nobody inside; too soon.

I played the light over the walls. It was a small cell, about eight feet square, a very necessary item in a place like this, with a wooden bench running down one side, and a stinking wooden pot in one corner, the sort of place where some recalcitrant sailor might be thrown when he made himself a nuisance, until the cops or his shore patrol came to get him. It presupposed the presence of bouncers, and I wondered how many of them there would be.

I went back to the tool box, found a screwdriver; and unfastened the four screws that held the lock in place. With the blade of my pocketknife, I carved out the wood around the lock socket. I helped myself to a handful of flour, mixed it with wine—there was no water—to make a heavy paste, and plastered the lock back into position just as it had been before; it would set hard in fifteen or twenty minutes. I went back to the main cellar, closed the door gently, used the bent wire to lock it again, and examined it carefully to make sure that it was holding its position correctly: I held it firm for a little while, just to make doubly sure.

Then there was the window to take care of. I found a heavy log of wood and went to work on the bars, bending them—easily now, with the leverage—back and forth until they broke off, and there was nothing but an open, three-foot wide window that could be negotiated in a hurry. I cut six dowels, which were more or less the right thickness—not exact, but close enough to survive a cursory glance— and wedged them into position. At the end of half an hour, I stood back and surveyed my handiwork, and there, framed against the moonlight, the bars looked exactly as they had been before. It was a neat and tidy job; and it wouldn't keep anything in, or out.

I looked at my watch; it was just past one o'clock in the morning, a time of night I am particularly fond of, with the new day just beginning and the old one tucked firmly into the historic pattern it will remain in forever more. (Out here, as a matter of purely academic interest, the Somalis refer to one o'clock in the morning as *sa'a saba'a,* or seven o'clock, because it's seven hours after their day begins, at sundown). But for me, it was the beginning of the day, and an excellent hour of the night. And there was still plenty of time.

I went back to the window, took out two of the wooden bars, climbed through, replaced the dowels carefully, and continued my exploration of the tiny island. I was sure there had to be a boat somewhere.

I found it on the northern side, in a small cavern underneath the flat rock that was the building's verandah. It was a natural cave at water level, with adze cuts showing in the soft rock where it had been artificially enlarged. A wooden platform—that exquisite porcupine wood again, which comes from the coconut trees on the mainland— had been built there, sloping down into the sea where the water lapped over it gently. I switched on my flashlight.

It was a fourteen-foot Crosby 141 Sled, an American boat, with a muscular four-cycle Bearcat outboard mounted, a trifle too heavy for the type of boat, but some people like it that way. It would put out, no doubt, about fifty-five horsepower at fifty-five hundred revs, an overhead cam engine that would push the little runabout through the water at very high speed indeed, providing the waves weren't too troublesome. Twelve-volt battery ignition, dual side-draft Tillotson carburetion, and a compression of 9.1. It was nice to know that I wouldn't have to swim back with Connie in tow; I'd have enjoyed the exercise myself, but Connie would probably have been scared stiff of the sharks, most people are, they've been conditioned by too many fishermen's tales. I took off the cover of the motor, opened up the distributor, slipped the rotor out and hid it, and put the cover back on again.

Everything was ready now, and I could comfortably afford to show myself and get into some trouble.

I clambered up onto the verandah, said to the waiter: "I'll have a bottle of champagne, please. Bollinger '59 if you have it, if not, Cordon Bleu '64. Two glasses." He stared at me in surprise for a moment, wondering where I'd come from, and then recovered his professional composure, and smiled broadly, and said: "I call Madame for you, M'sieur."

"Yes, do that."

He bowed and moved away silently on bare feet. He passed the other waiter and whispered to him, just a very brief word, and the second waiter looked at me and nodded, and then padded over and brought two highly-polished champagne glasses and a bucket of ice, and bowed and fussed, straightening the red-and-white checked tablecloth and brushing away some imaginary crumbs.

And in a moment, Madame was there. Behind her was a small, tough-looking, wiry young man with a barrel chest and black, black close-cropped curly hair and a neat little Van Dyke beard, dressed in khaki pants and a blue denim shirt with a red scarf at his neck. His shirt-sleeves were rolled up high over his excellent biceps, and the Lion of Judah was tattooed on his forearm, a forearm as thick as an Arkansas ham. His feet were bare, and he padded along behind Madame with the silent assurance of a cat; the bouncer; an Ethiopian.

Madame was about forty years old, though looking older, an Arab woman, comfortably dressed in a sort of muumuu with a cord belt at her waist, and high-heeled shoes she didn't seem very comfortable in. A pleasant enough sort of woman, with rather sallow skin and *kohl*-darkened eyes and gold earrings. She held herself well, with the slightly indignant near-hostility of someone whose home has been...not invaded, exactly, but intruded upon; it was as though she were ready to be quite hostile but wanted to get her facts right first, in case I were a good customer whose presence only *seemed* surprising.

I stood up and inclined my head and said: "Bon soir, Madame."

She looked at me quite hard, ready to smile if the occasion arose. She said: "M'sieur; would you mind telling me how you got here? The ferry arrived a long time ago, I didn't see you on it?"

I said: "No, I don't suppose you did. I ordered champagne, Bollinger '59, I wonder if you'd care to join me?"

She said stiffly: "I don't drink with the customers, M'sieur. Would you kindly present yourself?"

"Cabot Cain."

"And you came here...how?"

I said: "Well, that doesn't matter for the moment. Madame Leilani, isn't it?"

She inclined her head almost imperceptibly, just enough to tell me, with Arab reserve, that such really was her name. But it wasn't yet time for her to give way. She said: "I cannot serve you, M'sieur, unless you can explain your presence here." She didn't like this unexpected appearance at all; it was worrying her greatly.

I said: "I am not a policeman, if that's what you're worried about."

She raised a very cool eyebrow, "Worried? About the police? Why should I be? The Chief of Police here is almost a personal friend, and I know that you are not one of his men. Now, M'sieur..."

"Why don't you tell the waiter to bring me my Bollinger?"

She hesitated, and then made up her mind and sat down, and signaled the waiter. "*Le Bollinger cinquanteneuf.*" He nodded and moved away.

I looked at the Ethiopian and said affably: "*Te'ena yistling,* God be with you."

He folded his arms and looked up at me, appraising my size and knowing quite well that he had absolutely nothing to fear. His face was cold and expressionless, but he couldn't hide the thoughts in the dark intelligent eyes. There's nothing an Ethiopian likes more than a fight he can win except a fight he can't; he knows he's going to win it even so, and he likes the challenge. This one was already composing the triumphal song he would sing, at the first opportunity, to his little circle of friends, other Ethiopians, as they sat around the brazier drinking their *tej*, the mead they make from honey. The triumphal song is very important to them: "A lion of a man twice my size and three times my weight, and I broke his back and threw him to the sharks..." He would spread his great arms out wide, and dance on his flat, splayed feet, and they would clap and tell him what a lion he was himself, and it would all be very pleasant and charming. So, he stared at me and waited for Madame to say: "Take him."

I sat down and said to Madame: "You can dismiss your bodyguard, you know. You surely don't imagine I'm here to do you personal violence?"

She said calmly, very much in command of the situation: "We will soon find that out, won't we? You are a very big man, M'sieur Cain, and since you speak Amharic, if only to say 'God be with you', I can assume you've met a few Ethiopians and that you therefore know they can be quite dangerous. In spite of your size, my man will easily throw you out if I tell him to. Now, you were telling me how you came here, and what it is you want. I have an idea it's not what most people come here for."

I said: "I am looking for a woman named Constance Delorme, an American girl."

She looked surprised. "Here? All my girls are either Somali, or Arab, or Greek, or Italian. I have no American girls, I'm happy to say."

I said: "She is a friend of your husband, Ahmed Fellawi."

Now she really was worried. But she said coolly: "My husband? I have no husband, M'sieur."

For one alarming moment, I had a sudden vision; in it, Madame Chanson was making up the kind of story he thought I'd like to hear, and it was all a parcel of lies, and I was making a fool of myself with a perfectly innocent woman who'd never even heard of Ahmed Fellawi... And then I remembered that Fenrek trusted Jo, and Jo trusted Jean-Louis, and the horrific vision disappeared again and there was only logic—or likelihood—in its place.

So I said: "She came here looking for your husband, for Sheikh Ahmed, and I want her back. She's mine. I bought her from your husband, and now she wants to go back to him. It's all very simple."

She said, murmuring: "What makes you think I even have a husband? And that it should be this man Ahmed Fellawi?"

"She told me. Constance Delorme."

"And how did *she* come to this astonishing conclusion?"

I shrugged: "I don't know. I'll find out from her; if I have to, but it doesn't seem important now. I just want her back. And I must insist."

There was no one else but a waiter on the verandah with us, and for a moment I thought she was going to signal her bouncer to start something. But then the other waiter appeared swiftly and silently with the champagne. And it's strange how the incursion of a simple social amenity can change a mood so quickly. In one instant, there was the definite possibility of a little set-to, and then the next, simply because the champagne bottle was being twirled around in the ice bucket, all the danger had gone and we were back to the moment of gentle, polite inquiry.

The waiter popped the cork and poured the two glasses, and I picked mine up and raised my glass, all very formal, and said: "Your health, Madame."

She sat back in her chair and sipped the wine, and looked at me and said slowly: "So, you think your girl is here. Did she come of her own free will?"

"On the ten-thirty ferry, of her own free will."

"And will she, of her own free will, return with you?"

"Why don't we ask her?"

There was a secret smile on her face, the same sort of secret smile I'd seen on Connie's when she'd so easily offered to help. I wonder if people realize how easily they give themselves away when they do that! And I knew what she was thinking; she wasn't at all sure that she was faced with the simple matter of a triangle, one man trying to get his girl back when she wanted to run to another. As I'd hoped, it didn't seem real to her, she was quite sure there was more to it than that.

Again, there was the beginnings of a movement in the direction of the Ethiopian, almost, but not quite, a signal. I tensed my calf muscles, ready to get to my feet quickly if he should make his move. But then her motion stopped almost before it began; one of the French officers had opened the door to a room just across from us, and was coming out, the light streaming out behind him, his arm round the girl he'd been with.

This was not the place for a battle.

She smiled then, and said: "All right, you think she will return with you, so if you insist, we will ask her." She pushed it a little hard, and said severely: "But I want your promise. If she prefers to stay...then you make no trouble, is that understood?"

She got to her feet, giving in very easily. I wondered if she'd take me down to the cellar on the pretext that Connie was there. It didn't worry me very much. She said, still smiling secretly: "Come with me, M'sieur."

I followed her into the room that led to the balcony, a small restaurant, well-decorated in simple porcupine-wood paneling with plain polished tables and comfortable chairs. There was another bar here, all incised glass and polished oak, lit with concealed neon lights. Four or five French officers, and three or four civilians stared at me as I followed Madame Leilani through, and the three young girls seated on stools at the bar turned and watched; one of them winked at me. We went out into the hallway, and into another, smaller room with two comfortable divans in red velvet, and gold velvet drapes over the windows, and an old upright piano in one corner. The hi-fi set was here, and it was playing now Mysliwecek's Trio in B-Flat Major, Opus number one; I thought her taste in music was remarkable, but there's no reason why a cultivated Arab shouldn't appreciate the best in Western entertainment.

And Connie was there, lying on the sofa and looking up at the ceiling with a sort of bemused look in her eyes; her pupils were constricted, and when she looked round at me it was with a quick, jerky, tell-tale motion that spelled out a drug of the morphine group.

The Ethiopian was behind us, and he shut the door with his heel and then pulled the sound-proofing curtain over it. And Madame Leilani said quickly, in Amharic: "Both of them, down to the cellar."

I turned as he made a move towards me, and she said sharply: "No! The gun!"

He stepped back, a very light and easy movement, though I could well have taken him before he got the gun out. It was under his belt at the back, and he held it in a very professional manner, close in to his belt at his side, his elbow behind him. It was a Luger, nine millimeter, a nice weapon if you know how to use it and can control its bucking.

She said: "Make sure he's not armed."

Obligingly, I raised my hands and let his left hand pat me in the usual places, very, very warily; he circled round behind me to do it, and twice I could have taken the Luger from him before he could have fired with any hope of accuracy. It just isn't possible to search a man and keep him properly covered at the same time, and from the look in the Ethiopians eye I felt he knew this and didn't care anyway.

I said mildly: "I guess I sort of walked into something, didn't I?"

The searching was over, and he stood back, and I looked at Connie and said, keeping up the pretense: "You shouldn't have come here, Connie!"

Connie moved her head round and looked at me blankly, and then said, her voice a little hoarse: "Oh hello, Cabot, Cabot, Cabot, Cabot..." She blinked her eyes rapidly, as though the words were uncontrollable and she couldn't understand why. But it was not that, exactly. Her eyelids were drooping, and I knew what it was they'd given her.

I said to Madame Leilani: "If you're fooling around with morphine, I hope you know what you're doing."

She smiled, quite delighted. "Not morphine, M'sieur Cain. Simple cannabis. Hemp. You were going to ask her if she wants to come with you."

I sat on the edge of the sofa beside her and took her hand; it was hot. "You want to come back with me, Connie? Or you want to stay here?"

She blinked her eyes at me again, rapidly, the morphine look. "I want to stay, and wait for Ahmed." She'd passed on the message correctly, then. Good.

I said: "It might be some time before he gets here, we can come back if you really want to see him. But I want to be there with you when you ask him, can you understand that?"

She was shaking her head, jerkily: "No, not long. Tomorrow."

A little piece of useful information creeping out...

Madame Leilani said sharply: "All right, that's enough! This way."

She pulled aside a curtain, and there was a door behind it, a heavy door of solid teak. She unlocked it and threw it open, and said: "Take the girl, and get down there. And quickly, my patience is getting very short."

I did not move, and she said: "Unless you want to get badly hurt."

I gave in. I picked up Connie's limp, unresisting form, and carried her down the stairs to the cellar. The gun was never once close enough to touch me, but I could feel it, none the less, could hear the soft padding of those splayed bare feet.

At the bottom of the steps, she switched on the bare lamps that lit the cellar, and indicated the door to the cell. "Over there."

I carried Connie over, and stood aside while she unlocked the door, keeping my fingers crossed that the lock would hold firm in its flour-and-wine plaster. I took Connie inside and put her down gently on the wooden bed board, and Madame Leilani said: "Tomorrow, we will talk again, and this time Ahmed will be here to see that you tell me no more lies." She peered up at me and said: "I want to find out just who led you to me, you understand? Ahmed will want to know too, and I think you would be very well advised to answer his questions." She laughed shortly. "As it is, he will probably kill you anyway. So sleep on that, my friend."

She slammed the door shut; I winced at the sound of it, but the plaster still held, and then the key turned again and there was only silence. I thought I'd better give them fifteen minutes.

It was absolutely black in there, and the stench from that bucket was appalling.

I felt for Connie's hand and held it, and she said: "Cabot, Cabot, is that you?" as if there were fifty men in there with us.

I said: "It's me, are you all right?"

"Yes, I suppose so. I feel...sort of restless."

"They've drugged you. Just lie still."

"All right."

"Did you give them the message?" I knew, of course, but I wanted to find out how far away on her trip she was.

She said slowly: "I think so."

"Take off your shoes."

"All right." As she began to slip them off, feeling for them, I said gently: "All right, put them back on again."

"All right." She put them on. I said: "Touch your two index fingers together."

There was hardly enough light, but I could just make out the clumsy, inefficient movements. That, and the blind, unquestioning obedience...it meant a dose heavy enough to be very dangerous. I said gently: "All right, just lie still and close your eyes."

We waited for a little while longer, and then I said to her: "Well, we're going home now, so just hold my hand and do as I tell you."

"All right." She didn't even want to know how we were going to get out of there.

I put my shoulder gently to the heavy door and eased my weight into it. The plaster around the lock came off and the socket dropped to the ground without too much noise, and then we were out of the stinking confines of the little cell and into the large and airy cellar. We crept quietly across to the window, and I removed the dowels that looked like bars, and lifted her through, then followed her.

Outside, the air was fresh and cold after the stifling discomfort of the tiny cell. I took her hand and we walked quickly but quietly along the rocks to the cave where the boat was. She said: "It's a beautiful night, isn't it?" and I whispered: "Don't talk, Connie, just keep quiet."

"All right."

I sat her down in the little runabout, found the rotor, replaced it in the distributor, and started the engine. The roar of it in the confined space was shattering, but it didn't matter now. I swung the tiller over, opened up the throttle wide, and we shot out of there fast, heading for the distant lights, low on the horizon, that were Djibouti and our temporary home.

And fifty-three minutes later, at a quarter past four in the morning, I was knocking on the door of Jo's comfortable apartment.

She wore a pair of dark-blue silk pajamas and a white shantung robe when she answered the door, and I said: "Wake him up if he's asleep, we've got to plan our defenses now."

But Fenrek wasn't asleep. He came out of the bedroom as soon as he heard my voice, wearing only his fancy red velvet dressing gown, and he took one look at Connie and hurried to her and lifted a closed eyelid and said briefly: "Morphine, a heavy dose, do you know how much she's taken?"

I said: "Cannibis, actually, by injection, and she's taken quite a lot. But she seems to have a fair tolerance for it, so twenty-four hours good sleep and she ought to be over it. And by that time, Ahmed Fellawi will be here, looking for her, for me, for us."

He shook his head with relief. He growled: "You took a damn awful risk, Cain. You're lucky it came off. If, indeed, it has come off."

I shrugged. "The only way to look for a needle in a haystack. You use a magnet. Now, get back to bed, and I'll take care of Connie."

He nodded. Jo went into the bedroom and came back with a blanket, and opened up the sofa into a bed, and said: "Anything you're going to need?"

"Just tell me where you keep the cognac. And maybe some milk I can put on the stove if she wakes up in the night."

"Cognac in the cupboard there, milk in the frig. Anything else?"

"No. Go to bed. I'll manage."

She took Fenrek's hand and said, scolding: "Don't look so worried! She'll be all right. Come to bed."

He hesitated, then went with her back to the bedroom. I stripped off all Connie's clothes, stretched her out carefully on the sofa bed, and covered her with the blanket. She wasn't asleep, or in a coma; she was just quiet, and unresisting, and resilient, letting the world pass her by and do with her what it wanted *en passant*.

I said: "Go to sleep now. You'll feel fine in the morning. If you wake up, I'll be right here beside you."

I helped myself to a large glass of cognac, set some milk on the stove with the gas turned down to its lowest, then stood and looked at Connie for a while. She opened her eyes and blinked them once or twice, and then closed them again, and tossed the blanket a little aside. I finished my cognac, took off my shoes and my jacket, removed my tie and loosened my belt, did a hundred and fifty push-ups, and then lay down on the bed beside her.

She threw her arm over my chest, breathed a deep, long, sigh, and in two minutes was fast asleep.

CHAPTER 8

It's always a mistake to suppose that the other side doesn't have its own Intelligence Service—or that it might not be a very good one; and that's a mistake I've trained myself never to make.

All I'd learned about Fellawi predisposed me to the belief that he might be something more than the average run of the slavers, who are usually merely bums, outcasts, degenerate adventurers, call them what you like. His varied background, his education, the ease with which he kept his movements secret, all these things indicated a mentality we'd be foolish to underestimate.

I said to Fenrek: "I have a feeling the time has come for some official protection for both Jo and Madame Chanson, just in case Fellawi decides to cut off the limbs before he goes for the head. Starting with Madame Chanson. Let's not assume he won't find out we've been talking to her."

As always, he was aware of my thoughts long before I'd spoken them. We were sitting on the wide balcony of Jo's place, overlooking the big-main square, quite empty at this time of night, except for a couple of drunken sailors staggering back to their ship. There was the sound of running water—Jo was filling the bath, the washbasins, every possible receptacle while the water, brought in exposed pipes across the red-hot desert, was cool. That's the one snag with living in Djibouti; the cold tap *steams* after eight o'clock in the morning, and if you want cold water for a bath you have to run it during the night. We sat in wickerwork armchairs, the two of us, and sipped cognac, and listened to the distant sounds that came from the ships in the harbor. Connie was in bed, sleeping off the effects of the drug.

He said calmly: "It occurred to me when you first broached the idea"—only Fenrek talks about *broaching* ideas—"that if your somewhat tenuous scheme had any merit, it could easily bring down a massive reprisal on our heads. So I had a word with the Chief of Police. There are three men watching Jo, another three keeping an eye on Madame Chanson's place, round the clock."

"Good."

"Not that I think the scheme is going to work, but it just might, and it pays to be careful."

"It also pays to be rash, once in a while. As soon as Sheikh Ahmed comes running to Guani, to find out just how Connie tracked down his *pied-a-terre* so easily, he's going to find out that there's some monkey business going on, and he's got to learn what it is. I made our escape from her nice little brothel look as though it had been carefully planned, and even before we escaped Madame Leilani was quite convinced it wasn't as simple a matter as it all seemed to look. So, since he likes his security to be watertight, he'll track me down and quite probably try to kill me."

"He just might consider that too dangerous to attempt." Fenrek, as always, was trying to find holes in the argument, nothing more.

I said: "He lost thirty percent of his slaves crossing Africa, so we can assume that human life is not particularly valuable to him. And those slaves, incidentally, were carrying picks and shovels, dozens of them, I wonder why?"

He shrugged. "Does it matter?"

"The inexplicable always matters."

He fell silent for a while, and Jo came in and joined us, the day's supply of water already warming up in the heat of the apartment. She wore black silk pants and a piece of string round her top, what there was of it, and she looked delightful.

She said: "Connie's still sleeping, her temperature's a little high, but not too bad."

Fenrek said: "What are we going to do with her now that she's started the ball rolling for us?"

I shrugged. "I don't suppose she'll go willingly, but as soon as she's over her *malaise*, we'll put her on a plane for home." He looked at me suspiciously; he never quite trusts anyone who wants to do what he thinks is best. I said gently: "At least, we'll try. She's a very stubborn woman, and it may not be easy."

"You still believe she's in love with this punk."

From a Hungarian, the word *punk* sounds impossibly comic; it comes out as *poonk*.

I corrected him: "Love isn't exactly the right term, you said it better last time; fascination. And it's the *type* she's fascinated with, not the man himself. The dark and handsome, suave and tough type."

He said: "People don't fall in love with *types*, they fail in love with individuals."

"This type of woman falls in love with this type of man, even though she knows very well he's a poonk."

He glowered at me and said again: "A poonk. How can she have anything but the utmost distaste for a man like that? A man who would beat her, rape, sell her...treat her like an animal?"

Jo looked at him and smiled; there was a very amused look on her face. She said: "You'll never understand the feminine mystique, will you? There *are* women like that. I think Connie may be one of them."

There was a knock on the outside, and Jo looked at her watch and frowned. And then in a flash she was on her feet, but Fenrek got there first, moving quickly into the room with a signal to her to stay where she was. She looked at me and I said: "A knock at this time of the night, it's always alarming, isn't it? In this business..." She smiled: "Well, at least they knocked."

I heard Fenrek open the door, heard him whispering, and then he came in excitedly and said: "Madame Chanson. They've made their move. And if you tell me I told you so..."

No good at all in being modest. I said: "Well, I did, didn't I?"

It was a young policeman who had called, and we left him there with the girls and hurried over to the salon. The street outside was thick with what the French call *flicaille*, which might be roughly translated as "a mess of cops."

There were four police cars there, three police officers, at least twenty men, a radio car, an ambulance, and the kind of controlled chaos that can only be found in this sort of emergency; they were all giving excited orders to each other, milling around like ants. An Inspector of the Special Squad was there, and Fenrek introduced us: "M'sieur Cain, he's working with me... Inspector Montand, what happened exactly?"

The Inspector, a grey and slender man with a sallow face, sharp, angry eyes and a thin, pointed nose, was about sixty years old, He saluted and said: "An attack on Jean-Louis Krok, a hermaphrodite who runs a dress shop. He calls himself... Ah, but you already know about him, of course. Well, he was attacked by two men who forced their way into the salon, two Arabs. Unhappily, they seem to have found a way, past our men who were watching the place." He looked at Fenrek, his mouth tight. "My apologies, Colonel."

Fenrek said nothing.

The Inspector went on: "But one of the men heard Jean-Louis scream, and he burst in with half a dozen men, and...well, at least they were in time to save his life. It was obvious that she would have been killed. As it was... Well, we got one of them, at least. The other got away, but we will find him, no doubt."

Madame Chanson was in her black and white marble room, sitting on one of the blown-up plastic chairs; the other, slashed with a knife, was collapsed and helpless-looking, and so was she. She wore a long yellow nightgown with a salmon-colored kimono all covered with dragons in reds and greens and blues, and her hair...I'd noticed before that the elegant coiffure was a wig, and now it was misplaced just sufficiently to make her look like a figure out of one of the comic operas. But there was a terrible gash across her face, and she was dabbing at it with a wet towel and moaning softly. A policeman was hovering over her solicitously, holding out a glass of water for her, and she said, weeping: "No, you silly boy, not water, get me some *Creme de Menthe*, it's in the cupboard there, under the lovely skull."

She looked at us as we came in and said: "Oh dear, are you part of all this? I might have known it, mightn't I?"

I dropped to one knee beside her. "Are you badly hurt?"

She shook her head bravely. "No, not really. But if those lovely policemen hadn't come in..." She burst into tears and said: "They were going to *kill* me, and I've never done anyone any harm, *anyone.*"

A thick-set, burly Arab was standing in the corner, his hands manacled behind his back, a policeman standing guard over him with drawn pistol ready; they always like to make a drama out of these things, the French police. He was tough-looking and heavily-built, and his left ear was torn-off and bleeding badly all over his shirt.

I said: "I suppose it's too much to hope that the other one was Ahmed Fellawi?"

She shook her head. "No, I don't think it could have been, an old man, very rough and uncouth, not a nice man at all. And they were... Oh, dear, they were going to *kill* me!"

I said: "That mess to his ear... You did that?"

She simpered, and touched her hand to her wig. "I'm not as young as I used to be, I suppose, but my teeth are still good. My own, too, all of them. Look." She showed me her teeth.

I said: "From the beginning."

"All right." She took a long, deep breath, "I am a very heavy sleeper, and I'd never have heard them, never, only I was awake because I'd just come back from the john. I was coming into my bedroom, and there they were, slipping in through the window. I wanted to scream, but one of them—that one—put his hand over my mouth and held me down on the floor, and the other one pulled out a knife and stuck it in my throat and said: 'Where is the big man, Cabot Cain?' I struggled and tried to get free, and he pricked me, here." She gestured at her neck; there was a nasty little scratch there. "Of course, I didn't tell them."

I could not blame her for the lie. She fluttered her eyes and insisted: "I didn't tell them a *thing*, and they said if I didn't they'd kill me, but I was terribly brave, and I said: 'You'll not get a word out of me, not a word!' And then they both started to beat me up, and one of them slashed me across the face—oh dear, do you think it will leave a scar?"

I said: "Do go on."

"Well, I got angry and bit his ear, and then I screamed, and all those nice policemen came running..." She looked at me suspiciously, as though the thought had only just struck her. "They must have been waiting right outside, were they expecting something like this?"

I said: "Not really. But it did occur to us that they might come looking for me, through you. So you had protection. It was just a little late meshing its gears."

She moaned and said: "Oh dear; if only I'd known, I could have gone away somewhere, I need a holiday so badly."

I said: "You didn't mention the name of my hotel? The Moderne?"

She shook her head vehemently, lying brazenly to salvage all the dignity she could: "No, no, I didn't. In fact, I'd even forgotten that you mentioned it."

I got up and looked at the Arab. A seaman, by the looks of him. He was in his thirties, with arms like steel hawsers and tight, taut muscles, the kind of man who spends his whole life in a constant pitched battle against the rest of the world, rough-housing it all over the slums and ghettoes of the Middle East. There was a sullen, stubborn look in his eyes, and I knew he wouldn't give very much away.

But the other man... I was glad he'd escaped; it promised well.

I said to the Inspector: "I don't suppose he's told you anything of value? By the looks of him, he never will."

Montand said grimly: "In the course of time, no doubt, he will tell us everything. But so far, he has remained absolutely silent, he won't even tell us his name. But one of my men recognized him from the wanted posters. He is Suleiman Sala'at, a sailor, a smuggler, a thief. We have been looking for him for a long time."

Fenrek—ahead of my thinking again!—said: "What's he wanted for in this territory, precisely?"

The Inspector shrugged: "For murder, M'sieur. For everything. Theft, burglary, smuggling, blackmail, arson... A list of nine or ten indictments."

I said: "So there's no question of a deal."

He looked at me coldly and said: "No, M'sieur."

"No. I thought not. It was just an idea. And if you're not

prepared to offer him a *quid proquo*, he's not likely to offer you any information, is he?"

His grey eyes were like ice. "No deals, M'sieur, emphatically, no deals."

Fenrek looked at me and grimaced. They have no real authority, the Interpol people; they can only advise and suggest, and suggestion wasn't going to get us very far.

I said to the Inspector: "If it helps you at all, this man is tied in with a certain Sheikh Ahmed Fellawi. Currently, he's interested in the slave trade."

He frowned. "Fellawi? Fellawi? Ah yes! There was an Ahmed Fellawi concerned in the Somali revolt of three years ago, he was supplying dynamite to the terrorists. Is that the same man?"

"The same. Just now, he's running slaves to Arabia. This man Sala'at is working for him. If we could find out from him just where Fellawi is now..."

He turned his long thin nose away and looked at the Arab, and when he turned back to me there was a faint smile on his face. He said: "To find that out, it will not be necessary to make any deals, M'sieur."

I said: "I'll make a small bet with you. You can beat the daylights out of him, and he won't open his goddamn mouth."

He said smoothly: "I will find out for you, M'sieur. And if there is anything else you would like to know?"

Fenrek shrugged. "We know what he was trying to elucidate. It might be of academic interest to know how he was so sure that Jean-Louis had that information. It might help us all to get a better picture of their Intelligence sources."

The Inspector nodded. He looked back at me and said, that thin, cruel smile on his face: "We will find out, M'sieur. No bets, no deals. But we will find out."

I just didn't believe him. Suleiman Sala'at was going to keep that blank, stubborn look on his face till the day he died, in jail. He was that kind of a man, and it showed.

We left the police to clean up, had a drink with Madame Chanson, gloating a little now that she knew more of what she was part of, and before we went out she said, pleading: "I really didn't tell them where to find you, M'sieur Cain."

I nodded. I didn't want to distress her any more. I said: "I believe you. Thank you."

The dawn was just coming up when we stepped out into the cool—relatively—morning air. There was that bright copper glow on the waters of the Gulf that you don't see anywhere but in the Red Sea, and some brown-sailed dhows were silently coming in from the Bab el Mandeb, the narrowest stretch of water between Africa and Arabia.

Bab el Mandeb, the Gate of Tears. For centuries, the predators have been sailing across the twenty-mile stretch of treacherous water, searching out human souls for slavery, as far back as man can remember; Arabs going west in search of Africans, and the Somalis, too, in the old days, sailing east to raid for Arab women and boys, each continent stretching out its tentacles to trade in tragedy; the tears had always been very real.

There were great sheets of red in a sky that soon would be on fire with the heat of the day.

And Jo was there.

It gave me a moment of shock, but then I saw that she was smiling, and a little ashamed of herself. She said to Fenrek: "You were so long... I was worried."

I said: "Connie?"

"Sleeping still, the policeman standing guard."

I said: "It's not enough. How do you protect a woman from an assassin's bullet?"

"She is well away from the window, there's no danger."

"I wasn't thinking only of Connie." I said to Fenrek: "Police protection doesn't really amount to much, does it?"

He said calmly: "No. It's a figure of speech, nothing more. A man on a rooftop with a high-powered rifle—all the protection in the world is not going to help."

"And you realize Madame Chanson must have mentioned Jo's name?"

He frowned. "But she swears she didn't tell them a thing."

"Wouldn't you lie under similar circumstances?"

"No, I wouldn't."

"Perhaps, not. But take my word for it, before she lost her temper and started using her teeth, she told them quite a lot."

He said angrily, sure that I was right: "You're guessing again."

I admitted it. "But it's a good guess."

And, at that precise instant, I saw the man on the rooftop, just as Fenrek had spoken of him, not a hypothetical case anymore but a grey shadow against the yellow-red of the sky, rising up like a ghost not more than two hundred yards away from us, just a little to one side. He was torn between letting us get ahead of him so as to take us from behind, and the more sensible idea that the brightest part of the sky should be in our faces. There was even time to see the rifle going up to his shoulder, and I waited a split second so that he'd be ready to fire, and then I lunged forward at Jo and sent her sprawling into an open doorway, the wide shadowy doorway of a courtyard under the portico. I heard the crack of the rifle, and the bullet slammed into the stone pillar and chipped a great chunk out of it, and then it was too late for a second shot, and two policemen right behind us were firing back.

I saw the man on the roof spin round, heard the gun fall with a clatter, heard the final, unexpected shot go off as the rifle hit the ground, and then the body came tumbling down and smashed into the pavement.

I ran to Jo where she'd fallen, and on the rooftop I saw another man running for his life, the bullets of the two police chasing him as he leaped from one roof level to another, briefly, and then he was gone from our sight, I wondered how many more of them there were.

Fenrek was on one knee beside us, almost brushing me aside in his efforts to help Jo. He picked her up and held her tight for just a moment, and he looked at me and said nothing, though I knew what he was thinking; one infinite fraction of time was all that had been between Jo and a bullet through her head, a fraction so small that the shot must have been on its way before she was thrust aside out of its path. It's the only thing to do; if you act too quickly, you're merely shifting the target while there's still time to re-aim.

He said at last, very quietly: "Let's get back, shall we? The police will take care of all this."

They were already swarming over the dawn-painted rooftops, and we could hear the dual sirens as two more cars came speeding in. The police here didn't like this sort of thing a bit; it upset the calm, relaxed privilege of their colonial position.

We went back to Jo's apartment and found Connie safely there, still fast asleep and breathing more easily now, with the young policeman on a wooden chair by the window, with his rifle between his knees, watching the outside like a hawk. Jo went to the kitchen and made us breakfast, and I looked at my watch and said: "I'd better get over to the Moderne, hadn't I? Chances are there's someone already there waiting for me to turn up."

Fenrek said calmly: "Not at all likely. Without a doubt, they'll suspect a trap, and *no one* will be there. They'll be quite sure the whole area's thick with police, all in hiding and waiting for the trap to be sprung."

I said: "Why do you think I chose the Moderne? It's far enough away from where every policeman in town is at this moment, chasing ghosts over the rooftops. And a dump like that, a safe-house for thieves and murderers, the police must know they can't get within a mile of it without being detected; and so, they won't try."

He said, grumbling: "You seem to know an awful lot about this town."

"It's my job to know."

Jo came in with a pot of coffee, some rolls and a huge platter of butter. She set them down and said: "If you're not really as bright as you're supposed to be, this just might be our last meal together, so let's enjoy it. The Moderne's a horrible place, a slum, a flop house."

"Just the kind of place we need."

She looked at me shrewdly. "If you think he's coming to get you, you could easily have arranged for him to come here. If we're going to fight, there's no reason why we shouldn't fight in comfort."

I said: "What, and get blood all over your pretty carpet?"

She grimaced. "Yours? Or his?"

"I hope it will be Fellawi's."

"He will probably send someone else."

"Perhaps. But I'm hoping it's got to the stage where he has to take over personally. All his underlings, so far, have lost out horribly."

"And you can't be sure that Jean-Louis told them where to find you."

Fenrek said, as though he'd thought of it himself: "He told them alright. He protested too much. And I suppose we can't really blame him." He glared at me. "I suppose it's no good saying I don't like what you're doing?"

"No good at all."

"Then, let me come with you." He added sourly: "To hold your hand."

"No. You have that indefinable air of authority about you, not very strong, but just enough to frighten them off. Fellawi's got to be sure that this time he can win, and that means I have to go alone."

We finished our breakfast, I took a last look at Connie, and went off to find the Hotel Moderne.

CHAPTER 9

A shanty-town is a sad place.

On the Rue des Negres, where the Hotel Moderne had been thrown together by an amateur builder fifty years ago—it was already falling to pieces—there were hardly any buildings more solid than huts; there were sheets of rusting galvanized iron clumsily nailed to sticks; there were lengths of old burlap stretched over frames; there were sides of old packing cases lashed together; and here and there an adobe shack had been crudely whitewashed and covered over with old cans hammered out and held in place with rocks. There was muddy, stinking water in what passed for the streets, with old melon rind, bits of coconut husks, and month-old garbage lying around everywhere.

And even at this hour of the morning there were kids playing in the fetid gutters; they stopped and stared at me as I passed by, their solemn, age-old eyes sad and bewildered. One of them whispered: "*Flic*, a cop..." A beggar nearby, who was crushing the lice in his clothes between calloused thumbs, raised his head back and clicked his tongue in the Arab gesture that means "No."

The hotel had a painted board outside to indicate that it gave lodging, and served meals, at reasonable rates, controlled by the Government.

What a dump!

It was the kind of place where people say they wouldn't be found dead; that's not a very happy reference. It was close to the water, where Arabs and Somalis and Danakil mingled together in mutual hostility, noisily arguing and cursing each other as they brought in the early morning's catch of sharks to be sliced open for the liver and skinned, in some cases, for the leather which would be made into shagreen.

They had a very simple method of catching the sharks; an old oil drum, sealed tight against the water, was towed out to sea at night and baited with five or six strong wires to which pieces of raw goat meat were attached on six-inch hooks at the end of them. The first shark to be hooked would tow the drum in his fury, helping to catch other sharks that tore into the meat as it dragged noisily and bloodily through the water. And then, at first light, the fishermen would go out looking for their drums, hauling the sharks in close and first prudently smashing their jaws with belaying pins before bringing them aboard. A wise precaution; a shark's a pretty harmless fish until his temper is aroused and he knows he is dying, and then he's still fighting, sinking his triangular teeth into any stray leg that's nearby, long after he's good and dead.

There were fights among the fishermen all the time. The Arabs against the Somalis, the Danakil against everybody else, and most of all one tribe of Somalis against another; there were often sudden knife battles, with the losing side tossed unceremoniously into the sea before the police—who preferred to leave them alone anyway—should arrive to make a nuisance of themselves.

The Moderne was an ancient two-story building, with a cafe-bar and office on the ground floor, though the office was merely a beat-up old table in a corner, where a huge and very fat Somali sat, his enormous belly hanging out over the tight belt he had around his brown cloth skirt, his bare skin gleaming, his chest sagging, a heavy stick across his knees.

He looked at me as I came in and said: "No foreigners." He used the word *frangi*, which strictly means anyone who's white.

I laid a ten-franc bill on the desk and said: "Let's not be racial, friend. I want a place where no one's going to look for me." I'd put on an old shirt and the slacks I'd been wearing out in the desert, still grubby, but I suppose I still looked splendidly dressed.

He grinned, looked at the money, and said: "Ten francs for the room, number three."

I said: "If anyone comes looking for me, you've never seen me, understand?"

He said: "Ten francs more." I gave him another bill, and he tucked the two of them into his waistband, and when I asked for a key, he laughed and said: "No keys. All honest men here." He thought that was a very funny remark indeed, and threw his head back and roared with laughter, his great belly wobbling like a mass of jello.

I said: "Anyone waiting for me, by any chance? In room number three?"

The laugh went at once, too fast, but he shook his head and played his part. He said: "Nobody wait for you, nobody find you, is okay." He spoke a sort of French, heavily laced with Somali words, and said: "You want I bring you coffee? Girl? Drink? Maybe I bring you bottle of good wine, what you say?"

I took the bottle that Jo had given me out of my pocket and showed it to him, the Algerian wine that sells for pennies, only it was filled with Pouilly-Fuissé 1964, and said: "Nothing, I can't afford your prices." He thought that was very funny too. The printed notice tacked onto the wall, old and torn and fly-blown but still legal, gave the price of the rooms at two francs, and of coffee, fifty centimes.

I found room number three and went inside. It was an incredibly dirty room, with a broken china washbasin and an old enamel jug of water on a stand that was so rickety it had been propped up with an empty beer crate. There was a wooden bed with the cord supports broken and hanging down, with a kapok mattress on it full of holes and greasy stains, with a blanket thrown carelessly over. There was a single wooden chair with an upturned barrel that had once held nails to serve as a table, and a window with glass so grimed that the only place you could see through it was at the jagged hole in the middle.

I took the wooden chair and its barrel table over to the window, where some more or less fresh air was coming through the hole in the glass. I drank a little of the Pouilly-Fuissé, set the bottle down, folded my arms, and waited. I didn't expect it would be very long. And it wasn't.

Outside on the street, the sea was blue and clean beyond the rotting hulls drawn up on the beach. Closer by, some naked children,

Somalis, were playing, dragging a dead cat around on the end of a piece of string. I heard the door open softly, and Hassan Tahari was there.

Behind him, men streamed in like a devoted line of cohorts. First, the fat Somali clerk, and then the Ethiopian from Guani, and a tall, bearded man with a scar on the side of his nose, and finally a young Arab boy of eighteen or so, with a shock of henna-dyed red hair. They all had the weather-beaten look of the dhow sailors, and they filed in and stood in a semi-circle round me, not saying anything, not openly armed, not even particularly menacing; but silent.

I looked alarmed and said: "Don't try anything, this place is surrounded with cops."

For a long time, they all just looked at me. And then, Tahari laughed and said: "No, no cops, you think we don't look? You think a place like this is good for you to hide in? You are a fool."

The red-headed boy had pulled out a dagger, ornate and carved in the handle, with three holes drilled in its blades he was paring his nails with it. The tall man with the beard looked me up and down as though he had been warned of my size, and said contemptuously: "Too big, big man doesn't move very fast, I kill him easy." Even the fat and flabby Somali seemed spoiling for a fight.

It was just the Ethiopian who said nothing, who made no threatening move; he stood there with his arms folded, staring at me and not betraying any emotion at all. Somehow, I rather liked the looks of him, a tough and decent young man earning a living but in with the wrong crowd. And I admired his stolid refusal to make more out of this than it was worth; to him, it was just another job to be done.

I said to Tahari: "We've got to talk. All right, I got the girl back, but if you're going to start a fight over that you can have her, she's more trouble than she's worth anyway."

He shook his head slowly. "We don't need her anymore. Not now. We don't need her, we don't need you. Once you interfere, maybe we just scare you away, but you don't scare too easy."

He spoke an extraordinary mixture of Arabic, French, and Somali, with an English word here and there; it was almost as if he were trying to prove that he too was an accomplished linguist, something to do with bringing your enemy down to your mark, or yourself up to his, before tackling him; a question of personal dignity. But the result was quite astonishing, though I'd frequently heard this ill-matched assortment of languages from people who have no real country of their own. In an educated man, this statelessness often results in an ease with languages, but with Tahari it was a deliberate effort to impress both me and all his minions.

He said: "You interfere two times, is too much already. So now you got bad trouble. Why you come to this place?"

There was a pointer there. I said: "To Djibouti?"

"No. To Hotel Moderne, is not good for rich man like you, why you come here?"

It ought not to have surprised him. I wondered if it was Fellawi who had raised the question, and had said: "Ask him why." Was he close by, then? Outside the closed door, perhaps, listening, to find out what he could learn before making an entrance?

I said: "If you don't need the girl, why did you bother to come here? You know she wants to go to Fellawi—or didn't you know that? I don't want trouble, he can have her."

"No. He don't need her now." He shrugged. "One girl don't mean too much anymore. Now, you tell me why you come here."

I said clearly: "I wanted to hide from Fellawi, until he was off my back." I shrugged; it seemed the right thing to do.

He just looked at me for a long time, trying to discover what it was I didn't want to admit, and deciding he'd have to find out the hard way. And then...there was no overt signal, just a slight nod of the head, the skipper telling one of the deck hands to go to work.

The tall bearded man made a rapid move, quite creditably fast, feinting with both hands clenched together for a drive into my face. It seemed polite to do what he expected me to do, so I pulled my head back and stuck my stomach forward, tightening the muscles and waiting for the kick, so that when it came, a flat foot driven hard at my solar plexus, I was quite ready for it. I fell down to the floor and looked up at him and said: "What the devil!" He picked up the chair and smashed it into my face, and then stood back as though he'd done a good job of work, and said: "*Ulli, ya ibn kelb,* tell me, you son of a dog..."

I said: "No."

He picked up the chair again, and I said: "All right, all right, I wanted to meet with Fellawi, tell him he could have the girl back if he wants her, she won't stay with me anyway."

He grinned at me, and said to Tahari: "Easy, you see? I tell you so."

The Ethiopian shook his head: slowly, his eyes quite unemotional. He said: "No. He is lying."

There was a long silence, then. Tahari looked from one to the other of them, and then looked hard and long at me. He said softly, at last: "I think you try to play tricks with me, no?"

I wiped some blood from my face, and said: "No tricks. I've told you the truth."

And then, the door opened and Sheikh Ahmed came in, smiling genially and trying to keep the genuine amusement out of his eyes. He wore a smart business suit now, grey silk with a dark blue tie that might have come from Charvet in Paris' Place Vendome; he looked like a highly successful gigolo.

I stayed where I was on the ground, and he waited a moment, smiling at me, and then said: "All right, Mr. Cain, you may stop fooling around now. It's very easy, isn't it, to impress these idiots with your incapacity. But I beg of you, please get up, it makes me quite uncomfortable to see you in such an undignified position."

I got to my feet and sat on the edge of that disgusting bed. I said: "Tell me why it is that *one* girl is no longer of any use to you?"

That's when he told me the truth—or part of it. He looked quickly at Tahari with an expression of shock on his face; as though Tahari's comment, *one girl don't mean too much anymore*, had given away the whole secret. It was a look of absolute fury, and told me he'd indeed been out there listening. And in the same instant, he realized that he could only hope to keep the rest of the secret by not showing that fury, and the look was instantly gone.

I said, smiling at him; "*That's* why I came here, Fellawi, I hoped you might tell me something about your future plans."

He recovered himself very quickly. He stroked his little moustache with the tip of his fingers and said: "You really *are* a devious man, aren't you, Mr. Cain? And now that you're about to die, I'm supposed to tell you all you want to know? I can't really believe you're such an abject idiot as to imagine that."

"It was just a thought. Oh well, some other time, perhaps."

He stared at me just long enough to let me realize that he knew now, knew that even if he had not told me what he was planning, he'd at least indicated that he was planning *something*; and that's always half the battle; you can waste a lot of time guessing what's going to happen, when what's going to happen is—nothing. He knew now that he'd given away just a little bit; and just a little bit was too much.

He turned sharply on his heel and went to the door. As he stepped outside, he turned back and said to Tahari: "*Yallah. Udrubu.*"

Udrubu... In his own language, it could have meant: "hit him," or "take him," or "go ahead"—or "kill him." I didn't wait to find out.

First I went for the bearded man who thought I'd be slow on my feet. I grabbed a handful of beard and pulled his head down onto my upraised knee and hit him just once on the back of the neck and he was out cold. The fat clerk—surprisingly fast for such a heavy man— swung his stick round hard at my head, and I put up an arm to deflect the blow, grabbed it, and rammed it hard into his gut. He yelled and dropped to the ground and doubled up, and the young red-headed boy was rushing in clumsily with his dagger held out at arm's length, aimed at my groin. I threw myself back and thrust out a foot and sent him spinning, then picked him up and threw him hard at the Ethiopian.

But the Ethiopian side-stepped with the speed of a leopard, and the boy went slamming into the wall; I heard his head hit. He was smiling now, the young Ethiopian, his hands held loosely in front of him, his feet wide spread. He stepped forward and thrust out his left hand, the fingers hard and pointed at my throat, and I just touched his wrist and grabbed his elbow as he went past me, and twisted it round and heaved, and he doubled up expertly and did a sort of somersault, and landed square on his feet and spun round to face me again, unhurt and still ready for more. I waited for him, and when he charged, his head down like a bull, the hard, hard top of it aimed at my solar plexus, I brought up my right fist and caught him under the jaw, so hard that I heard the bone break. There was a fleeting moment of regret as he went sailing through the air, clear off his feet, and when he hit the ground, I couldn't help wincing; I somehow, *liked* this young man.

But he was on his feet again in a flash, the pain of a broken jaw meaning nothing to him, and now—enough of unequal combat—the Luger was in his hand, the same Luger from the same place in the small of his back. He fired as I threw myself sideways, and before he could get the second shot off I kicked the gun out of his hand and sent it spinning across the room. The bullet had gone wild, smashing into the ceiling, and I brought my clenched fist down on the top of his wooly head, and that was that, though it was like hitting a concrete floor.

I turned to Hassan Tahari. He had not moved. He was staring at me in considerable alarm, not understanding how it was that his team had flunked their course. And then, like a shot, he turned and dived through the window. I watched him for a moment as he raced down the beach, and then walked out of there and left them all behind me.

I went back to Jo's place. I needed a shower.

CHAPTER 10

Fenrek was furious.

He subscribes to the philosophy that half a battle won is better than outright defeat, while I have always thought that if you wait around a little while, if you play your hand properly, and above all, if you know when to pull back and wait for a better opportunity, the rewards are always more substantial. But it's hard to convince him of this; patience isn't his long suit, though he'd like to think it is.

He said: "You let them get away, both of them! How could you have done such a thing? How could you?"

We were sitting cooped up in the little closet that Jo used for the high-powered equipment that belonged to Interpol—the high-frequency radio set, the scrambler for the telephone, the cameras, developing apparatus and micro-film gimmicks—while he tried to raise his Paris H.Q. on the short wave.

He said: "We could have spiked Fellawi's guns right there, and I can't for the life of me understand why you didn't at least attempt to take him." He turned and glared at me over his shoulder. "You could have, you know, if you'd really wanted to, and why don't you admit it?"

I said: "I do admit it, why shouldn't I? But you'll agree, won't you, that Fellawi has some other scheme up his sleeve? At a guess, he's got a few more gullible stewardesses on their way here, or perhaps about to join one of his notorious cross-Africa caravans? Do you expect me to leave them stranded there, if that's where they happen to be at this moment? We've got to find them, as well as him, if that should be the case. And it's a likelihood we can't afford to ignore."

He gave the sign-off signal by re-identifying himself with the letters PRG, and shuffled his code books around uselessly.

He said grudgingly: "It's a possibility, I suppose, but we can't be sure of it."

I said: "Change of plans, increased demands for American girls, something big in the works, even Tahari's comment that one solitary girl didn't count for much anymore—it all adds up to one inescapable deduction."

He glowered. "Well?"

"He's got a whole bunch of them either on the way here, or marked down for seizure. Agree that it's possible?" I deliberately didn't tell him it was a likelihood, or even more than that; no sense in antagonizing him.

He said: "Possible, I suppose, but a bird in the hand..."

"You coin a phrase very well, for a foreigner."

"Oh well, what's the point of arguing? It's done! And what are we going to do now?"

I said: "Go down to the beach for a swim."

The air in the tiny closet was stifling, and I can't stand bad air or confined spaces. He raised his eyes to Heaven, imploring; they never understand, at Interpol, that there comes a time when there's nothing you can do but wait; they always want to be up and following clues; me, I'm a great man for waiting. "Wait and see," Lord Asquith used to insist, and that's how he got to be Prime Minister.

So, we found swimming trunks and went to the hot white sands in Tadjoura Bay, where the coconut palms were hanging over the edge of a brilliant blue and white surf, and the sound was pleasant and refreshing after the squalor of the night's activities. And by special request, mine, Jo took along her little transistor radio.

It's a special pack that Interpol Field Agents use, limited in range but extremely powerful. Not much bigger than a small attaché case, it can bring in a station four thousand miles away, and transmit just over half that. I wanted to keep in touch with Khartoum, Beirut, and the closest Interpol Coordinating Station, which happens to be high on a secluded mountain top just above Nicosia, on Cyprus. We had told them to check with the airlines in the Middle East and in Africa for any missing stewardesses. It wasn't sure, of course, that if Fellawi were really looking for a group of girls, he'd limit himself to the manner in which he'd already been initially successful; but if I were spiriting American girls off to the harems of Arabia, then I would probably make a beeline for the airports too, they offer a very satisfying potential; the girls are attractive, they are bored and therefore vulnerable, and they're already halfway to their destination. (Under normal circumstances, it might be days or even weeks before Interpol would be informed of the kind of disappearance we were anticipating, but Nicosia had agreed to keep in constant touch.)

So we lay on the beach, and waited. The girls stretched themselves in the filtered sun under the palm trees, while Fenrek and I went for a long swim out into the deep water, keeping an eye on the shore for any signal from Jo. We came back after less than two miles when he started getting puffed; he's not really as fit as he pretends to be. And we lay back on the hot white sand and relaxed.

Connie had quite recovered from her introduction to cannabis. She said: "For God's sake, people take that stuff for kicks?"

She wore a brown suede costume that Jo had found for her, and with the sunburn disappearing now she looked quite lovely, her long slim legs just getting that natural gold color and her hair streaming down over her shoulders. Jo wore the smallest bikini I'd ever seen, two pieces of black string, and Fenrek, even though he'd just spent the night with her, couldn't keep his eyes from wandering over her near-naked body, a smug, proprietary look on his face.

I moved the dial of the radio to the local station, which was broadcasting a selection of the old Somali war chants. The striking, out-of-the-past war chants were coming to an end, with the monotonous ululation that the Mahmoud Issa tribe used to scare the daylights out of the Hassan Mohameds, their deadly enemies. All Somalis, but Somali enmity starts at the family level, goes on up through the clans and into the tribes, increasing its venom as the group gets larger, tribal jealousy and dispute honed to its finest edge. They are bright, bright people, the Somalis, and good to look at; but they hate each other's guts.

Two of their women were strolling along the beach now,

picking up pieces of flotsam; they moved like gazelles, with their graceful, slender bodies articulating in a manner which no other African has. Come to that, the Somalis don't call themselves African; they still think of themselves as Asians, even after six—or ten—centuries. Which gives them, they believe, reasonable grounds to hate all other Africans, even more than they hate each other.

The two women looked at us as they passed by. Slim shoulders, rather large behinds, small breasts tightly confined in their cloth, under-the-arm dresses, legs straighter than most; and attractive Phoenician faces with huge eyes against the burned-coffee color of their skin. One of them spat as they moved on.

The war chants came to an end, and the announcer said: "Now, the day's events..."

Fenrek said: "See if you can find us some Hungarian music. No one plays Hungarian music anymore."

Jo got to her feet and dusted the sand out of her little navel, and staggered over in the way people do, even gorgeous women, when they're walking barefoot in ankle deep sand, and the announcer was saying:

"An Iranian Airlines Plane, a Caravelle, has been hijacked en route from Beirut to Athens, by two men armed with sub-machine guns and hand grenades. Twenty minutes after takeoff, the pilot reported to the Control Tower in Nicosia Airport that a gunman had forced his way into the cabin and had ordered him to turn south and land at Ma'an for refueling. The pilot warned the Control Tower that the gunmen had threatened to kill the co-pilot and the steward if any attempts were made by the Jordanian police in Ma'an to interfere with the flight in any way..."

Jo was standing there by the set, propped up in the sand, looking down at it, waiting for the item to come to an end before switching channels; her breasts under the tight piece of string were like hard-boiled eggs, halved. Staring at the set as though it were a human being, she said: "Here they go again, every hour on the hour, the jet-age pirates."

The announcer went on: "The plane is a charter from Iranian Airlines, and the fourteen passengers are all members of the Hollyoak Beauty Pageant now touring the Mediterranean area for their sponsors, the makers of Hollyoak Cosmetics. A spokesman in Beirut for the New York based company has stated that the young ladies were en route to the Cosmetic Manufacturers' Convention in Delphi, where preparations for a Trade Show are now being made..."

I said: "My God, fourteen members of a Beauty Pageant, what a haul."

Fenrek sat up straight and said sharply: "What? It's not possible!"

Jo had already started turning the dial, and I said: "Get the news again until the end of the item, then straight over to Nicosia."

She, too, said: "I don't believe it."

The announcer's voice came fading in again: "...and the plane is expected to arrive at Ma'an at eleven-thirty local time this morning, There is a dispatch just coming in...." We heard the rustle of paper over the mike, and I saw that Fenrek was still staring at me in disbelief.

I said gently: "Ma'an, it's almost due south of Beirut. An interesting direction for them to take. Next stop, Arabia?"

He frowned and shook his head. "No, it's quite impossible, absolutely out of the question." But he was already half-convinced.

The disembodied voice went on: "I've just been handed a dispatch from the newsroom. The Jordanian police have agreed that no overt action will be taken that might endanger the lives of the passengers or crew..." There was the rustle of paper over the microphone again, and then: "A dispatch from Nicosia has just come in over the teletype. It seems that the plane is headed for Merowe in the Northern Sudan, and the two gunmen, one of whom states that he is a pilot and quite capable of flying the plane if necessary, are both seeking asylum in the Sudan. The hijacker who claims to be a pilot has apparently shown his pilot's license to the crew in an effort to convince them that he will not hesitate to kill both pilot and co-pilot if any attempts are made at Ma'an to apprehend them, or if the plane is not permitted to proceed on to Merowe..."

Fenrek said, scowling: "Merowe? The Sudan? It doesn't make sense."

I said: "Ssshhh..."

The voice was detached, professionally casual: "The aircraft is under the command of Captain Carlo Sorrenti of Iranian Airlines, who has racked up an impressive total of fifteen thousand hours' flying time. Captain Sorrenti has informed Nicosia that he is convinced of the authenticity of the hijacker's papers, and that he intends to follow his instructions to the letter in order not to jeopardize the safety of his passengers and crew. The hijacker's license to fly is in the name of Nicolai Poulakis, and the other gunman appears to be an Arab from Northern Sudan, as yet unnamed.

"The Somali Youth Club in Hargeisa has once more pressed its demands for amalgamation of French Somaliland with the Republic of Somalia, and the Somali Ambassador to the United Nations has once more threatened to take his case..."

Jo was already switching the set to transmit, on the high-frequency channel for Nicosia. Fenrek took it from her, and as he waited for them to give the letters CGQ, he looked at me and said quietly, a small smile at the corners of his mouth: "Nicolai Poulakis, that was the name of the charter pilot who left his plane in the Rub al Khali. It seems you were right."

"As usual." No good pretending otherwise.

"We can take a plane from the airport straight to the Sudan, and be in Merowe before they land there. They have a couple of Caravelles on charter there, I believe."

"Not a Caravelle. A helicopter."

He frowned. "A helicopter won't have the range, anything like the range..."

"We're not going to Merowe. We're going to Khadir again."

He said into the mike: "CGQ? Hold on just one moment, PRG but hold." He looked, at me and said slowly: "A lot hangs on this, Cain. We've got to make the right decision. And we've just been told, clear as day, that it's Merowe."

I said: "A red herring, nothing more."

"We can't be sure of that. There's no reason at all why they should try to hide their destination."

I said: "There's a major guerrilla war being fought around Merowe, the Egyptian Army against the Sudanese guerrillas. Two days ago, the town was in the hands of the Egyptians. Today, it might be anybody, they couldn't be sure what sort of reception they'd get. They are just trying to throw us off the scent."

"Too tenuous."

"They wouldn't land in the Sudan and face that long haul over the desert, if they're headed for Arabia, as we're sure they are."

He frowned. "Better, but still not enough."

I said: "Hundreds of picks and shovels in the hands of a hundred slaves in Khadir. They're going to make an airstrip."

That did it. He said into the mike: "PRG, but I can't scramble, I haven't got the equipment, how do you read me?"

It was a Greek at the other end, and his accent was thick and guttural: "I have you loud and clear, PRG, have you trouble with your scrambler?"

Fenrek said patiently: "No trouble. I'll be calling you again in half an hour. I want all the information you have or the Iranian Airlines hijack, over and out."

Fenrek gathered up his towel, put on his bathrobe, and said: "And we'll look like a lot of idiots, won't we, if they really are on their way to Merowe?"

"They're not."

"Looking for asylum. And we're out in the middle of the Rub el Khali wasting away into mummies."

The girls were gathering up the odds and ends that women always seem to collect on beaches, and we hurried over to Jo's ridiculous little car and squeezed ourselves into it, dripping sand all over the place.

Now the decision was made, the die was irretrievably cast, Fenrek was worried again. He said: "For God's sake, we might be making absolute fools of ourselves. Shall we tell Nicosia where we're going, just in case?"

I said: "No. This is just between the two of us."

He muttered: "Well, I hope you are right."

"Of course I'm right! Everyone will be waiting hopefully for news of a plane landing in Merowe, but once it leaves Ma'an we shall hear absolutely no more of it. Fourteen young ladies who've nothing better to do than smile their winsome smiles all around the world are going to get the shock of their young lives, and find themselves in the middle of Arabia. Fourteen of them, all at once, that's quite a haul, wouldn't you say?"

Connie said, looking at me: "Fourteen *houris*."

"Worth building a minor airstrip for, especially when all it costs is the price of a few shovels. A smooth strip of sand eight hundred yards long, a red-and-white canvas wind-sock... Take my word for it, we're heading in the right direction."

Fenrek muttered: "He'll never get away with it!" Then he grunted, and said: "Yes, he will, if we don't stop him. It's just the audacity of it. It's incredible, and therefore not easily believed. If you know what I mean. And yet..."

"Yet?"

He looked at me accusingly, as though I knew that this very thing was going to happen. He said, growling: "You've been waiting for this all along, haven't you?"

"For something very like this. Yes, I have."

The little car was bouncing along the broken gravel road, flat out at sixty miles an hour, the tied-back rag top (I couldn't have gotten in had it been closed) flapping in the wind. There was almost no traffic on the road, which was just as well; the way Jo was driving, we'd have all finished up in hospital.

Fenrek said: "A full load of fuel in Ma'an would take him to Khadir, certainly. And it's a fair assumption that once he's airborne after refueling, that's the last we'll hear from him. He'll put the radio out of action, or hit the pilots over the head and toss them out of the plane. An easy landing in the desert outside Khadir, a camel caravan waiting... Yes, he could get away with it."

"But there is a problem, isn't there? To get the Royal Arabian Army into the act, even if they agreed to help us. There isn't time. The nearest police or military post is in Khadir itself—our old friend Lieutenant Osman—and he's firmly in the slavers' pocket. That means we're on our own, the two of us." Jo said firmly: "The three of us." And Connie spoke up and said: "Four."

I let it ride, and so did Fenrek, though he looked at me surreptitiously when he thought the girls wouldn't notice.

I said: "It's not much of an army, is it? Not if Lieutenant Osman's men are in there in force."

"Why should they be?"

"Because, on the last lap of the race, he won't want to run any risks at all. He'll have protection."

Fenrek said: didactically: "No. Precisely because he won't run any risks, he won't let anyone else in on the deal. Even Lieutenant Osman, even one man not paid off properly can ruin the whole deal. And it's too big a deal for that kind of risk. Ergo, Fellawi will handle this alone, and we can take him."

"You are jumping to conclusions on insufficient knowledge of the man's character. And you're quite wrong."

"I'm absolutely right."

It's impossible to push him when he gets like this. It's something to do with asserting his authority when he feels it getting away from him. I said: "And the last of the white slavers will take his gaggle of beauties on their merry way, dropping them off the caravan like so many birthday presents, one here, a couple there, half a dozen someplace else. Christmas day in Arabia, with all the rulers rubbing their hands and waiting to open their parcels."

We took the southern road to the town, and stopped off at Jo's place to get in touch with Nicosia once again. I said: "We'll need the radio when we get there, and we can't carry the scrambler."

Fenrek nodded. "I thought about that."

"Good. Ask for a Relay Officer who speaks Hungarian, a language not many people know."

He said stiffly: "Hungarian happens to be one of the world's most important languages. But I will find a way to overcome the difficulty."

I could see the wheels turning the problem around in his mind.

He smiled then, and said very softly: "Ah, I know the answer exactly."

He waited for me to question him, so I didn't. We told Nicosia we were standing by to be in constant touch with them, in clear, and the Greek operator said again, worried: "How is it that your scrambler is not working, PRG?"

I said, prompting him: "See if they can find out where General Hishara is at this moment, will you?" He relayed the message, and the Greek asked for more information. Fenrek ought to have known, but he looked at me and I took the mike from him and said:

"General Hishara, Supreme Commander of the Arabian Desert

Armies, poet, philosopher, scholar. He is somewhere on the Arabian-Yemeni border, fighting a frontier skirmish. I would like to get in touch with him, so see if he can be located and put in touch with a radio set, will you do that for me?"

The Greek said at once: "Who is that speaking?" It came out "*Khoo* is that..." Fenrek took the mike back and said into it sharply, his patience exhausted: "If he is on my set, and obviously with me, you'll accept his instructions. Get that information back here priority." He switched over the off-button and whispered furiously—whispered!—"Now they'll know where we're going, that's very bad security."

I said: "Not at all. Just tell them to let Hishara know that Cabot Cain would like to discuss with the General, over the air, his translation of the General's epic poems. That will bring him rapidly to the radio whatever he's doing. And as far as your H.Q. is concerned, it has nothing to do with a hijacked plane."

Fenrek sighed. But he relayed my message, and then said: "And tell Professor Selegrit I'd like to have him standing by as my Relay Officer. Get him there as soon as you can." He looked at me and grinned, a secret up his sleeve.

We took time out to check the radio over, took along a few things we thought we might need, and Jo called Inspector Montand to let him know we were leaving town and to tell him what we wanted. And by eleven forty-eight, we were in the office of the Airport Controller, waiting for a helicopter that I could fly to be wheeled out for us, destination undisclosed. They couldn't be party to an illegal excursion to the unfriendly, almost hostile shores of Arabia.

The Peninsula was only a matter of forty miles or so across the water, over the Narrows of the Bab el Mandeb; but it was a world away in time and essence from the modern, sophisticated city of Djibouti. Over there was just the fringe of arid coastline dotted with a few scraggly palms, and inhabited by sad and impoverished nomads; on this side, there were paved streets and a railway line, good restaurants and a few night-clubs; there were even a few avant-garde *salons*, which sometimes got violently assaulted when the old world clashed with the new.

Just a matter of forty miles; but the Bal el Mandeb, the Gate of Tears, was a chasm that separated the two territories by a thousand years and more.

We argued for a while, not very hopefully and more as a matter of principle than anything else, with the two girls.

With Jo, there wasn't much of a problem. As an Interpol Field Agent, Second Class, Grade Three, she was well-trained in all matters relating to security. I'd attended their Executive Course myself, and it is thorough and immensely comprehensive; it lasts eight months, with a ten-hour day at the Institute and three hours of homework every night, and you come out of it a very capable operative indeed. She'd be familiar with all kinds of weapons (and a crack shot, or she wouldn't have got past Grade Six), and most of all she'd be highly competent in the essential art of looking after herself—the art of self-preservation which is thoroughly drilled into anyone attending these courses. "A dead agent," they tell you, "is a bad agent, so don't get killed whatever else you want to do. You are just too damned expensive to replace."

And with Connie... I had reasons of my own for wanting Connie along. Fenrek said accusingly: "I knew you never intended to send her home."

There was that give-away smile on her face again, half-hidden. I said: "If she wants to go, we'll put her on the first plane out of here, but she doesn't."

Connie raised her eyes and looked at me sharply; the smile was gone, even though she didn't know it had been there. She said: "You are goddamn sure you know what's in my mind, aren't you?"

I said: "Yes, I am. Always. But if you want to go home...? Do you?"

She said nothing for a moment. Then she looked at Jo and said sarcastically: "All right, doll, you're another one who knows what side is up all the time. Do I want to go home? Or don't I?"

Jo said: "Well, if you had my brains, or his, or his...you'd go home, right away. But you won't. So, you want to come along, and most of us know the reason, don't we, *mon pauvre petit*?"

Fenrek said: "Oh God."

Connie's smile was there again, and it transformed her completely. She laughed and said: "The poor Colonel doesn't know what the hell's going on, he only understands women who are so transparent he can see right through them. All right, yes, I want to go along."

Fenrek gave up. He said: "Provided you put yourself completely under Jo's authority. If she says jump, you jump." He thought he knew what was up my sleeve, too, and he didn't really like it, though admitting its value, if only to himself. He glared at me and said: "We're a couple of bloody nursemaids; we shouldn't be taking women along at all. Jo, maybe, but an outsider..."

Jo said, the argument settled: "I've been in touch with Montand. For the weapons."

We didn't have a gun among us, except the little .32 that Fenrek always carried. A .32 is a good little pistol if you know how to use it accurately, if you can be sure of hitting precisely what you're aiming at and don't intend to blast away at a thousand yards' range. But against the private army that Lieutenant Osman just might have waiting for us, it wouldn't have been much use.

As though reading my thoughts, his favorite trick, Fenrek looked at me and said: "And I don't really believe that Osman will be there at all. A trick like this, Fellawi will surely want to handle it on his own. He just can't afford to let anyone else in on the secret. We'll have to deal with Fellawi, with Poulakis the pilot, and one other hijacker. Nobody else, I'm sure of it."

I said: "No."

And a little later; while they were fueling the helicopter; a police car turned up with three rifles and a shotgun. Montand was there, a fistful of papers in his hand for signature. He was much too adroit to ask what the weapons were for; Interpol had asked for them, and that was all he was expected to know. But he had to have the signature, in quadruplicate.

I said to him: "Did I win my bet, Inspector?"

His thin lips were tight. "It's a little early, M'sieur, for this matter to be decided."

"He's told you nothing, your prisoner?"

"Nothing. *Yet.*"

"And how hard have you tried?"

He smiled. "I'm sure you're not really interested in such purely departmental problems, M'sieur."

I accepted the putdown; he was right.

There were three rifles, one each for Fenrek, Jo, and me; and for Connie, there was a shotgun. All you have to do with a shotgun is point it vaguely in the right direction and pull the trigger, and it's defensive in battle rather than offensive. I thought Jo was showing a good deal of common sense.

The Controller came bustling in to tell us the helicopter was ready. He was a thick-set, cheerful Marseillaise, a stubby-fingered, black-haired; grey-mustached man in his forties. He scratched the top of his head when I couldn't produce my license to fly (it was back home in San Francisco), but he waved Montand's authority at himself and. said cheerfully: "Well, if you crack it up, I can always blame the police, can't I? Nothing more satisfying than giving the police a bad time once in a while."

His assistant was carefully rubbing a cut potato over the inside of the Perspex hatch, to get rid of the heavy condensation, and within three minutes we were up circling, taking a last look at the sleepy town below us, with its bright green ring of trees and its red-tiled, whitewashed houses, heading northeast over Obock, which used to be the capital, before the Administration found they couldn't cope with either the heat or the Danakils there, and so moved across the bay to build Djibouti.

And the hot stretch of bright blue water spread out below us, both shores clearly visible from up here in the crisp, dry air, was Bab el Mandeb.

We were on our way back to Khadir.

CHAPTER 11

Down below there on our right, we could see the western extremities of the dreadful Rub al Khali.

The sand dunes rolled on and on and on, forever, their crescent points curled away from the prevailing westerly winds, their half-moon shapes decided over the ages by the never-changing course of that wind; it was as though their points indicated the line of their steady, infinitely slow march. As a matter of academic interest, the dunes in differing deserts move at differing speeds, and in this particular area it happens to be two point three five inches a year, constant and unchanging; and that's a bit of the most otiose knowledge I have ever picked up, but there are earnest men who go to great pains to measure these things. Even so, it's still fast enough to cover, once and for all, the fertile fields that had once been there.

I kept a course close to the coast, making a wide circle east to miss the airstrip at Assab, then swinging north again over the barren islands of Kabir Hanish and Zugar. I made another wide sweep to the west when a Yemeni patrol boat came out from the airport on Karaman Island to take a look at us, and then went in very low over the long stretch of white beach that lies south of the Jebel Hejaz, to find the barbed wire coils that mark the frontier and to check my bearings.

It's strange; in all these barren miles you'll find nothing that lives; and then, unexpectedly, there's an airfield. Usually it's no more than an oven of a building, built of clay bricks and covered over with galvanized iron or aluminum sheets, but the short-range jets land there with their loads of pilgrims on their way to earning their green *tarboushes* at Mecca. And the oil-rich sheikhs like to have ready access to the luxuries of Beirut and Damascus.

Now was the time for caution, and it had been less than an hour since we had left Djibouti behind us. I followed the wire, flying at zero feet and hopping over the dunes and hillocks, with not a tree nor a shrub in sight; and there was el Arish coming up far to the left, a collection of mud huts and rush-roofed *dukas* where the Bedouins could trade the skins of their dead camels for cloth. Sa'ada in Yemen was there on our right, and it was hard not to wonder how or why anyone should live in this terrible land; what were they doing here? How could they even survive? The boulevards of Paris and Rome, the steep hills of San Francisco, had never seemed so very far away.

We swept over the dry river-bed of Wadi Harauna, which once every seven years floods with wasted water in this dry land and pours its wealth, unused, into the Red Sea. It was here that Seneferu built a great series of dams (they had more ambition in those days) and you could still see the huge stones, broken now and slipped away, marking the work he so laboriously had done.

There was the red tint of copper in a gully here (how had Seneferu managed to find it?) and a small patch of that brilliant green-blue that meant water in the honeycomb rock, then a ruin of sandstone blocks that might once have been a Phoenician lookout tower... And then, the mountain ridge beyond which lay the Oasis of Khadir.

I swung the chopper hard over to the east, over into the Rub itself, and Fenrek said: "I was just going to tell you, we're getting close."

Connie broke her long silence. She said: "Rulers of the desert, here we come. An avenging army led by a soiled virgin."

Jo said: "Who? You, *mon petit*?"

Fenrek said: "The wind's from the northwest. Keep to the east, or they'll hear us."

I said: "Uh-huh."

I slowed down, then finally hovered, looking for a valley I could travel in. We were too close for comfort, really, and it occurred to me that Osman might have some of his patrols out, even as far south as this. There was a dark, shady gash in the grey mountain, and I took the craft in there, the walls towering high on either side of us, dark red, streaked with grey, and foreboding, great jagged spires of burned-out rock where nothing could live but lizards.

For eight miles I followed the rift, very slowly; at times, the blades were no more than a foot or two away from the rock walls, and once Connie said plaintively to Jo: "Does he know what he is doing, do you think?"

I hovered again, and said to Fenrek: "By your reckoning, how far away are we from the oasis? Ten miles?"

He nodded. "Just about what I'd make it."

"All right, let's try for six, it's hot down there."

I followed the valley again. Two and a half miles further on, it petered out, and I climbed the rise very slowly, the skids just a few feet off the ground, worrying about the sound in the still air. What wind there was was blowing from the west, as Fenrek had noticed, and the sound would have been carried away. But it's wise to be sure; in the desert, a sound like that can travel for ever and a mile, and if the wind changed...

I said to no one in particular: "Look for a nice easy spot to put her down."

Jo pointed: "There."

It was the tabletop of a small mountain, flat as a pancake, smooth and clear of rocks.

I said: "No. If we have to make a run at any time, let's run downhill, not up."

"There then."

To the south, a thousand yards away, there was a patch of hard, unblemished sand. I nodded, swung round, and gently put the chopper where I wanted it.

We all clambered out, checked over our guns, hoisted the water containers on, their straps over our shoulders, two gallons each for Fenrek and me, a quart for each of the girls, and set off across the red-hot rock, climbing slowly and easily, taking our time, up to the peak that gave a clear view of Khadir oasis and everything around it.

We reached the top in less than two hours, hot and exhilarated by the climb, and ready for the first sip of water. I found a hollow in the rock, not really a cave, where the jagged spires of grey granite were some sort of protection against the sun's hottest rays, though even in the shade, even at this height, the heat was murderous, bouncing up off the Rub as though challenging us, daring us to brave its intemperance. To the west, eighty miles away, the sea itself was a white-hot sheet of shimmering blue.

Connie volunteered to climb up with the antenna wire, much to my surprise; now that there were four of us together, with plenty of water and a way out assured (I hoped), the desert seemed to have lost the terror it previously held for her. Jo fiddled with the transistor set, and I lay down on my belly and used the Trinovids, scouring every inch of the land that lay below us.

You can buy a fair pair of binoculars for twenty or thirty dollars, if you're not very particular, and the Leitz Trinovids cost three hundred dollars or so a pair. But it's at times like these that you realize their value. The view down into the desert was tremendous, all reds and yellows and burnt-umber and copper, with streaks of grey-blue where the granite was, and long patches of bright yellow sand, with not a tree in sight, except at the oasis itself. It was four miles away, and in the thin clear air it could have been, through the glasses, not much more than a thousand yards.

Behind me, I heard the radio crackling, and then the voice of the Greek operator responding to Fenrek's question. He said: "Yes, I have Professor Selegrit here, he is ready to take over."

Fenrck was looking very smug again, as though he'd pulled off a masterpiece of subtlety. He said: "Put him on, then."

The Professor's voice was a thin reed, the voice of a very old man, troubled with bronchitis; he sounded cheerful and delighted, and he said: "Colonel! It's very good to be talking to you again. Where are you?"

He was talking in a strange dialect of Lapp, which had me worried for a moment because I couldn't place it precisely; but if anyone had a police-band radio in this part of the world, this was one of the least likely languages he'd understand. Its phrasing was strange, and there were a few words that weren't immediately clear to me, though I speak Lapp, of course. I used to teach it in my student days when I had a passing interest in that small and strange group of languages known as Finno-Ugrian. It is one of the most interesting of all the language families, comprising the southern dialects of Scandinavia and Finland, with Estonian, Mordvin, Zirian, Vogul, and Magyar—which Fenrek has gotten around to calling Hungarian.

He was beaming at me delightedly, and I realized I must have been frowning. He said: "Ha! So you don't understand it, do you? It's Lapp."

I said: "Of course I do. Just missed a word here and there. And you're quite wrong to call it Lapp, you know. Correctly, it's Samelat, the old dialect of Lapland, almost extinct now, quite close to Magyar but with its own peculiar syntax. Not many Samelats around these days, how did you manage to find one on Cyprus?"

He said peevishly: "Yes, of course it's Samelat, and Professor Selegrit is not a Lapp at all, but as pure a Hungarian as I am. It so happens he's a student of philology, too, an old colleague from the School of Comparative Linguistics." He made a desperate attempt to rescue his dignity, "You probably haven't noticed that he uses the soft *rh*, which is more Vogul than Samelat."

I said: "I noticed. The long sibilants also, just as in Zirian."

He said: "Poof." Sooner or later, he was bound to say something like that.

The two girls had spread, so help me, a white tablecloth on the sand and were munching cold chicken drumsticks and pieces of celery while we waited. Jo waved a stalk at me and said: "Have some, nothing to do till the Caravelle comes in, and that'll be hours yet." Connie was quiet and self-contained, and she looked at me solemnly with those big, pale eyes, and said nothing.

Fenrek went back to his Samelat and spoke into the microphone: "This is for you only, Selegrit. We believe the plane is headed not for Merowe but for Khadir, on the border of Yemen and Saudi Arabia, and that's where we are now, but we don't want that information passed around. I have absolutely no authority to be here, and there'll be the devil to pay sooner or later, so let's put that off for as long as we can. What's the news of the plane now?"

Selegrit cleared the frog out of his throat, and his voice went up another pitch or two: "It took off from Ma'an, with fuel on board, at one twenty-three local time, on a course of a hundred-and ninety-two degrees, which would take them a trifle east of the Gulf of Aqaba, over

Lower Egypt, and more or less directly to Merowe, though I understand the commercial flights don't really take a direct course, they fly further to the west to pick up the Nile and follow it down."

I said: "Just trying to convince us that Merowe is their destination."

Selegrit went on, the voice going up again: "There was only one police officer present at Ma'an, they were very cooperative, although they wanted to attack the plane and arrest the hijackers, and didn't really like it too much when we insisted. The police officer states that one of the two hijackers, believed to be Nicolai Poulakis, was standing in the open doorway clutching a hand grenade with the pin apparently drawn. He was holding one of the two stewardesses and threatening to drop the grenade if his orders were not carried out."

I said: "Two stewardesses, grand total sixteen young lovelies for the harems, a nice catch."

Selegrit's voice was positively squeaking now. He said: "They tried, in Ma'an, to persuade the hijackers to release the passengers, but the man we believe is Poulakis said no, they were needed as hostages and would be released unharmed in Merowe, where he and the other man are seeking asylum. Why do you think they're heading for Arabia? The Arabians will have them both shot, there's no doubt of that at all."

Fenrek said: "If we are correct, this is not at all a simple hijacking. We believe the women on board are being kidnapped."

"Oh dear. Oh dear, how very distressing for them." There was a momentary pause, and then he said: "Ah, now I understand. Your request for communication with General Hishara, everyone in the office was wondering about that."

Fenrek looked at me, and I nodded and took the mike from him. I said: "My name's Cabot Cain, Professor Selegrit, nice to be talking Samelat again, and nice to meet you."

He was surprised, as he should have been. He said, hesitantly: "A Zirian, Mr. Cain? I thought I detected a slight accent."

"Not a Zirian. What's the news on Hishara?"

He cleared his throat; up a pitch once more: "We have been in touch with him and given him your message, and I must say, he seemed extremely surprised and also delighted. He seemed to know of you and is anxious to talk. In about an hour he'll be close to a radio again, his Command Post, apparently, and he'd be glad if you'd call him on ninety-one point eight five, can you do that? He'll be ninety-three six."

"Splendid. And where exactly is he now?"

"He wouldn't tell us that, Mr. Cain, something to do with what he called an intelligent military security. But the radio men here pinpoint him about thirty miles or so south-southeast of Wadi Habauna, if you hold on a moment I'll give you the coordinates, though they are only approximate, of course."

"Don't worry. I know where he is. He's ten miles south of the border wire, beating up the Yemienis in their own territory. I'll talk to him in an hour's time, I hope, we may need..."

He broke in, excitedly: "Hold on a moment, the plane's been sighted."

"Good." I waited a moment, and then he said:

"An American radar vessel has just reported an unidentified plane flying low eight miles off their starboard side, too low for proper identification, but they think it might be a Caravelle. The course is a hundred and seventy-eight now."

"And where is the radar ship exactly? Did they say?"

"Yes. They are stationed off the island of Sinafir, that's east of the Straits of Tiran."

"Good. They've begun to change course then."

It was a relief. Now there could be no doubt at all where they were heading; the last possible chance that the Sudan story was correct was gone.

I gave Fenrek back the mike and said: "They should be here in an hour and a half."

I took a leg of chicken from Jo and went off with the glasses for an inspection. I lay on my belly on the ridge of hard sand and looked down to the desert that lay to the east of the oasis.

It took a little while to discover the airstrip, and if I hadn't known where to look I'd never have found it. But they'd cleared and smoothed off a stretch of sand about a kilometer long, and there were two soldiers there, squatting on the ground with their legs tucked under them, making coffee over a tiny charcoal fire; their horses were wandering nearby, legs hobbled.

In the oasis itself, two miles beyond the strip, everything seemed normal. I could make out the tiny figures wandering around, the shimmer of the water in the major pool, the heavy loads of dates pendulous on the palms; it all seemed very quiet and peaceful. In the yard of the barracks, a dozen men were drilling, the grey dust hanging over their heads, their bare feet stomping as they marched and counter-marched under the command of a Sergeant.

I went back to where the others were. Selegrit was saying: "...Yes, it would be wonderful to see you again, if you can possibly find the time. And, incidentally, a lady was asking after you only last night, isn't that a coincidence? She asked me to be sure to give you her love when I next saw you, and here we are chatting already. Maria Christophorous, a charming young woman, I met her at the Club last night, and she really spoke most devotedly of you."

Fenrek looked over at Jo (her ears pricked up now), and murmured: "Maria Christophorous? I don't think I remember her." He quickly changed the subject and said: "We don't have a man in Riyadh, do we?"

Selegrit said: "No, of course not, was there something on your mind?"

Fenrek said vaguely: "No, only we're in Arabia illegally, and if we reported our presence it might raise a diplomatic problem. On the other hand, if the Arabian government wanted to help us, which is quite unlikely, I'm afraid, it would take days before they'd agree to act, and by then it would be far too late. Within a few hours of the plane's landing, I'm very much afraid that the young ladies on board will be well beyond any hope of rescue. So we will have to make our apologies afterwards, when they find out we've been here. That's why I want this thing kept as quiet as possible. There are going to be all kinds of protests, I'm afraid. A man in the Capital to smooth over our difficulties would have been very useful. Ah, well."

With the fate of sixteen young women at stake, Fenrek was still a hell of a man for protocol. But he was right; the chance of getting help in time, officially, was nil. The government's policy, quite correctly, has always been to support the desert rulers, and even if the delicate matter of slavery had been raised in Riyadh, no action would have been taken until it could not possibly do the rulers any harm.

There was only Hishara; I wondered if we could count on him. Wadi Habauna lay less than ten miles from us, and somewhere out in the desert beyond it, just the other side of those hills, Hishara was fighting one of his little guerrilla wars.

I went back to watch the oasis. Now, a long line of camels was moving out, towards the airstrip, twenty-one of them with twelve horsemen on the flanks. Out in front, on a brown and white half-Arab pinto, was the little plump figure that could only be Lieutenant Osman, though now he wore the *keffia* instead of his cap, and a long camelhair *jurd* instead of his uniform. Beside him, in a flowing brown robe and the regal *hattar* and *agal*, was Ahmed Fellawi. Ten or eleven cameleers were walking beside the camels, leading them, and sixteen of the camels had been fitted out with the bamboo-frame sedans, covered over with cloth, that would protect the girls from the hot desert sun on their long trek through the Rub al Khali. Sixteen sedans, for sixteen girls, he had it figured exactly right.

I called Fenrek over and handed him the glasses, I said: "They're getting into position now. Twelve soldiers, one Lieutenant, Ahmed Fellawi himself, a dozen or so cameleers, and two hijackers, all armed to the teeth. Against them—you, me, two girls, and possibly the Hollyoak Beauty Queens, if they are fighting mad enough. How do you like the odds?"

He stared at the column, aghast. He never had believed that Fellawi would make sure of his protection by bringing the troops into the act; he'd been absolutely convinced that Fellawi would act alone; he'd even half thought that the two hijackers, once they'd served their purpose, would be quickly put out of the way, the old-fashioned pirates buried with the treasure chest, and I'd not been able to convince him that Fellawi's enormous self-assurance would make him certain it didn't matter *who* was in on the plot with him. After all, once that plane landed in Arabia, Fellawi was practically home free; and he wouldn't take any chances at this late stage of the game.

But convincing Fenrek of that was quite another matter.

He said nothing now, but just looked at me accusingly as though I should have warned him and hadn't.

But Jo was smiling broadly. She said: "A little trouble ahead of us, no? What are we going to do about it?"

I looked at my watch. "I'm going to talk to General Hishara. And then, we'll wait for the plane."

Connie was staring with a strange, almost hurt expression on her lovely face. Her eyes were on Fellawi, and she was very close to tears.

I left them there and went over to the set, and Selegrit cleared his throat noisily, and said: "Ah, Mr. Cain? We have just heard from General Hishara, he's at his Command post now, if you can reach him. Ninety-one point eight five, and ninety-three point six, I'll leave you to it."

"Thank you, Professor, we'll be in touch."

The closest point of the Yemeni border was only a few miles away, to the southeast of us. I had seen through the glasses where the wire petered out and came to an abrupt end, as though it wasn't worthwhile to mark the frontier any more. Beyond the end of the wire that started at the sea and went inland, the great waste of empty sand might have been anybody's territory, anybody who wanted it, and it was hard to realize that anyone should think it worth fighting over.

But they did. For three years the Saudi Arabians and the Yemenis had been at each other's throats over this ill-defined border, skirmishing along the dunes, killing each other over an unmarked line in a desert.

Sometimes it was one Camel Corps against another, and sometimes it was horses and foot soldiers; and occasionally it would be a few half-tracks or vintage tanks which the Americans, the British, the French, and the Russians regarded as essential military aid.

And somewhere along there, they were fighting now. Somewhere out there, General Hishara was our closest ally—if we could get him on our side.

I turned the dial round to the twin frequencies and locked them in, and there was the deep base voice of the Commander, calling genially: "So where are you, my dear fellow, come on in, come on in. This is General Hishara calling Cabot Cain, and I'm not prepared to wait here very much longer."

I said: "Hello, General, my compliments on the battle you have undoubtedly just won."

He said: "Ha! Mr. Cain? Delighted to have the opportunity to speak with you, dear boy, and the battle isn't half over yet." His English was sooth, easy, immaculate, the English of a man who'd spent his formative years in the English schools and universities. He'd been at Charterhouse, I remembered, and then at Oxford. He said: "What are you doing in Nicosia? Delightful place, they tell me, never been there myself, too many damn foreigners there." He sounded like a retired British General in his Club in St. James'.

I said: "Not Nicosia. Quite close by you. I'm just outside Khadir, as a matter of fact."

There was a little pause. "Khadir? Then why the devil didn't Riyadh tell me you were coming to Arabia? I'd have laid on a suitable welcome for you. It's quite monstrous. I'm coming over immediately, and we'll have a feast. I'll have them bring some lambs, and we'll roast them over an open pit, and we'll spend the rest of the day and the night in talk, it's going to be very exciting. And we'll compose a letter to the Government between us, giving them hell for not letting me know."

I said: "Riyadh doesn't know I'm here. There wasn't time to inform them. I'm afraid I'm here quite illegally."

"Oh, well, that's a formality we can soon straighten out. Was that your helicopter my scouts reported? Flying dangerously low, they said, as though trying to avoid detection. Can't believe it was that, though?"

"Yes, I'm afraid that's what it was."

The pause again. Then—with a touch of hesitance to the geniality—he said: "And what are you engaged in here? I seem to remember you're an amateur archeologist, are you not? But you are supposed to get Riyadh's permission for digging here, you know."

I said gently: "No, it's not that. I'm a sort of one-man anti-slavery commission."

Now the pause was a very long one. The Anti-Slavery Commission of the United Nations has always given Saudi Arabia a very bad time; it's a touchy subject with them. He said at last, very carefully: "Would you kindly repeat that, Mr. Cain?"

"Certainly. I'm chasing a slaver named Ahmed Fellawi."

"Fellawi? Ah yes, that pimp who calls himself a sheikh, which of course he isn't. But that's hardly any of your business, Mr. Cain.

And if you're operating in my territory illegally, if you are really concerning yourself with such a delicate matter, then, *wa'Allahi...* But I can't really believe you'd do such a thing?"

"I'm afraid that's precisely what I'm doing, General. Fellawi's on his way to the various rulers in the Rub with a wagonload of women, and I'm here to stop him."

He said again: *"Wa'Allahi,* by God! I never heard anything like it! You have the impertinence to try and impose your immature philosophies on us here? I've no time for the likes of Fellawi, but none the less..." The friendliness was quite gone; there was a hard and ruthless man talking now. He said: "Your association with my literary work gives you special privileges, Mr. Cain, but all I am prepared to say at the moment is the devil with your privileges, you'll not abuse them in my territory! Now, stay where you are, I'm coming over."

I said: "I rather hoped you would. Kindly don't forget the lambs for roasting." I could almost hear him snorting.

He said: "Do I detect a note of arrogance there? Is our first meeting going to be a hostile one? I must warn you, Mr. Cain, I am not a man you can easily trifle with, as you may know. Stay where you are. And you'd better have a very good explanation of your extraordinary behavior before I get there. I never heard anything like it!"

I said patiently: "We need your help, General Hishara, and when you get here, I think you'll agree." But I heard the click as he shut off the connection at the other end.

Fenrek was standing beside me, a very worried look on his face. He said gloomily: "They'll put you in jail, of course, for ten years or so. But what will they do with me? A senior official from Interpol, crashing through frontiers like a common criminal."

I said: "Cheer up. There's the plane we've all been waiting for."

We could hear it quite clearly now, coming in from the north, though it was too early to see anything, even with the Trinovids.

Connie, the expert, said: "A Caravelle."

"Then that's it." I said to Fenrek. "You'd better stay here and talk to the General, if and when he arrives. I'm going down to the airstrip." I looked at Connie. "Would you like to come down there with me?"

Fenrek stared. He was almost in shock. He exploded angrily: "No! I won't allow it!"

Even Jo seemed worried, I held Connie's gaze; no surprise there at all. She looked at Fenrek and said: "Yes, I want to go down there. He knows why, he's always known."

For a moment, Fenrek did not answer her, and Jo said anxiously: "It's a terribly dangerous thing to do."

"Yes, it is, too dangerous," Fenrek said. "Fellawi will put a bullet through her brain if he even thinks she's helping us track him down, and that's what it looks like, that's exactly what he will think. No. I can't allow it." He doesn't really have any authority over me, though that's by mutual consent more than by the rules of the game, but I didn't want to push him too hard.

The sound of the plane was closer now, and we looked and saw it far to the north, coming in very low and very fast, I said:

"Now, a crucial matter of timing. First, brush away all the tracks we've made, very carefully, and then get deep into the cave and hide. Hide that goddamn tablecloth too, I don't want them to know you're here until the right time."

He said patiently: "Which is when, may I ask?"

I spread my hands. "I don't know. It will become apparent. They'll search, and when they've finished searching, that's when you start to move down to..."

"Why should they search up here?"

"Because I want them to, I want them to be sure we're alone. May I go on?" He grimaced. I said: "Then, when you think the time is ripe; move down to the hillock over there, where you can cover us and still be well hidden. You and Jo stay there, keep your rifles ready. They are not likely to give us much trouble until they're sure they know what the score is, and that will take a few minutes' talking. So, just keep us covered, and keep your rifles aimed."

Fenrek gave up. He said, irritably: "And Hishara?"

"I'm hoping he'll get here in time." Fenrek was still terribly upset. I said, giving him something else to worry about: "Don't forget that Arabia is not a signatory to any of the Interpol Agreements, so you'd better not throw your rank around Hishara."

He said stiffly: "I realize that, of course. And it's all very improper."

"Give us *time*, don't be hasty. Time, time, and more time. And above all, watch your footprints, they can spot the track of an insect."

He nodded miserably. I've never seen an unhappier man. I took Connie's arm and we moved off down the hill towards trouble.

CHAPTER 12

The camels had their long necks craned, their eyes immovably fixed on the approaching plane, each and every one of them.

It's a strange thing about camels. Where nothing moves except the life that is around them—the cameleer, a stray goat, a hawk swooping on a lizard—they watch out only for signs of food or water. And then, the moment something unaccustomed moves, however far away, they lift up their heads and *stare*.

They lock their eyes on whatever it is that has attracted their attention, and hold them there, unmoving; to the Bedouin, it's a warning of the approach of danger even before their own sharp eyes have picked it out. Living between distant horizons, spending their days with nothing close by on which to focus their eyes, the Bedouin are unbelievably far-sighted; but the camel can spot—and worry about—the slightest movement of a *jerboa*, the desert rat, at better than a mile away, even though it is colored precisely as the sand is colored and is no bigger than a domestic mouse.

If you go anywhere near a Bedouin camp, they're all waiting for you, because their camels have spotted you hours ago, the moment you crossed the horizon; and they are still staring when you get there, wanting to know who you are and where you came from.

And then, in concert, their heads all swung round and they stared at us instead, a greater danger, as Connie and I moved over the brow of the hillock and came into their range of vision.

Almost immediately one of the camel drivers gave a shout, and three of the soldiers broke formation and came galloping over, fast, flat out over the soft sand, yelling excitedly. One of them swung up his rifle and fired a shot, not really at us, but in our general direction, a warning. I heard Connie gasp, and I said: "It's all right."

She was remembering another time, when they'd been trying to bring us down in the dunes not too far to the east of here. I held my own rifle high and waved it, a friendly gesture.

And then they were reining in the horses hard, prancing elaborately around us; even at a time like this, they can't resist the temptation of equine drama. The babble of their shouting was quite incomprehensible, and I shouted back: "Keep your shirts on, there's nothing to be scared of, I want to see Sheikh Ahmed."

And then Lieutenant Osman was coming in fast, his plump body nicely balanced in the saddle in spite of his weight, and there were four more riders with him, angry, excited men all of them. He reared his horse not six inches from my nose and stared at me, not believing. He yelled: "*Inta! Shu biddak honn?* You? What do you want here?"

The last time we'd spoken, he was not calling me *inta*, 'you', but HADRAKAT, 'your honor'; times had changed, and attitudes had changed with them.

He reined his horse round hard, and looked all over the desert, and I wondered if Fenrek's head were showing over the rise of the hill behind me; I thought perhaps not, not yet. He was searching, and I took advantage of the indecision and said cheerfully: "You won't see them, Osman, but they're all out there somewhere, my private army. *Keef haalak, ya habibi,* how are you my friend, my brother, my esteemed uncle?"

He was remembering the indignity he'd suffered when we'd last been together, in front of the Sheikh. He swung his rifle at me savagely, gripping his horse with his knees and using both hands on it, and I grabbed the stock with one hand as it came close to my head, twisted, pulled, and sent him sprawling in the dirt. There was a violent fury in his eyes, and he looked at the soldiers as though to ask why they weren't already engaged in killing me, but I knew the answer to that, even if he didn't.

I said gently: "Better not, Osman, until your boss gets here."

He looked back at the Sheikh, cantering out now at a leisurely pace, not deigning to hurry. His mouth was set in a hard line, and he was trying hard not to look surprised. He stopped and sat his horse and looked down at me, avoiding Connie's eye, deliberately counting her as nothing. And then be grunted, a sort of self-deprecating snort.

He said calmly: "I should have stayed to make sure you were dead, that time in Djibouti."

Osman took his cue and yelled, and a soldier grabbed at my rifle to wrest it from me. I merely held on and let him swing on the barrel, and I said to Fellawi: "Tell him to let go, or I'll break both his arms." I spoke Arabic, and the soldier, not waiting for orders, fell back, not understanding quite why it had seemed so hard for him. Fellawi, too, was now looking carefully at the hills behind us, and Osman said, fearfully: "He says there's an army out there."

Fellawi said contemptuously: "What army?" He looked at me and laughed, and said: "The government at Riyadh has sent a thousand men, no doubt, to put an end to a business the government not only tolerates, but actively promotes. They left the Capital, six hundred miles across the Rub, on a forced march, what...a month ago?" He was really quite ingratiating when he laughed; his charm was very real, and it was always an effort to see the evil that lay below it. He said: "It's a question of *time*, isn't it? Even if they permitted you to interfere in a purely domestic problem. A problem, I might say, to you only. This whole operation has taken me two days exactly, so tell me where your army sprang from, will you do that? Perhaps it's a United Nations army, they're the only people who really disapprove of my activities. This is my home country, Mr. Cain, and you are a foreigner among xenophobes. And you are a fool."

I sighed. "Well, it's hard to convince you, isn't it?" It seemed necessary to get the searching over and done with, before Fenrek made his move.

Fellawi looked hard at me, and said to Osman: "Send two scouts up onto the hill, a wide arc around the airfield, see if they can find anything of interest."

Well, there it was, and about time too. Soon, Fenrek would be moving out of his hiding place, and I didn't want him spotted, not yet. There was the helicopter, of course, visible from the top of the hills; no problem.

Osman nodded and yelled an order. Two of the horsemen galloped off, heading for the hills, and Fellawi said curtly: "This way." He paid no attention at all either to my rifle or to Connie's shotgun. Why should he? A man of his arrogance; a couple of quick shots at the nod of a head was all that was required, and the odds were so insuperably in his favor that his contempt was clearly showing. Underestimation, the old weakness.

The plane was circling now, high above us, and on the little strip a couple of the soldiers were hauling on lines that raised the pole to which the windsock was attached. I shielded my eyes against the sun and saw that the plane's undercarriage was still up; I wondered if Captain Sorrenti, with fifteen thousand hours of flying time, was trying to pull a little trick of his own up there; he knew where he was, no doubt, and a little simulated trouble on board just might have given him a chance to try for the airport at Qizan; not much of a hope, but if that's what he was doing, I admired him for the effort. The hijackers, no doubt, would insist on a belly landing if the carriage wouldn't go down; but it was a nice try.

Some of the camel drivers had set up a small tent for the Sheikh, a Persian carpet spread out on the shady sand under the raised flap. He got down from his horse and said: "Now, if you don't mind, I will take your weapons." He'd made his point, and now was the time for him to be careful.

I swung my rifle slowly by its strap onto my shoulder, and said: "No, I'll keep it, if you don't mind."

For a moment, I thought he might give that nod of the head; two of his soldiers had their rifles pointed at my belly. But he merely shrugged and said: "You don't really believe you'll be able to use it, do you?"

It was politic to give him a little victory, so I said: "No, I don't suppose I will." I handed it to one of the soldiers, and Connie... Connie made quite a gesture out of it. She held out her shotgun, not to the man who was reaching for it, but to Fellawi himself. She said: "Take it, Ahmed. I don't want to do you any harm."

It was almost the first time he'd looked at her, and it was a hard, long look, as though he'd never been sure about her, about the effect his professional charm had on her. He even touched that little moustache as though making sure it was still there. He said: "Well, it seems you can't get the desert out of your blood... What made you come back here?"

"To be with you." Her voice was low, urgent, pleading.

"I have a better use for you now. You can join the others, wouldn't you say that's a good idea?" He said, mocking: "If you really want to serve me."

She said clearly: "I'd rather stay with you."

"Yes, I don't doubt you would. But I'd rather have the money you'll bring me. That's my vocation, I'm a slaver, why should I saddle myself with my own surplus merchandise?" He looked at me and back to her, and said: "Some other man's cast-off whore."

It didn't faze her at all. She reached out a hand and touched him, and said: "Please, Ahmed...Please?"

Quite slowly, he drew his foot from the stirrup, bent his knee, and was about to plant his sandal squarely in the middle of her face and shove. I reached out and took hold of his foot, and just held it tightly, and I said: "No, Ahmed. Beat her up and she'll only love you all the more, that's what this is all about, didn't you know that?"

Above us, the engine of the plane was coughing badly, the jets spluttering. I wondered what Captain Sorrenti was up to. I saw Fellawi wince at the pressure on his ankle, and then he raised his riding crop and brought it hard down, aiming for my head, an angry, futile blow. I let go of his foot and warded it off easily. I said: "Why don't you take her again yourself, Fellawi? She's willing enough."

He said again: "Another man's cast-off whore, good enough for the Rulers, but not good enough for me." He turned to a passing cameleer and called out: "You there! You want *baksheesh*? You want to take this woman? You and the others, till the caravan is ready?"

The cameleer grinned, wiping his hands on his greasy *felabieh*, but he hung back when he saw me make a move towards Connie.

Osman laughed, and said: "And him? What about him?"

The undercarriage of the plane was down now, the engine firing nicely, and it was coming in on the final run. Fellawi said: "Yes, about him..."

There was still something worrying him; and that's all it needs sometimes, a little bit of indecision. He looked at me, and then out into the desert again for my mythical army. I wondered if it were time to tell him about Hishara, dressing up the story a little, and then the two horsemen he'd sent out to search were galloping in and pulling up energetically close beside us. One of them, a Corporal, pointed with his crop and said: "A helicopter out there, eight, ten kilos away." I'd been hoping they'd see it from the brow of the hill; we'd made no attempt to hide it.

Fellawi said: "So that's how you got here. I was wondering." To the Corporal, he said: "*Zrir? K'bir?* A small one, or a troop-carrier?"

The Corporal shook his head: "Not a troop-carrier, *ya Sheikh*. Maybe two, three places, maybe hold three, four men, no more." The horse was prancing, dancing its feet lightly in the sand, throwing back its head and whinnying, then rearing back to paw the air with its hooves.

Fellawi said, irritably: "But you checked their tracks, you fool?"

He shook his head. "No tracks, *ya Sheikh*, the ground is hard there."

Fellawi still wasn't very sure. He looked at me thoughtfully and said: "It wouldn't make much sense for you to come alone, would it? I wonder if your Colonel—what is his name, Fenrek?—is out there hiding somewhere? And even if he is, one man, two of you against my men? No, you've got a hidden card somewhere, haven't you, Cain? I wonder if you'd like to tell me what it is?"

Osman said suddenly: "General Hishara."

Fellawi turned to him and frowned. "Hishara?"

"His Excellency is on the Yemeni border. He's a friend of Cain's, he told me so."

"His Excellency told you?"

"No. Cain told me."

"A lie. He's full of lies, don't you know that? And even if it were true, the General would undoubtedly have him shot for what he is doing." He laughed suddenly, very sure now. He said to me: "Do you know exactly what the *legal* position of these young women is going to be, the moment that plane lands? They're illegal immigrants. The

Kahdi's Court will set heavy fines for them, and they will legally become the property of anyone who pays their fines. That's the law here, Cain. So General Hishara is hardly likely to take your side if it comes to a showdown, is he? Even if he weren't occupied with the Yemenis at this moment. And that means that your hidden card is a bluff, and nothing more."

That's the secret, of course; you tell a careful mixture of fact and fiction, and it's the best way to confuse the enemy; there's nothing like seeding confusion when the flashpoint is approaching.

I said: "That plane's going to crash."

Startled, he swung round. The plane was coming in much too fast, even for a Caravelle, and it hit the ground and bounced crazily, then swerved and found its course again; one wing scraped the dirt and set up a cloud of dust. It occurred to me that the expert Captain Sorrenti might no longer be at the controls.

Fellawi yelled to the Corporal: "Tie him, hold him here!" and then he drove the spurs into his horse's flanks and raced off towards the plane.

The Corporal got down from his horse, slipped a saddle rope of soft camelhair from his bag, and gestured to me to hold out my wrists. Three of the others were ready, their rifles aimed. I held out my hands and let him tie them, and Osman said: "Her too." The cameleer was still standing there, waiting, wanting to paw at Connie and not daring to until I was well out of the way. He looked up at Osman, and back to her, and at Osman again, wondering if he had the courage to remind the Officer of the Sheikh's promise. He spluttered a little, and said: "*Ya effendi...*" It was just a reminder, nothing more, a plea for a promise to be kept.

Osman kicked out at him and sent him sprawling, and said: "After me, *ya ibn kalb*, I'll tell you when." The man whined.

The Corporal used his dagger to cut off the ends of the rope, dyed a bright red with cochineal, and tied Connie's wrists, and we stood there, the rifles not moving from our backs, and watched the plane bouncing along the strip.

Osman was racing towards it now, and Fellawi was already beside it, spurring his horse to keep up and not succeeding, and three or four of the other riders were charging off to join the party. The plane was slewing around horribly, and a wing tip caught the pole that was holding up the windsock and sent it flying, and then the brakes slammed on and it swerved and came straight at us. It was doing well over a hundred miles an hour, the wheels slipping in the sand, and it swerved again and headed past us and then stopped with a sickening lurch; the tail end tipped up quite slowly, the nose touched the ground lightly, and it stayed there, immobile, for a second; and then it tipped back into position.

It wasn't more than fifty yards from us. The whining engines cut, and in the sudden silence, the door was flown open and an Arab tumbled out, under the tail, and fell to the ground, picked himself up, and ran. He ran for a hundred yards or so, and then pulled up and looked back at the plane, sheepishly. The second hijacker?

The hatch of the pilot's compartment was thrown back, and a dark and swarthy face looked out, the huge black moustache looking almost comic, and then Fellawi was galloping up, swinging his horse round the nose. He looked up at the face and yelled:

"Poulakis! What happened?"

He yelled back, in execrable French: "The Caravelle, I am not trained to fly it, I had to make the landing."

"What happened to the pilot?"

Poulakis drew a finger across his throat. He said: "He try to make us go to Qizar, he say the undercarriage no good, get stuck, so I think maybe he is dead now, I don't know for sure. I bring the plane in, is okay now."

"All right. Get everybody out. Hurry."

The swarthy face disappeared. In a moment, the passengers started streaming out from the tail end, climbing unsteadily down the aluminum ladder, looking as though they'd had a very bad time indeed, and no wonder; by rights, that plane should have smashed up the moment it hit, then burst into fire.

The horsemen, as though drilled for the event, were circling the plane, keeping fifty feet away from it and from each other, cantering their horses and making them prance, showing off their expertise for the benefit of anyone who wanted to watch. And then, Poulakis was running through them, hurrying over to where the Sheikh, his master, sat his horse and waited, close by to us.

He was a slight, hairy man in khaki shorts and shirt, with a red scarf at his neck, and quick, nervous movements; his skin was the color of camel leather that's been too long in the tanning, a red-bronze, parchment kind of skin, and he had a two days growth of beard. I wondered how he'd managed to get on board the plane in the first place; any skipper in his right mind would have taken one look at him and thrown him right off.

He looked at me with a sudden interest—had he seen me when he was flying Fenrek's plane? —and I said to him, a question of tying all the ends together: "Did you hide in the can when the plane took off, Poulakis?"

He grinned and said: "What else?"

A loader; then; it wouldn't have been hard for him to get assigned to the baggage in Beirut, a few piastres in the right hands...

Fellawi said impatiently: "Get the luggage unloaded and onto the camel train, take everything that might be of value. What about the pilots? The steward?"

Poulakis spat onto the sand and looked around him: "I need a drink, what a god-awful country this is. The pilot is maybe dead, I don't know, a bullet in here, in the chest." He tapped the area over his heart and shrugged: "I don't know. Co-pilot is nothing, little bullet hole in leg is all, they both stay in cockpit, they don't go no place. The steward, he don't count for nothing, is there." He pointed, and I saw the steward, his face as white as his jacket, helping one of the girls; they were both of them almost in tears, his arm around her, he was trying to give her comfort, but he was visibly shaking.

"No other men on board?"

Poulakis spat again and shook his head. "And I need a parachute."

One of the men had dragged a brown-covered bundle up and was standing by it, waiting to be told what to do.

Fellawi said: "The parachute's here. You'd better take a course for Lufaiya, you know where that is? It's about eighty miles from here, and if you stay three miles north of the village you'll miss the radar at Qizar, but keep low, just to be sure. There's a dry river bed, easily recognizable, and twenty miles up it you'll see the truck waiting. There will be a smoke pot so that you won't miss him. That's where you jump. The truck will take you to the edge of the dunes, and there's a camel there for you, so you should be in here before nightfall."

"And the money?"

"When I know that plane's in the sea."

The realization was slowly dawning on Connie. I watched her and said nothing, letting it sink in, and when I saw the tears coming to her eyes, I said gently: "That's the kind of man he is, Connie, aren't you ever going to realize it? The two pilots, both of them dying, as far as we know, the steward... He's going to bury them in the Red Sea. He doesn't need them anymore, he doesn't need you either, just the money."

I saw her look at the cameleer Fellawi had offered her to; it was this more than anything else. I said: "He doesn't really look so romantic anymore, does he? The Son of the Shiekh, Rudolph Valentino, you still think that's the way it is?"

The women were crowding around us now, talking and saying nothing, babbling to each other because they still didn't believe what was happening. They were seeking the tiny patch of shade that was outside the tent, as though the sun was all they had to worry about, keeping in little groups of three or four, seeking comfort from their own particular friends. One of the two stewardesses, a tall, thin girl with auburn hair and freckles, was looking at me curiously, wondering about the bright red rope at my wrists; she was not from the Beauty Queen mold, a one-off model, with a white, anemic skin and intense, thoughtful eyes. She had less flesh on her than most of the others, the tendons at her wrists clearly visible, the fingers long and restless. She stared at me and said: "For God's sake, where are we? What's happening?"

They were frightened, all of them, and I wondered how much they'd been told on the plane. There couldn't have been much conversation, I supposed, but Poulakis might have said something, though I didn't suppose it was very likely.

I said: "You are all off to the harems of the Rulers, this man is taking you there, and isn't that charming? He is going to sell you off, so many cattle."

Fellawi was just getting down from his horse, and the stewardess followed my glance and looked at him indignantly and said:

"Well, it's about time someone told you..."

It must have been the look on his face that shut her up, or perhaps the movement he made with his arm. He raised it quite slowly across his chest and shoulders, and then struck her a back-handed blow across the face, so hard that she fell down and lay there looking up at him in shock. I was conscious that Connie was ready to pounce; her face was livid with rage. She reached out with her bound hands and clawed at him, ripping her nails down his cheek, and I tried to grab at her, but three of the soldiers grabbed at me first, and it wasn't time for the fight to start, not yet; I hoped to God that Fenrek wouldn't get excited and put in a couple of quick shots before they were needed; to be fair, I didn't think he would.

But to be sure, to keep the rising tempers from turning latent anger into active violence, I yelled out:

"Hold it! Hold it everybody!"

Surprisingly, everybody did, even Fellawi. He wasn't hurt, just a touch of blood on his face; and it was beneath his dignity to start a major battle over such a trifle.

I wrenched myself free of the soldiers and held on to Connie, and said: "Cool it, for God's sake."

Fellawi looked at her with a great deal of contempt. He said coldly: "You very nearly got killed, both of you, do you realize that?" I half expected her to spit at him, and I tightened my grip on her arm.

I said to Fellawi: "She's just fallen out of love, you know how women are."

He transferred his gaze to me, and held my look, and then there was a very humorous sort of smile on his face; it almost made him attractive. He showed his teeth and laughed, and said: "Yes, I do believe you are right, Mr. Cain."

Somehow, I was glad he was using the 'mister' again.

Osman had been hanging on the edge of the circle, not knowing whether to start shooting without orders or not, and Fellawi said to him; "All right, get the women lined up, I want to look at them."

There was a lot of bustling around as the soldiers pushed the girls into some sort of order. They stood looking frightened and bewildered, the phony smiles all gone, just simple hometown girls, torn away from the sycophancy and trite hedonism of their chosen careers; they weren't beauty queens anymore, just thoroughly scared kids. Several of them were weeping; one or two looked bright and intelligent, but most of them didn't. I couldn't help thinking of the stories they'd have to tell when they got back home to Peoria or wherever.

Fellawi walked slowly before them, and even now he couldn't resist the temptation to smile and show his nice white teeth at them. He nodded his head wisely, a General inspecting his troops and finding them all satisfactory. Osman marched stiffly behind him, the Officer of the Day; and Poulakis was there too, smirking. They went to the end of the line and back again, and I could almost see the calculations going on in that venal mind of Fellawi's. As they came past us, he jerked his head in my direction and said to Poulakis: "He goes on the plane, too."

Poulakis lost his smirk. He looked me up and down, looked warily at the red rope round my wrists, and said: "You will have to kill him before he get on board, I don't want no trouble up there. That kind of man is going to make trouble, I don't want it."

Fellawi nodded nonchalantly; it was part of his arrogance not to make a fuss about it. He said, off-handedly: "Yes, I think you're right."

He looked at Osman; and I was ready.

CHAPTER 13

Fellawi had remarked that it was all a question of time; more correctly, it was a question of *timing*. The timing was full of imponderables, but at least intelligent guesses and even calculations could be made; and I'd made them.

How long does it take an irate desert warrior, on a good horse, to get where he's going to in a hurry? How fast could Hishara's men move when their Commander was driven by his own indignity? I reckoned that it should be about *now!*

And it was.

The camels saw them first, of course, and craned their inquisitive necks to look at the two horsemen riding down towards us, just breasting the rise of the hill and coming down the slope, not fast, just taking it easy; but there was white foam on the horses' flanks; they'd been driven hard, and the slow walk was a deliberate effort, a clear attempt to formulate a decision.

Fellawi was staring too, and so was Osman, and there was a look of shocked alarm on the Lieutenant's face, because he knew already that he was going to have to make a terrifying decision, a decision he couldn't avoid, not with his master there beside him; it was already too late for wiggling out.

I was thankful that it was just two men; whose idea, I wondered, Fenrek's or the Commander's? Or the two of them acting together? They were in full uniform, the two riders, with khaki *keffias* wrapped around their faces, bound with black *agals* of goats' hair rope, and their rifles were slung over their shoulders.

It was a trap, a trap for Fellawi, and I knew it, a bait held out for him to take, and condemn himself—or reject, and save his miserable life.

Fenrek's idea or Hishara's? It didn't really matter very much.

I said to Fellawi: "You didn't believe me, did you? Only two men, but that's all we need." There was a look of fury on his face. I said again, making the lie thoroughly believable: "Just two solitary soldiers, but they're army men and you haven't the guts to fight them. And they know it, they are not even in a hurry, not even protecting themselves."

It didn't take him long to make up his mind. Why should it? A small patrol could disappear in the desert easily enough, it happened all the time, a common enough occurrence. He said coldly, the fury replaced now by a controlled dispassion:

"Osman."

Lieutenant Osman did not hesitate. He too never guessed the truth. He raised his rifle and fired. At that range, he could hardly have missed, but the horsemen weren't fools either, and they'd been briefed. As soon as the rifle went to Osman's shoulder, I saw them rear their mounts back and slip from the saddles, smoothly and efficiently, not waiting at all for the shot to sound, and they dragged their horses down with them and dropped behind their flanks, and started firing back.

And then the fun started. It was even better than I'd expected.

Osman yelled: "Fire at will!" and his men dropped to the ground and opened up, but the two cavalrymen were highly trained, the best in the desert, Osman went down at once, a bullet through his shoulder which had shattered his wrist on its way there, and one of the soldiers dropped, and then they were all firing, and the women were screaming and running for cover, only there wasn't any...

I shoved Connie with my bound wrists, and half-pushed, half-dragged her down behind a hobbled camel, its left knee tightly bound to keep it down where it was supposed to be. I went to work on the ropes with my teeth, pulling at the knots.

And now, behind the wide sweep of the hill's brow, the men I was expecting suddenly appeared, a line of eighty, ninety, a hundred of them, cresting the top of the dune and standing there, momentarily, on their horses and camels, getting the two lines straight, the horses in front, the camels in the rear.

Against the skyline, they made a splendid, awe inspiring sight, with their veiled faces and their long black cloaks and the bright reds and blues and greens and yellows of their horses' trappings.

And riding slowly, quite slowly, through the twin lines, was the man who could only be General Hishara.

He *looked* like a desert fighter. He sat on his horse as straight as an arrow, a tall, red-faced man with a grey moustache, in a well-cut uniform that might have been made in Savile Row, his *hattar* ringed with the gold and white *agal* to which he, no doubt, was truly entitled. He rode fifty paces in front of his men, looked back to check the dressing, and I heard him shout:

"Up on the left..."

The left flank of the lines moved forward a trifle, and stood there, waiting.

Osman was on the ground, staring in shock and horror, clutching his bleeding arm and shoulder. I looked at Fellawi and saw the wild anger in his face. I heard him yell: "Down! Down, and keep firing!"

It was too late for anything else, he'd already committed himself; that was the purpose of Hishara's bait, and now that he was trapped, all Fellawi could do was fight. I chalked up at least one virtue in his favor; he had guts.

The soldiers hesitated; they had no stomach for fighting their own army, but I knew that it wouldn't be more than a minute or two before they'd have to, like it or not.

Then, Fellawi grabbed a rifle from one of them and started pumping it furiously, firing at the line on the top of the hill; I saw one man fall from his camel. The Corporal raised his gun and fired, and yelled at his men, and then all of them were firing desperately, knowing, as I had known, that the damage had been done once Fellawi had ordered that first shot at the probing patrol. They were committed now, and if they couldn't live, at least they'd die shooting. They must have known the Commander even better than I did.

And then, out there, the General raised his arm, and so help me, there was a curved sword in his hand, I heard him shout the order, and the twin lines started moving forward, at the walk first, for fifty yards or so, then at the canter for another hundred; and then, when they were less than two hundred yards away—the old-fashioned lead-in to the charge. They broke into the gallop and tore down onto us, a thousand-yard arc of cavalry, their lances held high; we could have been back in the nineteenth century.

Behind them, the slower camels were trotting in with that smooth but ungainly gait that racing camels have, the riders armed with rifles, swinging their weapons round now and preparing to fire through the ranks of the horses ahead of them. They fired three volleys, and then broke to the flanks, half on one side and half on the other, the old desert tactic for cutting off any of the enemy who might break and run.

I heard the General shout the order: "Lower Lances!" and the long line went down in one smooth movement, the points shining in the sun. They came right through us, through the screaming women, missing them expertly, through the line of Osman's soldiers and not missing them at all; I saw three of them die with lances through their bellies, and then the horses reared up and swung round for the counter-charge, but it wasn't necessary. Osman's men were yelling desperately, the fight gone out of them after that one magnificent charge, their hands held high in the air and their rifles thrown to the ground. I heard a young officer with Hishara give the order to regroup, and within two minutes the twin lines were in formation again, sitting their mounts and awaiting orders. The charge over, they began to loosen the *keffias* from their faces, untucking them and letting them hang loosely. The horses were restless with the smell of blood, and even the camels were trumpeting.

And there, behind them, Fenrek and Jo were running in, panting with the exertion, trying to get in there before everything should move on without them.

The General swung his horse lightly around and walked over to where I was standing, waiting for him. He wore the brown cloak of the desert Arab over his Savile Row uniform, thrown open and back over his square shoulders, with breeches and dusty but highly-polished riding boots that looked as though they'd been bench-made in London too. His grey moustache was full but neat, and curved upward in the

British Cavalry manner, and his jaw jutted out as though challenging the whole world. He moved with an easy, controlled vigor, a very autocratic look in his black eyes, the look of a man who knows exactly what he wants, and isn't about to waste unnecessary time in getting it. He had an enormous dignity and presence. His curved sword was still in his hand, and I noticed with pleasure that it was one of the old Ispahan blades, heavily decorated, the scimitar that the Turks brought into Poland and Hungary in the eighteenth century.

He reined in and looked at me and said: "Mr. Cain, no doubt. I am General Hishara." His manner was both correct and courteous, and even genial. Good; it meant that Fenrek had already done the explaining. I couldn't take my eyes off that beautiful scimitar.

I said; "I didn't know that soldiers still fought with the *shimshar*, General. That's a splendid blade you have, there. Ispahan, isn't it? About seventeen eighty or so?"

He said: "Ha!" And then again: "Ha! So you know about swords, do you? Try the balance."

He tossed it to me with a quick and easy flick of the wrist, and as I caught the handle the continuation of the movement almost sliced my leg off at the knee, a sword with a mind of its own, which is what distinguishes the great blades from the bad ones.

I took it gingerly and examined it. The inscription around the pistol grip, recurved in the opposite direction of the blade—something the Western swordsmen had never learned—was written in the old cuneiform letters of the Achaemenid Kings, inlaid in gold and enamel: *Let my enemies stand in fear.* And along the fine watered blade itself the words were incised: *Had Shafi borne his blade with honor, the kings would have bowed down before him*, a quotation from the great 10th-century Persian poet known as Firdousi, though his real name was Abu el Kassim Mansour; he once wrote an epic history of his country in no less than sixty thousand verses.

I said: "A very rare and valuable weapon. Isn't it the work of Darwish Mahmoud?"

"Ha! Yes, indeed it is. Seventeen eighty-three, two years before he died, the greatest sword-maker the world has ever known, That sword has a twin somewhere, with the rest of the Firdousi quotation on it. I've spent a lifetime trying to track it down, but it's lost, I'm afraid."

I said: "It's in the Izmir National Museum,"

His eyes bulged. He said: "What? Ha! Really? Are you sure? Ha!"

"The Curator there is an old friend of mine. I'm quite sure the government could be persuaded to part with it."

"Good Heavens! Astonishing! Ha!"

I handed the scimitar back to him, and he slipped lightly off his horse and sheathed it, and looked around and said: "Your friend out there, ah, there he is. There they both are. What an extraordinary-looking young woman, more like a boy, isn't she? And these ladies..."

Fenrek and Jo finally reached us, puffing, and Hishara said: "Your Mr. Maximillian, as he likes to call himself... What did he say he was? An investigator for the Airlines? Ha! He told me just what the problem is. Must say, it's a bit awkward, isn't it?"

Maximillian is the name Fenrek uses on occasion when he wants to remain incognito. He'd heard the phrase "likes to call himself," and he looked pained.

The General smiled and said gently: "You're far too well-known, Colonel Fenrek."

Fenrek sighed. He said: "Excellency, a matter of protocol, I fear considerable apologies are demanded, but in view of the situation..."

"Yes, yes, of course." Hishara couldn't have cared less.

The Beauty Pageant was gathering itself together again, and although they didn't really know what was happening, they sensed that law and order was coming to their assistance. The General looked them over, his eyes gleaming, his moustache quivering. He was holding back his shoulders and pulling in an already taut stomach, preening himself as he looked at them.

Around us, a squad of his men was rounding up the prisoners, shoving them into a little herd, dragging the wounded along by their hair and dumping them out in the sun. One of the General's Sergeants was offering the girls a goatskin bag of *lebban*, the sour goats' milk the Arabs love so much, and the first of them sniffed it and grimaced rudely, and the General said: "Not *lebban*, you idiot, offer them water." The water would have been ripe with gypsum salts, and quite undrinkable for them, but it was a nice thought anyway.

He said, harrumphing: "American ladies, really is a bit awkward, isn't it? I mean, there'd be all sorts of questions asked at the U.N., wouldn't there?" He grunted, and said: "Got a brother at the U.N., did you know that? Bloody diplomat."

"Yes, I know of him."

"Lives in Manhattan." He took a deep breath of the desert air and said: "Can you imagine anyone living in Manhattan? Will that plane fly?"

I said: "The pilot and the co-pilot have both been shot, and we'd better do something about them, if they're still alive. Do you have a medic with you?"

"Not what you would call a medic, but we've got a fellow who knows how to dig bullets out of people, had lots of practice at it." He barked an order, and one of his men went running over to the plane.

I said: "I can fly it out of here if necessary."

"Splendid. Who shot the pilots?"

I pointed to Poulakis. "That man. His name's Nicolai Poulakis."

"Ha! Poulakis! That's the man who's been training those damned Yemeni pilots. Splendid!"

Osman was sitting on the sand, still clutching at his wounded shoulder. He tried to get to his feet as the General approached him, and one of the Commander's men thrust out a bare foot and kicked him back to the ground again.

The General said: "Lieutenant Osman, if I remember your wretched name correctly. You opened fire on my men, you know what that means, don't you? And you..." He looked at Fellawi and said: "And you fired on me personally, *wa' Allahi!*"

He turned back to the Beauty Pageant. "Extraordinary. Where did so very many young women come from? And they're all illegal immigrants, technically, aren't they? I'm tempted to post bail for them myself. What a splendid thought." He was looking at Connie, and he said: "Especially this one."

Suddenly, he held his hand out to her. "I am General Hishara, Madame," and I corrected him: "Mademoiselle". He threw me a look and said, harrumphing again: "Your lady, no doubt?"

"No. Nobody's lady at the moment."

Connie held on to his hand and said: "I am Connie Delorme, General. We owe you quite a lot, don't we?"

"Ha! Yes, indeed you do. You must have had a terrible time, and I'm delighted that I could be of some small service." So help me, he was brushing his moustache with a well-manicured finger. He said: "It's a terrible place he was bringing you to, the desert is a hard, hard master."

She said: "But it's so...romantic."

Oh God.

I said to Fenrek: "We'd better get the young ladies back on board that plane and get out of here."

He and Jo were just standing there, leaving everything to the General and to me. He said: "Yes. Yes, of course. If the General, that is...?"

The General said: "What? Ah, yes, I suppose you'd better leave us before I have to take official notice of your presence here, Mr. Maximillian. The young ladies, too, of course, and the sooner the better."

Connie's great solemn blue eyes were on him, and he smiled at her and said: "Why don't we have a little chat before you go, Miss Delorme? Are you interested in horses? I have a splendid stallion, half Arab, half Irish, the best of two worlds."

They were moving off together, and I said to Fenrek: "Well?"

He nodded, and we found the steward and told him to get the passengers on board, out of the broiling sun. The cavalry had reformed their lines and were preparing to march into Khadir, and the Camel Corps riders had formed up into two squads, one on each side of the plane, sitting their mounts and waiting patiently. A dozen men were roping the prisoners, and I saw that Fellawi was bound and hobbled, with a rope around his neck as well, the other end of it tied to the pommel of one of the camels. As I moved past him, he said quietly: "Do you have a cigarette, Mr. Cain?"

I shook my head: "I don't smoke." He smiled and said: "Just an idea. It's customary, isn't it?"

The women were boarding the plane, a herd of pretty sheep climbing the aluminum ladder and disappearing up the plane's fundament; a strange place for the hatch, under the tail of a Caravelle; disembarking passengers always looks like so many eggs being laid. Fenrek and Jo were fussing over them, and he looked over to where Connie was admiring the General's fine stallion, and he whispered: "My God, I believe he's got designs on her."

I thought it was a nice old-fashioned way of putting it. I said: "He's a good man, and she knows what she's doing."

We went on board and found the two pilots, still alive but not much use to anyone, their faces white and drawn, and the medic was grinning and holding up three spent bullets he'd dug out of them with the tip of his dagger.

I said to the pilot: "You think this plane will get off the ground again?"

He screwed up his eyes with the pain and nodded: "If that *disgraziato* didn't wreck the undercarriage, it will. But I don't know if I can...if I can..." He was gasping.

I said: "Don't worry about it, we'll have you in Djibouti in no time at all."

But he had already fainted.

We went outside again. Hishara and Connie were just coming back towards us, and now he was holding her arm. He said: "There's a helicopter out there, Mr. Cain. I'm afraid I have to confiscate it, landed illegally, that sort of thing. And it might come in very handy. You do understand, don't you?"

"Yes, of course I do. We'll settle with its owners when we get back to Djibouti."

"You're sure you don't mind?"

"Not in the least."

"There's one other question, isn't there? You really think you can talk your Curator friend into parting with the other Firdousi scimitar?"

"I am sure of it."

"Ha! Splendid! You're a good fellow, Mr. Cain."

"The word *good* is open to all kinds of interpretations, isn't it?"

"Ha! We have something on our mind, haven't we?"

I said: "We have indeed. Will you do me a good turn?

Yourself, too, perhaps, at the same time?"

He was already suspicious. But he said: "If I can, I will."

"There's a chain gang of slaves in Khadir, blacks from Africa that Fellawi brought here to build his airstrip. Set them free for me."

It was a sober moment. He said gently: "You're trying to impose your Western philosophy on me, Cain."

"Your Western education already did that."

"And how would it do me good?"

I said: "Somewhere in the Apocrypha, there's a line: *Do good, and evil shall not find you.* Do you believe that?"

"Ah yes, the Book of Tobit. But again, your religion, not mine. Slavery is...shall I say *covertly* legal here, as you must know. You're asking me to bend our laws, if not to break them, to satisfy your own idea of what is good."

"I won't argue. I'll only beg."

"And that's always harder, isn't it? But more sensible when the argument is untenable." He sighed. "All right, I'll do something about your slaves. Probably get me into bad trouble with Riyadh, but I'll do something,"

"Thank you, General. I'm grateful. We all are."

"Come to think of it, I haven't had a fight with the government for a long time. I'll rather enjoy it, show them who's in command in this part of the world." He said again: "You're a good man, Cain. Interpret the word any way you like."

"How kind of you to say so."

"And Miss Delorme has very graciously consented to accept my offer to, ah, show her my camp, to stay with us for a few days. If you have no objection that is?"

Fenrek was blinking his eyes a bit.

I said: "No objection at all. I'm sure she'll find it absolutely fascinating."

"My camp's in a little oasis at the edge of the Rub. A lot of date palms, Bedouin tents, the kind of thing any intelligent young woman would be interested in. Very, ah, colorful, all that sort of thing."

"Just keep her out of the Yemeni's line of fire."

He said scornfully: "The Yemenis! Ha!" There was the

greatest contempt in his voice, a contempt touched with a very real amusement. He peered at me then, and said: "Miss Delorme tells me you brought her all the way back here because you thought she had...some sort of feeling for this fellow Fellawi. To, ah, cure her of it. I can't really believe you thought that?"

I said: "What a ridiculous idea! I wonder where she got it?"

He grunted. "No man can understand the workings of a woman's mind, can he? Extraordinary."

Connie's blue eyes were on me, and she looked away and smiled that secret little smile of hers again. Hishara shot out his hand and took mine, and it was like a steel hawser being wrapped around my fist and tightened. He said: "You won't forget about the scimitar?"

"I certainly won't."

"And you don't mind about the helicopter?"

"Not in the least."

"Splendid. So I've come out of all this rather well, haven't I?" He turned to Fenrek and took his hand, and I saw Fenrek wince; and he's a strong man, too. The General said: "Good to have met you, Mr. Maximillian. Next time you visit us, I hope you'll be calling yourself Colonel Fenrek again. Army rank, y'know, mustn't treat it so lightly."

I had to keep persuading myself that his martial pomposity was all a pose; underneath all the bluster, this man was a fine scholar, and he knew that I knew it.

There was an amused lift to the corner of his mouth. He said: "Come back one day, Cain, and we'll have that roast lamb I promised you."

It didn't take too long to start the plane; the damage to it was slight. With a quick briefing from the wounded pilots, I took off in less than ten minutes, and when we circled the little airstrip and the oasis, we looked down and saw them there, the Camel Corps and the cavalry moving in formation into Khadir. Moving slowly in the opposite direction into the hills and the Rub al Khali, the two horses with Hishara and Connie mounted were circled by his personal bodyguard of eight riders, their horses brilliantly caparisoned against the yellow sand; they were, of course, prancing.

And forty minutes later, with ten minutes' fuel left in the tanks, we landed at Djibouti and the story broke.

* * *

It was two weeks later that I heard from the General.

He wrote to thank me for the scimitar, which had safely been delivered through Izmir, Istanbul, Riyadh, Taif, Qizar, and Khadir, guarded on the way first by two Turkish, and then two Saudi Arabian policemen, after I'd pulled a few strings with the Curator and the government.

I had to promise, in return, to send them all my research on the origin of the Seldjukides, an obscure tribe of Turks who grew into an immensely potent army and devastated all the provinces of Mahmoud the Ghaznavide; it was a very fair exchange.

It reached me, the letter, in Fenrek's Paris apartment that overlooks the beautiful green Bois de Boulogne. We were sitting on his verandah in the cool damp of the evening, sipping cognac and watching the world below us, the cars shooting by, the lovers arm-in-arm, the white-gloved traffic cops with their white-enameled batons...

As I read the letter, Fenrek stretched out his long legs and waited, and said at last: "Connie?"

I passed it over to him. The General had written, in part:

... and you'll be surprised to hear that I've decided to give up my Military career and devote my time to my writing. I thought I might start work on a translation into French of those Sabaean epics, so Connie and I will shortly move to Djibouti. She asks to be remembered to you with the greatest possible affection; and I expect you'd like to know that she's very, very happy...

Fenrek sighed. He said: "Ah, Djibouti, what an attractive little town that is! I really must go back there one day soon. I wonder how Jo's getting along?"

He stood up abruptly. "Well, I'd better get dressed."

I said: "Oh? Going out this evening?"

He nodded. "Professor Selegrit sent me some very interesting papers from Nicosia, by one of his special carriers. A lady named Maria Christophorous, as a matter of fact. I thought I'd take her to dinner and a show." He said politely: "Perhaps you'd care to join us?"

I said: "I wouldn't dream of intruding. And I've got some studying to do, anyway." I remembered the lovely Maria.

"Well then...?"

Soon, he went out, dressed to kill in his best tuxedo. I leaned on the railing, sipped my drink, and watched the lights, and listened to the sounds, that came up from the Bois de Boulogne.

It had never seemed a friendlier place.

THE END

ABOUT THE AUTHOR

Alan Lyle-Smythe was born in Surrey, England. Prior to World War II, he served with the Palestine Police from 1936 to 1939 and learned the Arabic language. He was awarded an MBE in June 1938. He married Aliza Sverdova in 1939, then studied acting from 1939 to 1941.

In January 1940, Lyle-Smythe was commissioned in the Royal Army Service Corps. Due to his linguistic skills, he transferred to the Intelligence Corps and served in the Western Desert, in which he used the surname "Caillou" (the French word for 'pebble') as an alias.

He was captured in North Africa, imprisoned and threatened with execution in Italy, then escaped to join the British forces at Salerno. He was then posted to serve with the partisans in Yugoslavia. He wrote about his experiences in the book *The World is Six Feet Square* (1954). He was promoted to captain and awarded the Military Cross in 1944.

Following the war, he returned to the Palestine Police from 1946 to 1947, then served as a Police Commissioner in British-occupied Italian Somaliland from 1947 to 1952, where he was recommissioned a captain.

After work as a District Officer in Somalia and professional hunter, Lyle-Smythe travelled to Canada, where he worked as a hunter and then became an actor on Canadian television.

He wrote his first novel, *Rogue's Gambit*, in 1955, first using the name Caillou, one of his aliases from the war. Moving from Vancouver to Hollywood, he made an appearance as a contestant on the January 23 1958 edition of *You Bet Your Life*.

He appeared as an actor and/or worked as a screenwriter in

such shows as *Daktari*, *The Man From U.N.C.L.E.* (including the screenwriting for "*The Bow-Wow Affair*" from 1965), *Thriller, Daniel Boone, Quark, Centennial*, and *How the West Was Won*. In 1966-67, he had a recurring role (as Jason Flood) in NBC's "*Tarzan*" TV series starring Ron Ely. Caillou appeared in such television movies as *Sole Survivor* (1970), *The Hound of the Baskervilles* (1972, as Inspector Lestrade), and *Goliath Awaits* (1981). His cinema film credits included roles in *Five Weeks in a Balloon* (1962), *Clarence, the Cross-Eyed Lion* (1965), *The Rare Breed* (1966), *The Devil's Brigade* (1968), *Hellfighters* (1968), *Everything You Always Wanted to Know About Sex* (*But Were Afraid to Ask)* (1972), *Herbie Goes to Monte Carlo* (1977), *Beyond Evil* (1980), *The Sword and the Sorcerer* (1982) and *The Ice Pirates* (1984).

Caillou wrote 52 paperback thrillers under his own name and the nom de plume of Alex Webb, with such heroes as Cabot Cain, Colonel Matthew Tobin, Mike Benasque, Ian Quayle and Josh Dekker, as well as writing many magazine stories.

Several of Caillou's novels were made into films, such as *Rampage* with Robert Mitchum in 1963, based on his big game hunting knowledge; *Assault on Agathon*, for which Caillou did the screenplay as well; and *The Cheetahs*, filmed in 1989.

He was married to Aliza Sverdova from 1939 until his death. Their daughter Nadia Caillou was the screenwriter for the film *Skeleton Coast*.

Alan Caillou died in Sedona, Arizona in 2006.

LOOKING FOR ACTION AND ADVENTURE
AUTHOR ALAN CAILLOU
NOVELS DELIVER!
WWW.CALIBERCOMICS.COM

AVAILABLE IN PAPERBACK OR EBOOK

DON'T MISS ANY OF MICHAEL KASNER'S HARD HITTING MILITARY NOVEL SERIES

BLACK OPS

Formed by an elite cadre of government officials, the Black OPS team goes where the law can't - to seek retribution for acts of terror directed against Americans anywhere in the world.

3 BOOK SERIES

Armed with all the tactical advantages of modern technology, battle hard and ready when the free world is threatened - the Peacekeepers are the baddest grunts on the planet.

4 BOOK SERIES

CHOPPER COPS

America is being torn apart as criminal cartels terrorize our cities, dealing drugs and death wholesale. Local police are outgunned, so the President unleashes the U.S. TACTICAL POLICE FORCE. An elite army of super cops with ammo to burn, they swoop down on the hot spots in sleek high-tech attack choppers to win the dirty war and take back America!

4 BOOK SERIES

FROM CALIBER BOOKS

www.calibercomics.com

DON'T MISS ANY OF NEIL HUNTER'S NOVELS FROM CALIBER BOOKS

Reporter Les Mason is completing an expose on the Long Point Nuclear Plant. But before he can finish he dies an agonizing death. The doctors are baffled—and there are similar cases to follow...Chris Lane, his girlfriend, and organizer of the Long Point Protestors, discovers Mason's notes, and decides to find out for herself what the plant has to hide.

2 BOOK SERIES

In middle of the 21st century America – over-populated decaying cities are ruled by hi-tech gangs pushing every vice and wastelands are controlled by bands of mutants. Ordinary citizens are oppressed and face a hopeless future. But Marshal T.J. Cade is a new breed of law enforcer. Teamed with his cyborg partner, Janek, Cade takes on these criminals and works in the gray areas of the law to get the job done.

3 BOOK SERIES

The village of Shepthorne England wasn't being gripped, but strangled by a winter's blanket of heavy snow and Arctic temperatures. The trouble began innocently enough with a massive pile-up of autos on frozen roads leading to and from the village. Then, from the sky, a military transport plane with its top secret cargo of devastation crashed down towards the center of the village. Hell was just beginning to touch Shepthorne and its unsuspecting citizens...

FROM CALIBER BOOKS

www.calibercomics.com

CALIBER COMICS GOES TO WAR!
HISTORICAL AND MILITARY THEMED GRAPHIC NOVELS

WORLD WAR ONE: MO MAN'S LAND

ISBN: 9781635298123

A look at World War 1 from the French trenches as they faced the Imperial German Army.

CORTEZ AND THE FALL OF THE AZTECS

ISBN: 9781635299779

Cortez battles the Aztecs while in search of Inca gold.

TROY: AN EMPIRE UNDER SIEGE

ISBN: 9781635298635

Homer's famous The Iliad and the Trojan War is given a unique human perspective rather than from the God's.

WITNESS TO WAR

ISBN: 9781635299700

WW2's Battle of the Bulge is seen up close by an embedded female war reporter.

THE LINCOLN BRIGADE

ISBN: 9781635298222

American volunteers head to Spain in the 1930s to fight in their civil war against the fascist regime.

EL CID: THE CONQUEROR

ISBN: 9780982654996

Europe's greatest warrior attempts to unify Spain against invading foreign and domestic armies.

WINTER WAR

ISBN: 9780985749392

At the outbreak of WW2 Finland fights against an invading Soviet army.

ZULUNATION: END OF EMPIRE

ISBN: 9780941613415

The global British Empire and far-reaching influence is threatened by a Zulu uprising in southern Africa.

AIR WARRIORS: WORLD WAR ONE #V1 - V4 *Take to the skies of WW1 as various fighter aces tell their harrowing stories.*
ISBN: 9781635297973 (V1), 9781635297980 (V2), 9781635297997 (V3), 9781635298000 (V4)

CALIBER COMICS PRESENTS
The Complete
VIETNAM JOURNAL

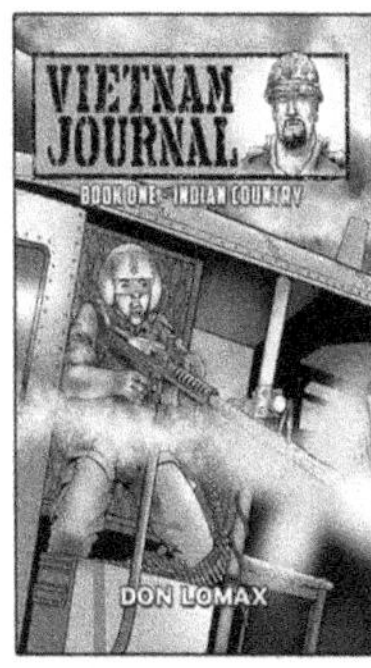

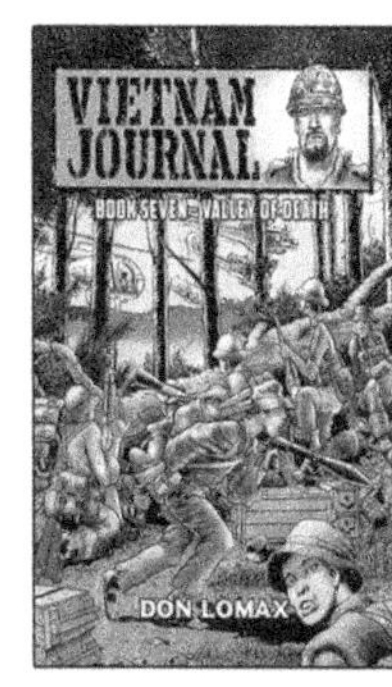

8 Volumes Covering the Entire Initial Run of the Critically Acclaimed Don Lomax Series

And Now Available
VIETNAM JOURNAL SERIES TWO
"INCURSION", "JOURNEY INTO HELL", "RIPCORD"

All new stories from Scott 'Journal' Neithammer as he reports durings the later stages of the Vietnam War.

CALIBER COMICS WWW.CALIBERCOMICS.COM

CALIBER COMICS GOES TO THE EDGE!
Science Fiction and Horror themed graphic novels

DEADWORLD
ISBN: 9781942351245

RENFIELD
ISBN: 9781942351825

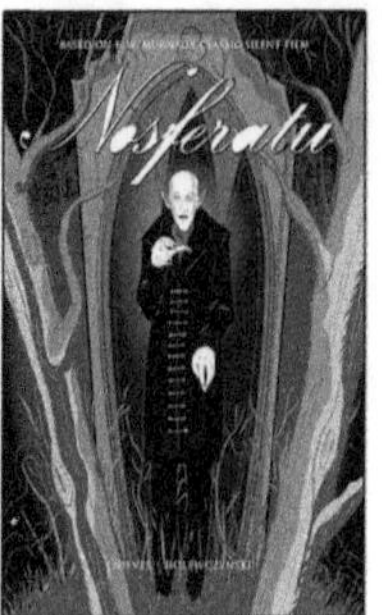

NOSFERATU
ISBN: 9781942351931

**LOVECRAFT:
THE EARLY STORIES**
ISBN: 9781942351634

**THE WAR OF THE WORLDS:
INFESTATION**
ISBN: 9781942351962

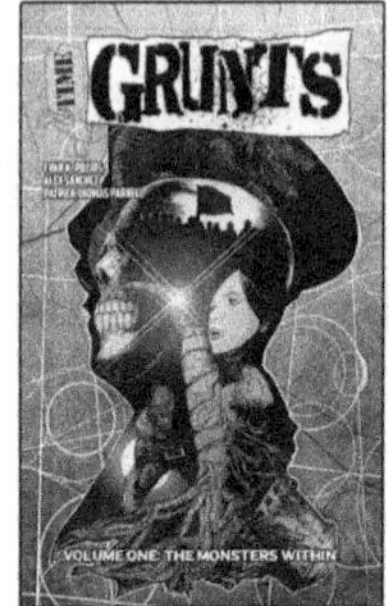

TIME GRUNTS
ISBN: 9781635299472

DRACULA
ISBN: 9780996030649

**DRACULA:
THE SUICIDE CLUB**
ISBN: 9781635299571

**JACK THE RIPPER
ILLUSTRATED**
ISBN: 9781942351917

THE SEARCHERS
ISBN: 9781942351979

A.A.I. WARS
ISBN: 9781635299168

**AUTUMN: TERROR IN THE
LONDON UNDERGROUND**
ISBN: 9781544624020

www.calibercomics.com

ALSO AVAILABLE FROM CALIBER COMICS

QUALITY GRAPHIC NOVELS TO ENTERTAIN

THE SEARCHERS: VOLUME 1
The Shape of Things to Come

Before *League of Extraordinary Gentlemen* there was *The Searchers*. At the dawn of the 20th Century the greatest literary adventurers from the minds of Wells, Doyle, Burroughs, and Haggard were created. All thought to be the work of pure fiction. However, a century later, the real-life descendents of those famous characters are recuited by the legendary Professor Challenger in order to save mankind's future. Series collected for the first time.

"Searchers is the comic book I have on the wall with a sign reading - 'Love books? Never read a comic? Try this one! ....money back guarantee..." - Dark Star Books.

WAR OF THE WORLDS: INFESTATION

Based on the H.G. Wells classic! The "Martian Invasion" has begun again and now mankind must fight for its very humanity. It happened slowly at first but by the third year, it seemed that the war was almost over... the war was almost lost.

"Writer Randy Zimmerman has a fine grasp of drama, and spins the various strands of the story into a coherent whole... imaginative and very gritty."
- war-of-the-worlds.co.uk

HELSING: LEGACY BORN

From writer Gary Reed (Deadworld) and artists John Lowe (Captain America), Bruce McCorkindale (Godzilla). She was born into a legacy she wanted no part of and pushed into a battle recessed deep in the shadows of the night. Samantha Helsing is torn between two worlds...two allegiances...two families. The legacy of the Van Helsing family and their crusade against the "night creatures" comes to modern day with the most unlikely of all warriors.

"Congratulations on this masterpiece..."
- Paul Dale Roberts, Compuserve Reviews

DEADWORLD

Before there was The Walking Dead there was Deadworld. Here is an introduction of the long running classic horror series, Deadworld, to a new audience! Considered by many to be the godfather of the original zombie comic with over 100 issues and graphic novels in print and over 1,000,000 copies sold, Deadworld ripped into the undead with intelligent zombies on a mission and a group of poor teens riding in a school bus desperately try to stay one step ahead of the sadistic, Harley-riding King Zombie. Death, mayhem, and a touch of supernatural evil made Deadworld a classic and now here's your chance to get into the story!

DAYS OF WRATH

Award winning comic writer & artist Wayne Vansant brings his gripping World War II saga of war in the Pacific to Guadalcanal and the Battle of Bloody Ridge. This is the powerful story of the long, vicious battle for Guadalcanal that occurred in 1942-43. When the U.S. Navy orders its outnumbered and out-gunned ships to run from the Japanese fleet, they abandon American troops on a bloody, battered island in the South Pacific.

"Heavy on authenticity, compellingly written and beautifully drawn."
- Comics Buyers Guide

SHERLOCK HOLMES:
THE CASE OF THE MISSING MARTIAN

Sherlock is called out of retirement to London in 1908 to solve a most baffling mystery: The British Museum is missing a specimen of a Martian from the failed invasion of 1899. Did it walk away on its own or did someone steal it?

Holmes ponders the facts and remembers his part in the war effort alongside Professor Challenger during the War of the Worlds invasion that was chronicled in H.G. Wells' classic novel.

Meanwhile, Doctor Watson has problems of his own when his wife steals a scalpel from his surgical tool kit and returns to her old stomping grounds of Whitechapel, the London

CALIBER PRESENTS

The original Caliber Presents anthology title was one of Caliber's inaugural releases and featured predominantly new creators, many of which went onto successful careers in the comics' industry. In this new version, Caliber Presents has expanded to graphic novel size and while still featuring new creators it also includes many established professional creators with new visions. Creators featured in this first issue include nominees and winners of some of the industry's major awards including the Eisner, Harvey, Xeric, Ghastly, Shel Dorf, Comic Monsters, and more.

LEGENDLORE

From Caliber Comics now comes the entire Realm and Legendlore saga as a set of volumes that collects the long running critically acclaimed series. In the vein of The Lord of The Rings and The Hobbit with elements of Game of Thrones and Dungeon and Dragons.

Four normal modern day teenagers are plunged into a world they thought only existed in novels and film. They are whisked away to a magical land where dragons roam the skies, orcs and hobgoblins terrorize travelers, where unicorns prance through the forest, and kingdoms wage war for dominance. It is a world where man is just one race, joining other races such as elves, trolls, dwarves, changelings, and the dreaded night creatures who steal the night.

TIME GRUNTS

What if Hitler's last great Super Weapon was – Time itself! A WWII/time travel adventure that can best be described as *Band of Brothers* meets *Time Bandits*.

October, 1944. Nazi fortunes appear bleaker by the day. But in the bowels of the Wenceslas Mines, a terrible threat has emerged . . . The Nazis have discovered the ability to conquer time itself with the help of a new ominous device!

Now a rag tag group of American GIs must stop this threat to the past, present, and future . . . While dealing with their own past, prejudices, and fears in the process.

CALIBER
C O M I C S

www.calibercomics.com